Patchwork Family

Book I

Steve's Song

M. H. P. Rosenbaum

BLACK BEAR PRODUCTIONS

For Ned, who made my dream of family a reality

Published by Black Bear Productions
815 Simon Greenwell Ln., Boston, KY 40107
mhpros@hughes.net

Cover Art by Rivkah Walton/studio-rw.com
Book Layout and Cover Design
by Maggie Pagratis/Custom-book-tique.com

Chapter 1.

Steve

S teve sat in the deserted playground, tapping the rhythms in his head onto the stitches in the heavy cloth of the swing seat. At thirteen he was too big for the swing, and he didn't know how to use it, anyway. *Whoever heard of a thirteen-year-old who didn't know how to play on a swing?* he thought. He thought things like that a lot; there was so much he didn't know. He didn't know what that cloth was called, he didn't know how to use a swing, he didn't know how to play or how to talk to people or how to be in the world.

Those months in the institution, they'd let him have his own room and stay alone most of the time, except in class and when he sat and talked to the lady doctor. Then last night she'd brought him to her big house with about a million rooms and what seemed like a hundred people—well, not really, just three girls and three other boys, and the three grownups, but he wasn't used to being around more than one other person. So this morning, after he heard the lady going out to work early, he'd gotten up before anyone else was awake and sneaked out of the house to be alone again for a while.

Steve scuffed his feet in the dust, turning so the chains of the swing twisted above his head. The hot sun on his short blond hair was starting to burn his scalp. He lifted his feet and found out the untangling chains would twirl him back around. He tried it again. *Is this what you're supposed to do on a swing?*

A car went by blaring the new Elvis song, "Loving You." *Third straight Number One album, title track. With the Jordanaires, and Fontana on drums. Scotty Moore and Tiny Timbrell backing Elvis on guitar.* Steve missed his radio. He wondered if there was one where he would live now.

Suddenly he noticed three guys leaning on the chain link fence, staring in at him. When they saw him looking, they pushed off and started in through the gate. *Don't think they're any of the people from the house last night.*

They were bigger than he was. They all had long sideburns, and greasy hair combed back on the sides like wings. One was wearing a black, shiny jacket even in this heat, and had a chain hanging from his belt.

Their boots clocked on the concrete as they came toward him, spreading out a little so Steve was more or less surrounded. They were smiling, though. *Are they friendly?*

"Well, what's this?" the one in the jacket said. "Little fresh chicken, huh?" *No, not friendly.* He sounded like Bert on a sober day, just before the pain would start. The other two made laughing sounds that weren't really laughing and moved a little closer.

Steve swallowed the bubble of panic in his throat and slipped his hands into his jeans pockets, hoping there'd be something there he could use as a weapon. *Nothing.* He could try to run for it, but he didn't think he'd get far, and he couldn't remember where the house was that he was supposed to be living in.

Black Jacket was right in front of him now, his knees almost touching Steve's. "Whatcha lookin' for, chicken?" he said. "Lost your balls?" His buddies started to make clucking noises and flapping their elbows.

Steve closed his eyes and tried to sink down into himself, to get to that secret place deep inside where he could pretend that whatever was happening was happening to someone else, someone far away.

One of them grabbed the swing chains and started jerking them, trying to tip him off onto the ground.

5

They were all making a lot of noise now, cackling and calling ugly names, but he could hardly hear them any more; they were like voices on the radio.

Then the chains stopped jerking and the hooting and clucking stopped. A new voice—a deep, grown-up sounding voice—said, "Back to the roost, jailbirds."

Steve opened his eyes. It was that big colored kid from the house last night. He had his hand on Black Jacket's upper arm; his dark brown fingers went almost all the way around, even over that thick sleeve. Steve knew a lot about what hands making somebody hurt looked like, and it didn't seem to him that this one was squeezing very hard, or much at all, but Black Jacket was holding himself at an angle as though he was scared and looking for a way out.

Another older kid from the house, the one they called Robbie—Steve remembered his name because he was the only other blond boy there—was holding the wrist of one of the other guys. But this hold would hurt, since he had yanked the wrist back and up between the guy's shoulder blades. "You hoods are cruisin' for a bruisin'," he said. "Why don't you just beat it, like Laurie said, before you get in some real trouble?"

"'Laurie'?" crowed the third guy. "He's got a girl's name?"

"That's right," said a girl's voice from right behind Steve. "And he's tough as a girl, too—even tougher than I am, birdbrain. So why don't you all just quit bugging our brother and get lost?"

Black Jacket wrenched his arm away from Laurie's hand. "Come on," he said to the others. "McAlisters are all a bunch of freaks. Leave 'em to their new little freak." The three of them walked away slowly, swinging their arms, trying to look like they hadn't been run off.

The girl behind Steve let her hands drop lightly on his shoulders and then away when he flinched. Laurie turned from watching the others go and hunkered down in front of Steve. "Ready to go home, buddy?" he said.

"H-home?"

Robbie said, "Hard to feature, isn't it? I remember how freaky it was for me, but I was just a tadpole."

Steve wasn't sure what he was talking about, so he put it away to think about later. He looked from Rob to Laurie; they were both smiling. "I thought 'bugging' means making somebody kind of mad."

"It does," Laurie said.

"But you guys don't look mad." Now they both looked puzzled. "She said," Steve tilted his head toward the girl who was still standing behind him, "'quit bugging our brother.'"

The boys looked at each other and the girl's hand found Steve's shoulder again. He tried hard not to slap it off. "Celia was talking about you, honey," Robbie said.

Nobody had ever called Steve "honey" before. *"Lovey,"* he thought. *Somebody used to call me "lovey."* He got up, pushed between Rob and Laurie, and stood the length of a room away with his back to them. He could sense them watching him and maybe signaling each other behind him.

After a minute they came up beside him, close but not touching him. Laurie said, "Come on, time to go, Stevie." Somebody had called him that before, too.

Chapter 2.

Wednesday, July 17, 1957: 8:45 a.m.

Steve

The house looked even bigger in the daylight than it had the night before. The sun made the white paint gleam, except under the trees where it looked cool and shadowy. It was cool inside, too, and quiet.

Steve could feel his heart slowing down when the heavy front door closed behind him and the other three kids, but then he heard voices somewhere in the house—up the stairs in front of him, he thought—and there were rooms around him, and he didn't know where he was supposed to go. The floor was covered with some soft gray stuff that went all the way up the stairs; it looked nice and felt nice, but how could you scrub it? *I wish I could just lie down in it and go to sleep, but that lady said she didn't want me to sleep in the daytime.*

Now here was the man from last night, way taller than Steve so Steve could just look at his middle and not have to see his face and how mad he might be. His heart started to race again, and his breath came faster. He looked at the shiny gold buttons on the man's dark blue jacket and waited to see what would happen to him.

"He was in the playground, Dad," Laurie said. "That j.d. Tom Varner and a couple of his hoodlum friends were hassling him."

"Ok," the man said. "Thanks for finding him, kids. Steve, will you come with me?"

He led the way into the room to the left of the stairs and Steve followed, starting to shake. *That side has windows, no bars, but if I jumped out, where would I go? What's behind that door? Oh, bathroom. No way out.*

The man closed the door behind them, walked past a couple of desks, and sat down on a couch in front of an empty fireplace. "Here, sit with me, Steve."

He didn't sound mad, but Steve backed away till he was jammed into the angle where the fireplace met the wall. "I didn't mean to," he said desperately.

There was a little silence. When the man spoke again, it was very slowly and quietly. "Didn't mean to what, honey?" There it was again, the second time someone called him that.

"I don't know," Steve said. "Whatever you're mad about. I didn't mean to go Outside."

"You didn't mean to go outside? How did it happen, then?"

"I mean, I just had to get away. I had to be alone. I know I'm not supposed to be Outside."

The man took a deep breath. "Ok, Steve, listen now. First of all, I'm not mad about anything. I was worried, but now you're back safe so I'm not worried any more. I'm just trying to understand. Will you come over here and sit by me?"

Steve moved slowly to the couch, watching the man's hands and his eyes. The man saw Steve's eyes flicking back and forth; the man's shoulders sagged and his mouth drooped down at the corners. *What does that mean?* Steve sat on the edge of the couch, as far from the man as he could. He tapped nervously on the couch seat. *Blue, like my blanket, but smoother.*

The man said, "There's nothing wrong with you being outside, Steve. There's nothing wrong with you wanting to be alone. Just, next time, will you tell us about it first?" Steve nodded cautiously, jamming one hand between the couch cushion and the back and hanging on.

"Good," the man said. "I know this is hard, and strange, and scary for you. It would have been better if we could have brought you here for a few visits, let us get to know each other, but they wanted to move you over into the juvenile justice system and we were afraid we wouldn't get a chance again." He tapped his fingertips together, thinking, then smiled at Steve. "But what we want is for you to be happy, and to feel safe here. This is your home, now. Try to tell us what you need, and we'll try to see you get it."

"But I don't know what I need! I don't even know who I am." Steve felt like a moron. *What does that even mean, what I just said?* But the man was nodding as though it made sense.

"We'll take it slow," he said. "We'll all try to help you figure it out. For now I'll just tell you that I think you're incredibly brave and strong, and—"

Steve was still scared, but now he also felt a wash of red rage come over him. "That's a lie," he said. "You're lying to trick me." Then he clapped his hands over his mouth, screwed his eyes shut, and waited for the hitting to start.

When nothing happened, he opened his eyes again. The man was still sitting there, looking down at his own hands in his lap. After a minute he looked up at Steve. *Are those tears in his eyes? They are! But he doesn't seem drunk.* Steve didn't know what to think.

"Steve, is it all right if I put my arm around you?" the man said.

Here it comes. But it was better than hitting, and at least the guy was asking. Steve nodded once and shifted a little closer, closed his eyes, braced himself, and started looking for his secret inside place. But the arm that had been looping around his stiff shoulders jerked away again as though it'd touched something hot. He could hear the man's voice pulling him back to the surface.

"Steve, Steve, please look at me. Steve!" Steve opened his eyes. The man was very close, but not touching him, and his voice was really calm. "Steve, honey," he said. "You don't have to say yes if you don't want to. No one is going to touch you if you don't want them to. And I am never, ever going to lie to you, or try to trick you, or hurt you on purpose in any way. I don't know whether you can believe that right now, but I'm going to keep showing you it's true until you do believe it. All right?"

Steve couldn't look at his face any more. His own chest felt like someone was sitting on it; he could hardly get any air. The man was saying, "Breathe, Steve. Come on, take a breath. Blow out and then breathe in." Everything that squeezed out of Steve's chest seemed to be jammed in his throat. He felt like he'd choke if he didn't let whatever it was out of there. He thought he might be sick.

He opened his mouth, but instead of throwing up he started crying, bawling out loud like a little kid. The man just sat there beside him, not saying anything or coming any closer but not going away. Finally the choking sobs trailed into silence, like a storm blowing away. The man handed him a Kleenex and Steve mopped his face off. He couldn't open his eyes.

There was a knock on the door, then the sound of the door opening and closing. "Sean? Steve?" It was the lady doctor from the institution, the one who brought him here. She came around to where they were sitting. Steve could hear her draw in a sharp breath when she saw them there side by side. *Is she going to be mad?* But her voice was still soft when she said, "Laurie called me. I came straight home. Are you all right, Steve?"

He nodded, but he couldn't speak to her. He still had trouble talking to more than one person at a time. "Is that what I call you, 'Shawn'?" he asked the man, copying the way it sounded when the woman said it.

"Yes, you can call me Sean if you want to. Or if it feels all right to you, now or some time down the line, you could call me Dad."

The woman sat down on the other side of him and put her hand on the back of his neck. He shivered, but he let her do it. "Well, you're calling me Mom," she said firmly. Steve's eyes opened.

Chapter 3.

Sunday, July 20, 1957: 3:00 p.m.

Robbie

Robbie McAlister sat on the floor between the twin beds in the larger spare room, picking out the new Paul Anka song, "Diana," on his guitar, humming under his breath. *Maybe I need to shift it up a little. Where's the capo?* He found the little woven strap with its metal bar halfway under a bed and hooked it around the guitar neck, effectively shortening the strings to raise the pitch. *Yeah, now we're cookin',* he thought, running through the tune again and singing along. He looked up to see the half-open door shift an inch. "Who's there?" he said. "Hello-o-o?" He sang the last word.

After a second the door swung open the rest of the way. *The new kid. Freaky. How long was he standing out there?* "Hi-ho, Steverino," he said. "What's the story?"

Steve edged into the room, eyes sluing around to the corners. *Does he think there's somebody hiding in here?* Rob wondered. *Or is he checking for an escape route?*

Steve's stare settled on Robbie's guitar. "Was that you playing? I thought it was a radio," he said.

Robbie gave a soft, scoffing laugh. "Yeah, I sound like Paul Anka. That's close."

"But there is a radio in here." Now Steve was staring at the table-model Telefunken on the dresser. "Does it get WHYL?"

"You fracture me, kid," Rob said. "Any radio around this part of Pennsylvania gets the same stations, you on my frequency here?"

Steve shrugged. "I didn't know. I just had the one in The Room. I don't know about any other ones."

"But you liked the sounds?"

"I listened to everything, but I liked Top 40 the most."

"Crazy," Rob said. *What's wrong? He looks like I hit him. Oh—* "'Crazy,' it's just an expression. It means, like, cool or neat, but with a little extra."

"Oh," Steve said, relaxing a little. "There's lots I don't know."

He keeps staring at the radio. "You mean, like, reading and all that jazz?"

"Yeah, that, but other stuff. Girls."

"Girls? You don't get girls? Let me clue you in, little buddy, nobody does."

Steve flushed. "It's not funny. I mean I never saw one."

Robbie's mouth fell open. "God, that's radical," he said. "You never saw a chick?"

"I guess I did when I was little, but I don't remember. I almost remembered when—"

"When what?"

"When you and that colored guy—"

"His name is Laurie."

"Ok, don't get mad, I never saw any of *them* before the institution, either. Anyway, when he called me Stevie, and you called me... 'honey,' maybe I remembered."

"You remember a woman calling you 'honey'?"

"'Lovey,'" Steve whispered.

For once, no easy words came to Robbie. After a minute he said softly, "Your mother?"

"Maybe." Steve shook himself all over, like a dog coming out of deep water, took a breath, and went on in a firmer voice. "There's other stuff I don't know about, too. Even, I mean, like food."

"Food? You had food before, or you'd be dead."

"Sure, but it was different. Like, everything here is hot. Well, not everything, but like the meat and the green stuff. Or those pancakes Dad made after church today. I didn't know food was supposed to be hot. At the institution, the food was sort of hot but it all tasted like glue so I didn't think about it."

"You never had hot food before Rolling Meadow?"

"Bert used to just give me whatever he didn't finish. Sometimes it was a little bit warm, but mostly cold, especially the pie."

"He gave you pie for dessert?"

"What's dessert?"

What's dessert? God. "Sweet stuff you eat after the main meal."

"No, this wasn't sweet. He said it was tuna fish pie, but it was hard and real cold."

"Those little frozen pies? In the aluminum tins? And he gave them to you without cooking them?"

"If I waited long enough, they'd get soft. But sometimes I was too hungry to wait, and maybe he'd take it away before I got a chance to eat it. Mostly it was his food, though. That was better, especially if there was no cigarette butts in it."

"That's unreal, man."

"You think I'm lying?"

Crap. Now he's mad. Should I tell him what I know about eating what comes your way, no matter what's in it? Not ready for that, yet. Better say something, though. "Steve, I just like this sort of jazzy hep talk. I don't mean anything by it. Junk comes into my head and spills out of my mouth, no brain in between—I'm a spaz that way, you dig?"

"Maybe."

"Can you just figure that I'm not putting you down, no matter what I say?"

"Ok." As they talked, Steve had drifted across the room and was now standing at the dresser, fingering the radio.

"Do you want it?" Rob asked.

Steve snatched his fingers away as though they'd had an electric shock. "I didn't say that."

Robbie scooted himself up off the floor and perched on the bed, setting his Gibson beside him. "You can take it into your room if you want, no sweat."

"Really?" Steve still wasn't looking at him.

"Why not? Check with Mom that it's cool with her, but this room isn't used much. I was in here because the music room upstairs is raunchy on a hot day like this, and Laurie's catching some z's in our room, but mostly there's nobody in here." *Now what, he looks mad again.*

"If nobody uses it, why can't I have it?"

"The room?"

"I have to share with that other guy."

"Jamie. Right, like I share with Laurie, and Celia shares with Joy."

"That blind girl doesn't share."

"You're really starting to bug me, kid. Beth doesn't share because she needs to know where everything is all the time, not have somebody leaving their gear in her way and mixing up her stuff. Anyway, there aren't enough rooms for us all to have our own. Why should you be the big cheese?" *Now he looks scared again. Cool it.* Robbie softened his voice. "I think the nitty is, they want us to share so we learn to, like, get tight with each other."

"I get so mixed up," Steve said miserably. "I didn't like being by myself, but I'm not used to being around other people."

"We all get that. You don't have to do it all like Speedy Gonzales, you know." Rob stood up. "Come on, let's move that radio. Hey, I like your new threads—uh, clothes."

Steve looked down at his striped t-shirt and chinos, then raised his toes in their high-top black Keds. "I'm still not used to wearing shoes," he said. "I wore Bert's old stuff before, but his pants and shoes were too big, so I'd just wear a shirt most of the time."

"Wow, what a drag. Never mind, you're going to get the whole ball of wax, whatever you need, from now on, honey. We'll have a blast." Robbie reached a hand out to pat Steve's shoulder, but Steve ducked away. *Right, right, give him room, give him time.* Steve looked at him sideways, cringing a little but ready to be mad again. Rob smiled at him. "I didn't mean to rattle your cage, kiddo."

Rob reached behind the dresser and unplugged the radio. "Let's get you situated."

Steve followed him out of the room.

Chapter 4.

Wednesday, July 31, 1957: 2:30 p.m.

Joy

Joy McAlister lay in the hammock reading *Catcher in the Rye* for the third time. She dangled one foot over the side and wagged it to keep the gentle rocking motion going. Red dye from the battered paperback cover had bled onto her sweaty palms; she dropped the book on her chest to rub her hands on her shorts and then just gazed up into the rustling leaves overhead for a few minutes.

A voice startled her. "Would you show me how to do that?" It was Steve, sitting on the ground by the lilacs a few feet away. She had to peer over the side of the hammock to see him. *How long has he been there?* He kind of gave her the creeps.

When he'd arrived two weeks ago, she'd been a little teed off that someone was coming into the family who was only a month younger than she was. At just thirteen, she was used to being the baby of the family,

23

the one everybody looked after and petted and thought was so cute. But she could see that this new kid really needed looking after and petting. He was cute, too, in a scrawny kind of way. But he hardly talked to anybody, and he was always popping up like this when you had no idea he was around.

Still, her parents had told them all that Steve'd had a really rough life so far, and they would all have to help him. And they'd all agreed they would. *Maybe it wouldn't be so bad, not being the absolute youngest any more. It might be nice to have a brother who needs my help.*

So she tried to sound extra friendly when she answered him. "Show you how to read, you mean? I thought the lady at the special school was helping you with that? I'm not sure I'd know how to—"

"No," he interrupted, looking straight at her for the first time that she could remember. His eyes were really, really blue, like deep ice on the lake. "I meant, show me how to do that." He flapped his hand toward her.

Joy scooted herself up to see him better. "I'm sorry, Steve, I don't get it," she said.

"That thing you're sitting on. It's like a swing, right? Robbie showed me how to use a swing the other day. But I tried to sit on that and it tipped over and I fell out."

"You sat on the edge, probably. This is called a hammock. You have to get your butt in the middle before you put your weight down. C'mere, try it while I'm sitting in it. That way it won't tip over."

Steve came over and stared down at the hammock. He looked a little scared but mostly stubborn. He started to raise his knee toward it. "No," Joy said. "Turn around with your back to it. That's right. Now put your hands on the edge." She curled up to one side and grabbed him at the waist with both hands. "Ok, now, just get your bottom as far back as you can and plop down. Don't worry, I won't let you fall."

He came down with a whoosh, unbalanced, and fell over sideways onto her. She laughed and wiggled out from under, while the hammock thrashed and they almost both got dumped out. "Hold still!" she said. "Just relax a minute." They lay there side by side, their combined weight bringing the canvas almost down to the ground. Joy could feel the tickling of the grass through the coarse weave. Steve was warm against her. *He smells a little like a puppy, like damp hair and sun on skin.*

"All right, I'm going to put my foot on the ground and start us with a push. Then just kind of shift your weight a little from side to side to keep the rocking going."

It took them a couple of tries to coordinate their movements, but soon they were swinging gently in their canvas cocoon, the sides pulled up around them, the trees above. Cicadas were trilling and there was a bumblebee somewhere near.

After a while, Steve spoke. "What's a j.d.?"

"Juvenile delinquent, a bad kid. Why?"

"It's what Laurie called those guys who were bothering me. There's lots of words I don't know."

"Lucky for you, I know lots of words. You can always ask me if you want."

"Good. Thanks."

"Steve?"

"What?"

"Can I ask you something?"

"Ok."

"I'm just wondering—I've noticed you kind of don't like for people to touch you much. I've kept away from you a little because of that. But you don't seem to mind lying here next to me."

"Because you're littler."

"You mean, because I'm smaller than you? Why does that matter?"

"You can't hurt me."

Joy felt like she might cry. "Nobody here is going to hurt you, Stevie. Not on purpose."

"I know they say that. I guess it's hard to believe."

Joy shoved her arm down between their bodies so she could take Steve's hand. "You'll start to believe it after a while. Everyone is so glad you're here."

"I don't know why."

Joy thought about it for a minute. "I guess it's partly that it's nice to bring someone else in, to share what we have."

"Seems like you already had enough people without me. Three boys, three girls—where do I fit?"

"Right in the middle, silly. I don't mean age, of course. But we all want to kind of surround you and keep you safe. Mom's been telling us about you—not private stuff from your sessions with her," she said quickly, feeling him stiffen, "but just how much she was getting to like you and admire you."

"Admire me?"

Oops, he sounds mad. "I guess you don't believe me. But I'm telling you the truth, Steve. We all think it's amazing that you can even stand to be here with us, after everything you've been through, the stuff that was in the newspaper."

Steve relaxed a little. "It's nice here."

"It is, isn't it?"

They lay quietly side by side for a few minutes, then the back door opened. Ruby Jones came out, carrying two double-scoop chocolate ice cream cones, a broad smile on her round brown face.

"Thought you kids might like a treat," she said.

"Ooh, thanks, Ruby." Joy tried to sit up, but Steve's weight made it hard to move in the hammock. Ruby laughed, handed her one of the cones, and hauled her up by the other hand. When Joy got free, she let Ruby take both cones again while Joy helped Steve out of the hammock—it took two tries, and he stepped on her foot, but finally he was up.

Ruby handed them each a cone and went back into the house. Joy sat down on the grass. "Let's not try the hammock with these or we'll end up wearing the ice cream instead of eating it."

But Steve looked like he was doing both. His head was bobbing up and down over the top scoop so his nose was hitting it. He looked like he was trying to attack it. Then he opened his mouth wide and chomped down on the ice cream. When the cold hit his teeth he gave a little screech and spat it out again.

Joy thought at first he was goofing around, but when he spat the ice cream out the truth hit her like a punch in the stomach. "Steve," she said, "let me show you how to lick an ice cream cone."

Chapter 5.

Saturday, August 10, 1957: 1:00 p.m.

Steve

It was a hot, rainy day; the air felt like a wet washcloth pressed over Steve's mouth and nose. The weather was interfering with his radio reception—the Telefunken on the table by his bed was crackling and fizzing as though someone had put in one of those Alka Seltzer tablets Mom gave him last week when his stomach was upset from eating too many of Dad's pancakes. Tomorrow would be Sunday again; he'd have to watch how much he ate. Sighing, he fiddled with the tuning knob. Maybe he could get some sports news on WHP. *Don't really care about sports, but if I can't get music, at least I can listen to something.*

Mom knocked on the open bedroom door and stuck her head in. "Steve, you can't be getting much enjoyment from that radio with so much static. And I'd like you not to spend the day in here listening to it, anyway."

Steve's stomach knotted as he turned the knob to "off." He didn't know how to say what the radio meant to him.

Mom looked like she understood, though. "Listen, Steve, I'll make you a deal. You try every day to talk to somebody or do something with someone in the family, and you can listen to the radio for three hours. Ok?"

She asks me, but I don't really get to pick, Steve thought even as he nodded his head.

Mom came around to sit on the end of Steve's bed. She'd gone into work this morning and was still wearing her suit, a jacket and skirt made of some light crinkly material with thin blue and white stripes.

She smoothed her hands over her skirt for a minute, looking down into her lap. Then she said, "When I was a little girl, I found a squirrel in a trap my foster father had set. He didn't want squirrels, he was trying to catch muskrats for their fur, so he let me have it."

"Why did you want it?"

"I wanted to have something of my own. I lived in twelve foster homes while I was growing up, so I never had anything that was just mine. And also I wanted something to take care of and pet and love."

Steve nodded. "I had a bug once, but Bert smashed it. What happened to your squirrel?"

"It had a broken leg, so I snapped a Popsickle stick in half and tied it on, pushing the little bone back straight. The squirrel struggled and bit me twice, but I knew what it needed so I held it down until I got the splint in place. Can you guess what happened then?"

"It got better and it loved you 'cause you saved it?"

Mom rubbed her thumb over her lips. "No, it died. It was already scared because of the trap, and my handling it and hurting it with the splint was too much for it. It went into shock, I suppose. The next morning when I went out to the shed to check on it, it was lying in the box, stiff and cold."

"I cried when Bert smashed my bug."

Mom nodded. "I cried over my squirrel. But I learned something, too. I learned that sometimes you can cause more harm than good when you're trying to help. I learned that you can't force your help on someone, even if you know better than they do what they need."

Steve thought about it. "…Me?" he said.

"You, that's right. When you were still at Rolling Meadow and I was just your therapist, we could talk about what was bothering you but it wasn't up to me to make decisions about what you could do and not do.

31

Now that you're part of our family, your dad and I have to make some of those decisions. But we don't want to force you or scare you. We do want you to try to trust us, though. Can you believe that we know at least some of what you need, and that we're on your side?"

Nobody's ever been on my side. Steve started to tap on his blue blanket, the one they let him keep from The Room, listening to the rhythms in his head.

After a long silence, Mom said, "Well, can you try to believe it?"

Steve nodded.

Mom smiled. "Good. Now, the reason I came in here is to tell you that today is Dad's birthday. Ruby will make a special dinner tonight and afterwards we'll give him our presents. But it occurred to me that you've only been getting an allowance for the few weeks you've been here, and you haven't had a chance to shop for anything. Would you like to give him something?"

"Sure."

"I thought you might. Come with me."

Steve followed Mom out of the bedroom into the hall and turned right into the smaller spare room. Laurie was in there, leaning over the bed and wrapping a bottle in some thin green paper. Steve shrank behind

Mom, seeing Laurie so close all of a sudden. *He's so big, and so—dark.* Laurie's smile vanished when he saw that, and Steve felt bad, but he didn't know what to do about it.

Mom didn't seem to notice. "What do you have there, darling?"

"Bay rum aftershave," Laurie said, tying a ribbon around the twisted paper at the top of the bottle.

"Good, he could use some more." Mom went over to the open closet door. Steve stuck close behind her. "Here, Steve," she said, pulling a box out. "When I see something on sale, or something unusual or especially nice, I'll sometimes buy it and stash it here for when someone needs a gift. Take a look and see if you spot something you'd like to give Dad."

Steve crouched down and started going through the box, pushing it farther into the room so he could see inside better. He saw a fountain pen in a special case, a couple of ties in boxes with clear lids, a doll in a fancy dress, some books, a big box of crayons... all kinds of stuff, just packed away in this closet in case somebody wanted it. "Are you rich?" he said.

Laurie stopped trying to tie a little card onto his ribbon to look at him and Mom stopped pulling a roll of wrapping paper off the closet shelf. Then she started pulling it out again and said, "No, we're not rich, but we're lucky enough to be comfortable. Dad and I both bring home paychecks, and his father left him this house and some money, so we don't have to worry the way some people do. Why do you ask?"

"You've got all these things just lying here, and there's always so much food, and so many rooms I can't keep track of them. I wish I was lucky like this."

Mom put the wrapping paper on the bed next to where Laurie was working and started to cut a piece off with the scissors that were lying there. Steve looked down quickly, away from the scissors. *Sharp.*

Mom said, "You are, Steve. You're a member of this family, now. Everything we have is yours, too."

Steve pushed the box away and sat back to think about that just as the blind girl, Beth, came into the room. Before he could stop her, she walked right into the box and tripped over it, falling onto her elbow on the foot of the bed and sliding to the floor. The box she'd been carrying popped open and a shirt with big bright flowers on it fell out. Steve put both arms over his head and closed his eyes. *Nonononono—*

The next thing Steve knew, somebody was touching his arm very, very lightly, like the moths that used to get into The Room sometimes. "It's all right, Steve," a soft voice said. "I'm all right, don't be scared." Cautiously, he raised his head. *It's like she's looking at me, but my head's right next to me or something.*

There was a silence, then Mom said, "Are you too scared to say anything to Beth, Steve? She can't see your face, she needs to hear your voice."

Mom sounds like she's being nice, but she's pushing me to talk, Steve thought. "She's a girl," he said. *Stupid, stupid, stupid.*

"When you hurt a girl, it's just like hurting a person," Laurie said, his voice cold.

When Steve spoke, Beth's face had turned so it almost seemed like she was really looking at him. Now she said, "He didn't mean to hurt me, did you, baby?"

Steve shook his head. *Stupid, stupid,* he thought again, *she can't see you.* "Uh, no, I didn't," he said. "I just meant, I'm not used to talking to girls."

"Joy said you talk to her," Mom said.

"Joy's different. I don't know why, she just is. Anyway, I, uh, I'm sorry I put the box there. I was looking for a present for Dad."

Beth smiled and gave him one of those little moth-pets again, this time on the knee. Then she felt around for the fallen shirt, put it back in the box, and got up, pushing her long blonde hair behind her ears. Laurie and Mom relaxed and went back to what they were doing.

35

"Have you picked out something to give Dad?" Mom asked, wrapping a book in the paper she'd cut.

Steve twisted around to push the box back into the closet. "It's not right," he said. "Everybody else really bought something. If I gave him something from the box, it would be like a lie."

Mom and Laurie looked at each other. *What are they smiling about?*

Beth said, "I know something you could give Dad, that would be really from you."

"What?"

"A hug."

"That's dumb. It doesn't even cost anything."

"Doesn't it?" Laurie said.

"He'd really like it," Mom said.

"I don't know if I can," Steve said.

Mom said, "Just try."

"I can't," Steve said. His hands were shaking.

"Tell him how you feel some other way," Beth said.

Maybe— "That paper I use for the special classes I go to, that's mine, right?"

"Right," Mom said, nodding encouragingly.

Steve left the room.

Half an hour later he was back, brushing eraser crumbs off a sheet of lined paper. Mom, Laurie, and Beth had finished up and gone. It was the two dark-haired girls, Celia and Joy, in the room now, wrapping their presents in bright paper with fancy bows. Steve stopped at the sight of Celia. *Another girl. I don't know what to say to her, I don't feel like I know her. Not like Joy. Celia stood up for me in the playground, though.*

But it was Joy he looked at, willing her to speak. "What's that you've got, Steve?" Joy said.

"Present for Dad." Now that it was done, Steve was filled with doubt. *This is stupid. He won't like it. I'm stupid.*

"Can I see?" Joy asked.

She's safe. She won't hurt me. He handed her the paper and looked over her shoulder as she read it. DERE DAD I AM HAPPY TO BE HERE THANKS YUR FREND STEVE. It was taking her a long time. *She reads faster than me, she reads whole books for fun. She thinks it's stupid, and she doesn't want to say.*

But when Joy looked up at him, she said, "This is going to be his favorite present, Steve. Can I show this to Cissy?"

"I guess."

Celia looked up after only a few seconds. "Joy's right, Steve. Dad's going to like this better than anything."

"It's not pretty like the other ones," he said.

"We can fix that," Joy said. "There are some colored envelopes in the desk." She went over and started searching through a drawer.

Celia said, "I'll get a bow to tape on the outside."

They're helping me. Maybe it won't be too stupid.

Chapter 6.

Wednesday, August 21, 1957: 9:00 a.m.

Laurie

It was Laurie McAlister's day off from his summer job in Dad's office at the Navy Depot. He'd slept so late, by the time he came down the back stairs to the big, old-fashioned kitchen everyone had gone except Steve, who was eating cereal in that funny gobbly way of his, and Ruby, who was washing the breakfast dishes.

"Morning," Laurie said, grabbing a mug of coffee, a bowl and spoon, and the box of Wheaties and plopping down at the table. He closed his eyes for a quick silent blessing, crossed himself, then said, "Pass the milk, please, Steve? What are you two up to today?"

"Oh, President Eisenhower's invited me to the White House to give him some tips on running the country," Ruby said. "He figures if I can manage this zoo I could whip Congress into shape in no time."

Laurie laughed as he sliced a banana onto his cereal. "I bet you could, too. But what would we do without you? Better tell the president you have more important things to do."

Ruby snorted and started getting things out of the refrigerator.

"What about you, Steve?" Laurie asked. "What's your plan for today?" He watched confusion come over the kid's face, and then panic. *Damn. It's so hard to know what's going to throw him off kilter.* "You don't have to have a plan," he said gently. "I just meant, what do you feel like doing?"

"Listening to the radio," Steve said.

"You know what Mom said about that."

"I know, three hours a day. But I don't know what else to do. Everybody's busy. Celia and Beth are taking Joy to get school clothes and Mom and Dad have to work and Jamie and Rob both went to the, what do you call it, the tooth guy."

"The dentist, Dr. Johnston."

"Yeah, him."

"Well, I'm not busy. Want to spend some time with me?"

The kid looked like Laurie had suggested jumping off a cliff. His eyes got big and his breath hitched a little and he shrank back on the breakfast nook bench. *Jesus, time to put a stop to this before it gets worse.*

"It'll be fun," Laurie said. "It'll be a chance to hang out a little. I'll be going to college in another year, so we should spend time together while we can. It's really nice today; we'll take a walk in the woods out back. I know you don't like going outside alone, after what happened in the playground that day, but you don't have to stay cooped up in the house on a day like this, not while I'm around."

Steve was doing that if-I-don't-look-at-you-maybe-you-can't-see-me thing again, but Laurie decided to take advantage of the fact that the poor kid never thought he could say no to anything. "Good," he said, "that's settled." He got up to bring his empty cereal bowl and mug to the sink. "Ok if I fix us a picnic lunch?" he asked Ruby.

"And what's wrong with the one I just made you?" she said, popping two apples into an already bulging brown paper bag.

"You're the best," Laurie said, kissing the top of her gray head.

"Yeah, that's what the president said, too."

Laurie took a canteen from a hook by the door and filled it at the tap. He turned, screwing the top on. "Ok, buddy, ready to go?"

Steve didn't say anything, he just slid out from the table and stood there like he was waiting for instructions. Laurie's eyes met Ruby's over the top of Steve's head. She gave him an encouraging smile. Laurie suppressed a sigh. *It's going to be a long day.*

One good thing about spending time with an unsocialized abused kid, Laurie reflected two hours later, *is that you don't have to use energy making conversation.* Steve hadn't said above a dozen words since they'd walked down the broad lawn behind the house and into the woods that sloped up toward South Mountain.

Steve seemed to like being under the trees more than out in the open, but Laurie thought being outside so long was starting to make him nervous. He was lagging behind some, too. *Maybe he's had enough walking for a while.* "Let's take a break," Laurie said, perching on a fallen hemlock. Steve sat at a little distance from him, letting himself down gingerly and starting to tap his fingers on the trunk between them. *He's always tapping on things. It's not because he's nervous that I'm sitting by him. Or is it?*

Laurie took a swig from his canteen and passed it to the kid. Steve stared at the mouth of it for a long moment, then started wiping it with the hem of his t-shirt, rubbing and rubbing at it. *Oh, great. Here we go.*

"I don't have cooties," Laurie said, more sharply than he'd intended.

The kid looked startled. "I-I always—" he stammered, "B-bert said never— I mean, it's got germs, right? It's not because you're a n-n-n—"

Well, this is getting to the point with a vengeance. "Say it, Steve," Laurie said harshly. "Say the word and get it over with." Steve started crying, but Laurie was implacable. "Say it!"

"N-n-nigger," he whispered.

He'd asked for it, but it still made Laurie feel like acid had been poured over the top of his head. He forced himself to breathe, and to unclench his fists.

Steve slid off the log and crouched on the ground with his knees up and his arms over his head, sobbing. *Oh, Christ. Now look at him.* It was such a pathetic sight, Laurie had to move. He knelt next to Steve and gathered him into his arms.

"Oh, sweetheart, it's all right, shhh, don't cry."

Steve heaved himself backward and punched Laurie on the jaw. Laurie swung his head back so the fist just grazed across it, but it stung in more ways than one. *Easy now, he's like a squirrel in a trap,* he reminded himself, watching Steve pull back and curl up, nursing his knuckles.

Laurie let go but didn't move away. "Sorry, buddy, I guess it's too soon for that, isn't it? I didn't mean to upset you. It hurts to hit someone, doesn't it? You should put some ice on that when we get back."

Steve went very still. "Aren't you mad?" he said.

"Don't ever lie to him," Mom had said. *"He was lied to for years; he has to know we'll tell him the truth. And he doesn't understand any emotions but fear and anger. We have to help him learn how normal people feel."* When she'd said it, it had sounded easy.

Laurie thought a minute about what he needed to say. "Yes, I am mad," he said slowly. "And my feelings are hurt. And hearing that word always scares me a little, too. But—"

Steve pulled farther away to look at him. "You're scared of me?"

"Not scared of you, scared of what makes you want to hit out at anyone who comes close. Scared of the hate that uses the word you said. Not mad at you, either, exactly. Mad at the world, mad at the man who taught you that word, mad at him because he was a monster who made you so afraid to say the wrong thing, who mixed up love and violence in your head. Do you get what I mean?"

"Not really. You don't talk like a kid, you talk like—like Dad."

Laurie smiled and shifted around so he was sitting next to Steve in the cushion of hemlock needles on the ground. "It's because I'm the oldest, I guess. I don't mean to be uptight. Let me try to explain. There was something that happened a few months ago. A man named Willie Edwards—"

"He drowned in the Alabama River. His wife says it was men from something called the KKK who made him jump off the bridge, but the police say there's no way to tell how he died."

Laurie was stunned. *Joy said this kid didn't even know how to lick an ice cream cone, but he knows all about Willie Edwards? Oh, wait—* "You heard about it on your radio?" Steve nodded. "Do you remember hearing about Emmett Till?" Steve thought for a minute, then shook his head. "He was just a little older than you, fourteen years old, when the same kind of people killed him in Mississippi a couple of years ago. And he and Willie Edwards and a lot of others have been murdered for the same so-called crime: they supposedly said something fresh to a white woman, and they had black skin."

Steve shrugged. The notion of people being killed for no good reason didn't come as a surprise to him. But there was something he did evidently find odd. "Your skin's not black, not really."

"You're right about that, just like your skin's not really white. It's a way of speaking. What we say is important, the words we use. But that doesn't mean I'm going to hate you for using the wrong word once in a while."

"I don't know the right word."

"You could say 'Negro'; some people like 'black' or even 'colored' better. But I'd rather you didn't use any word about my skin when you talked about me. I'd rather you just called me Laurie, and when you think about me, think 'brother.'"

"Can I touch you?"

"What?" *Surely the kid didn't mean—*

"There," Steve said, pointing at Laurie's hand, at his palm.

Understanding dawned. "Oh. Oh, sure, I guess so." Laurie held his hand out palm up and sat patiently as Steve's fingers traced the brown lines incised in the pinkish flesh. "It doesn't rub off," Laurie said.

"—Your hair?"

Laurie sighed. "Ok." He bent his head.

"It's soft," the boy said wonderingly. "I thought it would be... not soft."

"Look, Steve—"

The searching hands retreated immediately. "Sorry, I'm sorry, that was too much, wasn't it?"

"No, not too much. Just—enough, for now anyway."

"You're mad again?"

"No, I'm not mad. You know what I am? I'm hungry. It's a little early for lunch, but what do you say we get into that bag Ruby packed for us?"

There was no conversation as the waxed paper crackled off their sandwiches and the apples crunched in their jaws. No conversation to speak of on the long walk home, either. But as they drew in sight of the house, Steve shyly stepped closer to Laurie so they came home almost touching.

Chapter 7.

Wednesday, August 21, 1957: 12:15 p.m.

Jamie

Jamie McAlister sat in the bedroom window seat looking down on the back lawn as Laurie and Steve walked up to the house side by side, arms lightly brushing together. "Typical," he said aloud with a sneer. But he couldn't stop watching.

And what's that about, Hymie? he said to himself. He always called himself by his old name in his head—the name he had before he became a McAlister, an American, a ghost: when he was still Chaim Metzger, the rabbi's son. *You know they'd all love it if you'd let them get close to you. And so would you.*

He rubbed his jaw where the Novocaine was finally wearing off. What was he thinking? *Jedem das seine,* he reminded himself, seeing the sign on the iron gate in his mind, right where it always was. *You get what you deserve.*

He got up with a grimace and started sorting through his books for the coming term. Time to buckle down if he was going to get into MIT next year—a year early, but he was ready to get serious. He was halfway through the pile on his dresser when the door opened. Steve stopped in the doorway, the way he always did when he found Jamie already in their bedroom.

"Well? Are you waiting for an invitation? Come in and hide if you want. Quick, before somebody tries to be nice to you again."

Steve slid past him with a secretive sidelong glare and climbed onto his bed on the far side of the room. He curled up with his back to Jamie.

After a minute Jamie heard a soft sniffle. "God, kid," he growled, "you leak like a sieve."

There was a silence, then Steve said, "I don't know what that means."

Jamie gritted his teeth. "It means you cry any time somebody looks at you cross-eyed. What's the matter with you?"

"You know."

"Oh, yeah, poor little Steve and his poor little life. I forgot for a minute, you're the only one who's ever suffered."

"I hate you."

"I hate you back."

Steve rolled over to look at him. His eyes were narrowed, his face flushed. "I could kill you," he said softly.

"I know you could." Jamie's voice was matter-of-fact.

Steve sat up. "You think it's a joke?"

Jamie came around his own bed to sit on the edge facing Steve and pushed his glasses into place with a knuckle. "I know it's not."

"Why are you so mean to me?"

Jamie sighed. "A lot of reasons, none of them having anything to do with you."

"You're weird."

"Weirder than you know."

Steve pounded his fist on the pillow. "Would you just talk straight to me? I'm not smart like you."

"You're smart enough. You just don't know anything."

"Like what should I know?"

Holding his gaze on Steve, Jamie slowly unbuttoned his cuff and rolled up his left sleeve. He held his arm out, and Steve looked down at the six numerals tattooed there. "What do they mean?" Steve asked.

"They mean I'm a Jew," Jamie said.

"That's, like, a religion, right? The reason you don't make that cross thing on yourself when we say the prayer before dinner, like Mom and Dad and them do? Why do they make you put numbers on yourself in your religion?"

"Not them. The people who killed us."

"You're not dead."

"Really? Look who knows so much all of a sudden."

Steve's face scrunched up. "What are you talking about? You're saying you're—dead?"

"Maybe, maybe not."

Steve's hand went up to cover his mouth and he looked at Jamie's arm in sudden comprehension. "Are there more?" he asked.

Jamie's fingers started to move down the front of his lightweight summer shirt, undoing the buttons. This was a first. He and Steve ordinarily undressed alone in the bathroom their room shared with Rob and Laurie's room. He slipped the shirt off.

Steve gasped, then put out a shaky finger. He stopped, looking questioningly at Jamie; Jamie leaned forward so Steve could reach.

The younger boy's finger brushed across the shiny pink rope of scar that ran from Jamie's shoulder to his clavicle. "A burning beam fell on me," Jamie said.

51

"When they murdered my parents." *Tati, clutching the Torah scroll in the flames as* Mamme *screamed in* the *Hebrew* Jamie hardly knew except for prayers, *'Run and hide, Hymeleh. Don't let them catch you. Hide, hide!'*

"This?" Steve pointed at the hard reddish lump on the other side of Jamie's chest.

The stifling dark, the dust sifting into my nose as the heavy boots tromped overhead, clenching to keep from sneezing, from weeping, from breathing, from crying out as each footfall pressed the piercing pain into my chest. Then the silence and the hunger and the fear, waiting and listening in my own filth until the boards were ripped up and the brutal light blinded me. "Nail in the floor," he said.

Steve's finger moved to the silvery purplish channels running up Jamie's stomach into his dark chest hair. "Stretch marks, from when I had food again." *The American GI vomiting beside me, the delicious chocolate smell of the vomit.*

Steve got up and walked around to see Jamie's back, with the white wheals striping it. "Riding crop," Jamie said. *The* Blockführer, *the day before the Allies came, screaming like a demon, 'Die, die, Jew piglet!' Shaking for hours after the skeletal hands of the other inmates hustled me back into the barracks.*

Steve came back to stand in front of him. His thin face was pale even for him; his hair and eyebrows were almost white. *He looks like he's halfway to disappearing completely,* Jamie thought. *And his knuckles are red and swollen. What's that about?*

Steve grasped the hem of his long-sleeved t-shirt and pulled it over his head. He turned slowly and Jamie catalogued the marks on his skinny torso in silence. Cigarette burns dotting his arms and chest. Knife marks in long white ridges. Whip wheals, of course, curving around his ribs and disappearing into the waist of his jeans. A scattering of pinpoint marks—a belt buckle, maybe. A place on his upper arm where a hollow the size of a fist interrupted the swell of muscle and the skin covered nothing but bone. *God.*

Steve watched his face, then said, "You never cry, do you?"

"Only in my sleep sometimes. There's no crying in hiding. You don't want to be noticed."

"Bert liked it when I cried. He wouldn't stop till I did. Sometimes he wouldn't stop even then, but I always had to cry."

"Do you want me to say I'm sorry?"

Steve sat back on the bed. "No. You're the only one who isn't nice to me. I like that."

Jamie nodded. "Sometimes it feels like they're smothering you, doesn't it? Or like it can't be true, all that soft talk. And the touching, like they can't keep their hands off you." Steve was looking at him wide-eyed. Jamie went on, "It is true, though, and they do mean it, and it's good for us. You know that, right? We need to try to let them."

"I don't hate you really."

"Right. I don't hate you, either. Get your shirt on," Jamie said, putting on his own. "I have something to show you."

He led Steve out of the room, down the hall, up the stairs to the sunny music room, through the low door into the stuffy gloom of the attic. He went to one of the cabinets under the eaves, opened the door, and stood back.

Steve crouched down to peer in. Jamie knew what he'd be seeing: the sleeping bag, the battery lantern, the wind-up clock, the thermos of water. Steve craned back to look up at him. "You hide here?"

"Yes. When I can't take it any more. When I have to be alone." They were both whispering.

"Do they know about it?"

"Mom and Dad know I have a place. I had to tell them, because they kept looking for me. But they don't know where it is."

"Why did you show it to me?"

Because you're my brother. Because I love you. "You can use it, if you want."

Steve wiped tears off his face with his sleeve. "Sorry," he said. "I'll try not to, uh, leak around you. I—thank you."

"It's ok. You can only use it for an hour at a time, and you can't lock it or block it so that no one can get in. That's the deal I made with them. And no food, so there won't be bugs."

"Can I bring my radio? I could run it on the battery for a while up here."

"Don't see why not. Keep it low, or they'll hear where you are." Steve nodded. Jamie turned away from the gratitude in his face. "Let's go find Mom; she's working at home this afternoon, and they should know you're going to be using it."

They went down the narrow staircase from the music room in single file, then down the wide front staircase to the ground floor side by side, not touching. Jamie gave a single knock on the study door and opened it. Mom was sitting at one of the desks. Her face lit with a big smile as they came in. *She always smiles. You'd think she didn't know what the world is like.*

"Tell her," Jamie said.

"Uh, Jamie showed me his place. His special place. He said I could use it. I know about not locking it and not staying more than an hour and all that. Is it ok if I bring my radio there?"

"Yes, if you keep to our agreement about not listening more than three hours a day."

Steve was shifting from foot to foot. Jamie knew the feeling. "Can I go there now?"

"Yes, all right, sweetie," Mom said. The kid disappeared like he was shot from a gun. Mom smiled at Jamie. "That was very well done, son."

He stood rigid. "The kid didn't tell you what led up to it. I said—awful things to him. I said things to hurt him on purpose. And I never said I was sorry."

Mom's smile got a little watery but it didn't go away. "Of course you did, my darling."

Chapter 8.

Monday, September 2, 1957: 11:00 a.m.

Steve

S teve lay in the attic cabinet listening to the rain on the roof inches above his face. He could also hear Robbie playing guitar in the music room next door. He had already listened to his three hours of radio, two in his room and one on the battery up here, but the thought of starting school tomorrow had kept him from relaxing. It was hot here, but it felt safe.

I can't do it, he thought. *All those strangers. And I'm so far behind, they'll laugh at me. Maybe those tough guys will be there and they'll try to hurt me.*

He turned on his side and drummed his fingers on the blanket under him, his blue blanket from The Room, looking almost black in the light of the battery lantern. But no music came into his head this time.

Yesterday he'd felt so scared about going to school, he'd let Mom put her arms around him. *She felt so soft, softer than my blanket. It felt safe, like being here.* He'd buried his face in that softness, sitting on the long couch in the living room, and it had made him think about some other softness, a long time ago. *Lovey.*

The clock near his head said 11:00. His hour was up. He unlatched the cabinet door and slid out onto the attic floor, pulling the big radio awkwardly behind him. It felt much cooler out here, but the shadowy gloom under the rafters was scary. He turned off the battery lantern and carefully hooked the cabinet closed again. He tiptoed across to the low door that led into the music room and sat on the floor with his back to it. He couldn't leave with Rob out there, or Robbie'd figure out where the hiding place was. So he just listened to the music.

After a while he heard Laurie's voice from the stairs. "Robbie, Ruby says we have to do a better job on our room. No comic books under your nightstand, and we have to clear out the junk under the beds."

"Is she still on that kick?" Robbie grumbled. His feet thumped down the stairs.

Steve waited another minute and then came through into the music room. Rob's guitar was sitting on a chair. He stopped beside it, set the radio on the floor, and reached a finger to one of the strings. *Twang.* He snatched his hand back. *I'll get in trouble.* He stood frozen for a minute, but when there was no outraged call from downstairs he tried it again, then another string.

Each one makes a different sound, but they don't make a tune. He brought his other hand up and pressed down on the neck the way he'd seen Robbie do. This time when he flicked a string, there was nothing but a buzzing sound. *Did I break it?* Panicked, he leaned forward and tried again. This time he got a note. *It's because I leaned on it. You have to press harder.* He slid his finger farther along the neck, making a squeaking sound, and pulled the string again. A different note.

He was too nervous to pick the guitar up off the chair, but he stood there, trying different strings and different points on the neck, till Celia called up the stairs and said it was time for lunch. He raised his head, surprised. *I've been here all that time, and didn't worry once about school?*

On the thought, his fears came pouring back. He dragged his feet going down the back stairs to the kitchen. Ruby had made tuna fish pies for lunch, especially for Steve so he could taste what they were like hot. It was hard to swallow anything, though.

After lunch he went up to his room and started going over his school supplies. He'd already checked them ten times or more, but he thought if he had everything perfect maybe things would go well tomorrow. *I should have five books, one for each class.*

Jamie came in while he was checking his pencils. "You sharpened them all?" he said.

"I want to be ready," Steve said.

Jamie stood looking down at him, eyes hooded behind his glasses. "I cleared out this desk for you," he said finally. "I'll use the one in the spare room."

"Thanks," Steve said.

"It's quieter in there anyway."

He doesn't like me thanking him, but at the same time he sort of does. Steve kept looking at Jamie's face till the older boy turned away. "Get your books out of the middle of the floor," he said. "Somebody could trip on them."

"Ok," Steve said. "Sorry."

"You'll do fine," Jamie said, not looking at him. "You're smart." He left the room.

Steve lined all his pencils up in their new case so the sharpened points were exactly even. Then he started counting his books again.

They had franks and beans and corn on the cob and pickled beets on the screened porch that night. The rain had stopped, but everything was still dripping. "Some Labor Day picnic," Joy grumbled.

"Look on the bright side," Celia said. "Coconut cake for dessert. That'll give us a good send-off for school."

Steve's stomach felt like somebody was poking it with a stick from the inside. *Wish they'd quit talking about school.*

He looked up to see Dad watching him. "How about some music after dinner?" Dad said to the rest of the table. "Rob bring your guitar, and we can all sing for a while. It is a holiday, after all."

"Can we sing something besides those dopey songs you and Mom and Ruby like, though?" Joy said.

Dad gave her a look. *Oh, no, she made him mad,* Steve thought. *Now what's going to happen?* But Dad only said, "Perhaps you'd like to rephrase that, young lady?"

Joy's cheeks got red. "Sorry, sir," she said. "I just meant, could we please sing some new songs this time?"

"Seems like a reasonable request," Dad said. "Why don't you and Robbie teach us some later? Steve, too, if he feels like it."

The others started talking again, and no one seemed to notice Steve was shaking. But Joy squeezed his hand as they left the table.

That night the family sat for hours singing—folk songs, show tunes, pop hits from the past twenty years, spirituals, even rock and roll. Steve listened to the music and watched the faces. He didn't join in the singing; he didn't feel like there were any songs inside him that would be good enough. But his heart seemed to get big in his chest and his stomach calmed. *Someday I'll sing, too,* he thought. *Someday I'll have a song.*

Still, that night he waited till Jamie was asleep, sneaked into their bathroom, and scrubbed tiles till his fingers were raw.

Chapter 9.

Tuesday, September 3, 1957: 3:45 p.m.

Celia

Cecilia McAlister found herself hurrying the last few yards up the front walk to the house. She loved her house, the big gracious look of it, the sense that it had been there for generations and would be for generations more, the way it felt cool in summer and warm in winter. She loved the stillness of the upper floors on a snowy afternoon. She loved the comforting hive-like hum when everyone was home on a July evening and all the windows were open and the racket of the crickets and the peepers outside mingled with the twanging of Robbie's guitar from the music room on the third floor and the competing murmur from Steve's radio in his room on the second floor and the companionable voices of the adults in the screened porch downstairs.

She liked school, and she was a good student, but the first day of the year, with lockers clanging and raucous shouting in the echoing halls, always took a little getting used to. Now she blew a breath of relief as she stepped in the front door and stood in the spacious hall, sensing the house around her.

Quiet: I must be the first one home. She dropped her books on the hall table, ran her hands through her thick, dark bob, and followed her nose through the living room and dining room to the kitchen, where a pot roast simmered in a huge dutch oven. Ruby was nowhere in sight, but she'd left a bowl of pears, a covered cheese dish, and a basket of crackers on the table. Celia piled a sampling onto a paper napkin and started up the back stairs, munching as she went.

Coming into the bedroom she shared with Joy, she pitched her pear core wrapped in the now-empty napkin into the wastebasket, kicked off her flats, and stripped off her calf-length straight plaid skirt and green sweater set. *Wearing that was a mistake. I always think it's going to be cool just because school has started. Good one, Celia, starting sophomore year in a sweat. So attractive.* She pulled on jeans rolled to the knee and a worn checkered shirt that used to be Laurie's, pushed her feet into loafers, and started toward the bathroom between this room and Beth's to toss her discarded slip into the hamper.

She stopped outside the door. *What is that scritching sound? Joy has a scout meeting, can't be her. Is Beth home from Paoli, without waiting for the weekend? Something must be wrong for her to be back from school already—* "Bethie? Are you in there?" The sound stopped. A little nervously, Celia pushed the bathroom door open.

"Steve! What are you doing in here?"

Steve jumped and wheeled to face her, hiding something behind his back. "Sorry," she said. "I didn't mean to startle you, I was just surprised to see you in here. Is there something wrong with your bathroom?"

"It's already clean," Steve said. He brought his hand out from behind him. It was holding a toothbrush. Celia noticed that half the sink was scummed with a coating of suds.

"So you decided to clean the girls' bathroom? With that?"

"Is that wrong? It's what Bert always made me use, at night when he let me out of The Room."

"It's not wrong, exactly, it's just doing things the hard way. Where'd you get the toothbrush?"

Steve flushed. "I didn't take anybody else's, it's mine."

Geeze Louise. "You mean you're using the same brush you put in your mouth to clean the sink with?"

"I let the water run on it till it doesn't taste bad."

65

Don't let him see you're trying not to throw up. "Well, I think a sponge would be better. There are a couple under the sink. Here, I'll help you."

They scrubbed in comfortable silence for a while. Steve did a much better job than Celia usually bothered with, poking around the faucets and gouging out the crud lodged under the edge of the metal strip around the sink with his thumbnail. "You like to clean, don't you, Steve?"

"It makes me feel quiet inside. And when I was cleaning, I wasn't in The Room, so that was fun."

Fun. Criminey.

After a minute Steve said softly, face turned away from her, "And he usually didn't hurt me till after, so as long as I was cleaning it was ok."

Celia shivered and sat back on her heels. "Hey, Stevie, I think we've done a pretty good job in here. Let's go back in my room and listen to music or something. Oh, wait, put Beth's hairbrush back on the right-hand side of the sink, ok? Since she can't see, we have to be careful that all her stuff stays where she can find it when she's home on the weekends. Good, now let's quit."

He put the sponge down as though following orders and moved into the bedroom with her. He sat on Joy's bed, tapping on the chenille bedspread. Celia opened her record cabinet. "You like Johnny Mathis?"

"Sure. He's good."

She put the *Wonderful, Wonderful* LP on the turntable, flipped the record player switch, and set the needle on the first groove. The swooping strings of the intro to "Wild Is the Wind" filled the room, then Johnny's voice in deep-velvet mode. She tossed the empty sleeve next to Steve on the bed before dropping down on her own bed across from it.

He picked up the album cover and leaned back onto Joy's pillow, looking at the picture with interest. "I didn't know he was a n... a Negro. He doesn't sound like one."

"How does a Negro sound?" she asked, amused. "Like Laurie, for instance?"

"No, he doesn't, either. I meant like Chuck Berry or Jerry Lee Lewis."

"Lewis isn't, actually."

"No?"

"No, he's just poor and Southern, that's what you're hearing."

"So that's why Laurie doesn't sound that way? Or Ruby?" Steve shifted onto his stomach and looked over at Celia. "Is Ruby his real mom?"

"Mom is his real mom." *Careful, don't get crabby, he's just figuring things out.*

"You know what I mean."

Celia scrunched her mouth up. "I guess I do, and you're not the first person to think that about Laurie and Ruby. But his natural mother is dead, and so's his natural father. He's been a member of this family longer than I have, you know. He was abandoned when he was a baby, left outside the gate of Rolling Meadow where Mom had just started working, and Mom and Dad adopted him before I was born, while Dad was still on active duty before the war. Laurie's not just the oldest, he's the first."

"So he never knew his real parents?"

Let it go. "Not when he was little. When he was about my age, he started wondering about them. Mom got a policeman friend of hers to look into it, and they tracked down his mother and found out his father was dead. The mother was very sick; she died in this house a few weeks later."

Celia thought for a minute, then said, "It's a funny thing—she was happy to see Laurie and find out things were good with him, and of course it meant a lot to Laurie to know she gave him up hoping he'd have a better life, but it was Mom she really wanted to spend time with. It's like, that little baby she gave away was gone forever, but she and Mom would spend hours looking at photo albums and talking about him. Laurie as a big boy was never completely real to her, I think."

Celia stopped talking again, remembering the shy little black woman coughing out her last breaths in the bigger guest room, then went on, "And Ruby's been here forever, too. She helped raise Dad and Uncle Kevin."

The record was onto "No Love" by now, Mathis's voice in its higher register. They listened for a while, then Steve said, "But you're their real kid. You and Robbie, and I guess Beth."

"We're all their real kids, Steve. If you really have to know, Robbie and Beth are biologically brother and sister. Mom found them when they got sent to Rolling Meadow because they were living on the street in Harrisburg and Robbie was stealing food for them. He was only six, so he didn't do that great a job of getting away with it, but he had been doing it for a while when they caught him. Nobody knows where their original parents went, or why the kids were on the street. He's my age, sixteen now, and Beth's a year younger. Anyway, Joy and I are the only ones who were born into this family."

"Doesn't it make you mad, having all us freaks pushing in on your family?"

"You are my family, Stevie, I promise you. Like I said, it's been this way as long as I remember. We're like that quilt on Mom and Dad's bed, you know, the one with all the different colored squares? It's called a patchwork quilt, and if it didn't have all those patterns and designs in it, it wouldn't be so beautiful."

Celia rolled over and stared at the ceiling, considering. "Sometimes I wish things were easier, more like what people call normal, but mostly I feel luckier than my friends. Some of them have parents who drink too much, or are mean to them, or are never around."

She swung around to look at Steve again. "I don't mean our parents are perfect; they aggravate me a lot sometimes."

"How do they aggravate you?"

Celia fell onto her back and idly raised a leg, turning her foot in the air as she thought. "Well," she said, "they kind of focus on us more than most parents do. Like, a couple of weeks ago I had a fight with my friend Barbara. It was a dumb thing; it would just have blown over in a couple of days." She let her leg drop back to the bed. "But Mom caught on I was upset the minute it happened, and wanted to talk about how I felt about it, and Barbara, and life in general. And when I tried to brush her off she got Dad in on it, and he started in about strategy and tactics for getting things back on an even keel. It was just too much, them poking in my head and my life that way."

"So they aggravate you because they care about you too much?"

Celia leaned up on an elbow to gape at him. "Whoa, Steve, when did you get so sharp?" She shook her head, smiling. "You're right, I know. I guess that's just one disadvantage to this patchwork family—with so many kids, all with different backgrounds and problems, they're constantly on the watch for trouble. But they know how to listen. We can say anything to them, good or bad. And we can always show each other how we feel."

"Jamie says you can't keep your hands off each other. Not like him and me."

"That's true. We like to touch; nobody I know kisses and hugs their family the way we do. But you and Jamie are a little different, we get that. You two have had the hardest times of any of us. Dad found Jamie in an orphanage in France after the war when he was only five. He'd been in a horrible place called Buchenwald. I remember when he came here. He was so skinny! Skinnier than you, and scareder, and that's saying a lot. You've got a lot to deal with. But Mom especially thinks it's important for us to be open with our feelings, more than most people are. It helps hold us together."

As they talked, Celia could hear the front door opening and closing, and people talking, and feet on the stairs; the others were coming home.

The bedroom door banged open and Joy came bouncing in, her Girl Scout neckerchief pulled away from her throat and a light sheen of sweat on her forehead. "Gosh, it's good to be here in the coolth," she said. "Hey, Cissy. Hi, Steve. How'd your first day of school go? I wish we had lunch in the same period." She toed off her black-and-white bubble shoes, shoved him over on her bed, and flopped down next to him without ceremony, brushing her damp, straight, brown hair out of her eyes.

"It was ok, I guess. Better than the classes at Rolling Meadow before I came here. It was scary being around so many other people, so I pretended they were voices on the radio. My special class is a bunch of morons, but the teacher's nice."

"Mom says you're making fabulous progress," Celia said. "You'll be out of that class soon enough. You shouldn't call them morons, though."

Steve sighed. "I can't keep track of all the things I'm not supposed to say."

Joy nudged him in the ribs. "We'll keep hassling you about it, don't worry." Steve, daring greatly, nudged her back. *He really is making fabulous progress,* Celia thought.

The first side of the Mathis album came to an end. "How about some Pat Boone?" Joy said.

Celia and Steve both shuddered. "Pat Boone is crap," Steve said. "Do you have any Fats Domino?"

"Sorry, I don't," Celia said.

"Too bad. He's the real stuff."

Joy said, "You know everything, huh?"

"I know more than you about music, anyway," Steve said. Then an odd look came over his face. "This is the first time I ever told anybody I knew more than them about anything!"

Celia leaned over and kissed his forehead before he could shrink away, then she and Joy started tickling him and he tickled back till they all fell in a giggling heap. *Wow,* Celia thought. *Something's really happening here.*

Chapter 10.

Thursday, October 3, 1957: 4:30 p.m.

Joy

The temperature had dropped ten degrees since yesterday; finally it felt like fall. Joy was happy to be in the warm house, playing an afternoon game of Monopoly on the dining room table with Steve and Robbie and Rob's new girlfriend, Nancy.

Steve had picked up on the way money works amazingly fast, considering he'd never touched any before about six months ago. *It's like he sees the numbers in his mind. He can already make change faster than I can. Too bad he can't see words that way.*

Steve rolled and landed on Chance. "Ooh, let me," Joy said, snatching the orange card from him and acting like she was just being bratty and grabby. She hadn't liked the way Nancy looked at Steve last time he'd stumbled through reading a Community Chest card. "'Get Out of Jail Free'! Keep this with your property cards, Stevie, so you can use it when you need it."

Ruby came in with a basket of Ritz crackers and a bowl of onion dip. "There's bug juice in the fridge if you're thirsty," she said.

"Thanks, Ruby," Joy and Rob said, digging in and passing the snack to Steve and Nancy.

"Don't forget to clear this stuff up when you're finished."

"Yes, ma'am."

"Ruby, my jewel," Robbie added as she turned to leave, "you didn't forget that tomorrow's my birthday, did you?"

Ruby stopped and cocked her head. "Don't I always forget your birthday?" she said. "It's not like I would ever make, say, a yellow cake with chocolate icing just for you, is it?"

Robbie gave a playful poke at her midriff. "Just checking," he said. She poked him back and went into the kitchen again. "Hey, Jo-Jo, you going to roll the dice any time this year?" he said.

"Don't call me that," Joy snapped, and promptly rolled herself onto Go Directly to Jail.

That was the start of a string of bad luck. Before long, all Joy's yellow and maroon properties were mortgaged. Steve had houses on Boardwalk and Park Place plus all the railroads and both utilities, Nancy was holding her own on the red properties and the green ones, but Robbie was raking in the cash with his low-rent-property hotels on the whole purple and light blue side past Go.

"Good evenink, velcome to ze castle of Count Dracula," he said in a Bela Lugosi accent, theatrically rubbing his hands as Joy landed on Baltic Avenue. "Zat vill be four hundred and fifty simoleons, my little chickadee."

"I think you're getting your imitations mixed up," she said, gloomily handing over her $200 from passing Go and starting to liquidate her holdings.

Laurie pushed open the door from the living room. "Game Two of the Series is about to start," he said. "Don't you guys want to see if Milwaukee finally breaks the New York monopoly?"

"Nah, baseball's boring," Robbie said.

"Baseball's ballet, you philistine," Laurie said.

"Ballet's not my thing, either, and my name ain't Phil. Yuk, yuk, yuk," Rob cackled at his own sophomoric humor. "Basketball, now there's a game, brother o' mine. People actually, you know, moving their duffs and doing things to the ball. Baseball's just standing around on one foot most of the time. Besides, I'm in the middle of creaming this sorry crew and becoming Master of the Universe."

"I'll come and watch," Joy said. "I've lost anyway." Steve gave her a sideways look. *He doesn't want me to go. He's nervous with Nancy here.* She sank back into her seat. "Uh, on second thought, maybe I'll stay here. Just to make sure Robbie doesn't cheat."

Rob's indignant squawk crossed Laurie's "Suit yourself," as he disappeared.

Joy dragged her chair closer to Steve's. "I'll look over your shoulder," she said.

"Is that all right, if she helps me?" Steve asked Robbie.

"Honey, you're the one who's still in the game," Rob pointed out.

Nancy stifled a snigger. "Something funny?" Joy asked. *I don't think I like her.*

Nancy's fair skin flushed till her face was almost as red as her hair. "Sorry, it's just—I never heard a boy call another boy 'honey' before," she said.

"That's nothing," Rob said calmly, rolling the dice and moving onto one of his own properties. "That big galoot who just left calls us all 'sweetheart'."

"And you've got a brother who's a Negro, speaking of him," Nancy went on, picking the dice up but not rolling right away. "And another brother who's thirteen and can hardly read. And you treat the maid like she's your grandmother. At school you seem, like, normal. Here, it's—I don't know, weird."

Nobody said anything for a minute. *Robbie looks like he doesn't like her much at the moment, either.*

Then Steve spoke up. "I know what you mean," he said. "Seems weird to me, too. Nice, though."

"Yeah, it is," Nancy agreed, and they smiled across the table as she finally rolled. Rob and Joy shrugged at each other and the awkward moment passed.

Two hours later, they were sitting in the same places but the rest of the family was there, eating dinner. Dad and Laurie were hashing over the Milwaukee Braves' unexpected win that day. Celia and Nancy were deep in the pros and cons of the new chemise dresses. Jamie, Mom, and Ruby were discussing the high school in Little Rock, Arkansas and whether President Eisenhower's having sent the National Guard in to force them to accept Negro kids alongside white ones would help or hurt the next racial desegregation effort. Rob was pretending to snag the garlic bread off Beth's plate but she somehow managed to slap his hand away every time. *Weird but nice,* Joy thought contentedly.

She glanced over at Steve. He was struggling with his spaghetti, trying to get the slippery strands into his mouth before they slithered off his fork. Joy nudged him to get his attention, then slowly twirled her pasta around her fork into a nice compact mouthful. He copied her immediately.

Dessert was Ruby's home-canned peaches with ginger. Steve didn't have any trouble with those, and Joy noticed he was learning not to put his face down by the plate and shovel the food in. After a few bites, though, he stopped eating and dropped his spoon. His face went blank, his eyes closed. *What's happened?* Cautiously, Joy whispered, "Are you ok, Stevie?"

Mom's unerring radar kicked in; she stopped in the middle of a sentence and turned to look at Steve, concern furrowing her brow. But he looked up almost right away. "I had this before," he said softly. Then he said it again, louder. Everybody stopped talking. Steve turned to Joy as if there was no one else at the table. "It didn't have this yellow powdery stuff that sort of stings your tongue on it," he said. "But I ate this before, a long time ago. I remember."

"That's wonderful, darling," Mom said.

"Radioactive cool, honey," Rob said. Nancy smiled at Rob, then at Steve.

Maybe I do like her, after all.

Chapter 11.

Tuesday, November 5, 1957: 7:30 p.m.

Beth

It was Beth McAlister's birthday, Sweet Sixteen. Dad had made the two-hour drive to Paoli to pick her up at Bolotin, the school for the blind she boarded at during the week, so she could be with the family tonight.

Now she could feel the heat from the candles as Ruby put the cake in front of her after dinner. She leaned forward carefully, holding her long ponytail back behind her shoulder, and blew till the applause of the family told her she'd gotten them all. *What shall I wish? I wish that next time I have a birthday cake, I also have a boyfriend.*

Mom said, "Knife's on your right, Bethie, server to the left of the cake. Plates at ten o'clock."

She moved her fingers along the edge of the cake platter to find the corner. *Always sheet cakes in this family;*

too many people for a round one. "Who wants a corner piece?"

"Me, please," Robbie called, as she knew he would. She passed the top plate in his direction.

She cut and handed out a few more pieces, then skimmed her hand over the top of the cake. "Oh, here's a rose," she said. "This piece is for Mom. Steve, what kind of cake do you like, end piece? Center? Extra frosting?"

Steve's voice came from across the table. "I don't know. I never had cake before Dad's birthday this summer, and Laurie's and Rob's after that. They were all different. Anything's good, I guess."

That's the most I've ever heard him say at one time. "Well, I'll just give you the next one in line, so you'll have another example to keep in mind for next time." She cut it and passed it across to him, smiling. *Don't want him to think that's another chore or something.*

The others had started to talk among themselves, so she kept pitching her voice to Steve as she pushed the cake platter toward the middle of the table and began to eat her own piece. "How's school going?"

"It's ok. I still don't like being around all those strangers. At least I got out of that mo—uh, that special class. But I'm way behind everybody my age."

"I know just how you feel."

"You do?" Steve said.

"Sure. When I first came here, even though I was only five, I was still behind. The other kindergarten kids had all been read to by their parents, and most of them had at least felt Braille and knew what learning to read would be like. All I knew was how to hide when I heard voices and how to figure out whether something I touched might be good to eat."

"Really?" Steve said with his mouth full. He stopped long enough to swallow. "Did it take you a long time to learn?"

"Not too long. I really wanted to read, once I realized I could see the world in books."

"I don't think I'll ever like reading. I know I'll never be any good at it."

Don't lie to him. "Maybe not. Thirteen is pretty old to start; you may never feel really comfortable with it. But I think you're very smart—you can learn whatever you set your mind to. And if it's not reading, then you'll find something else you like to do and are good at."

"You think so?"

"I do." The others had all stopped talking to listen to their exchange.

Now Mom said, "The biggest job Steve has had this year is just learning to be around other people, not only us but strangers at school. He's doing a great job of that."

"I just pretend they're on the radio."

Everyone laughed but Beth. She smiled at him in a way she hoped got across that she knew it wasn't a joke. *Who knows. I probably made a face that looks like I have a stomachache.* She sighed and pushed her empty plate away. "Is everyone finished? Isn't it time for my piles of loot?"

"'Loot'?" Dad said. "Surely you weren't expecting presents on top of this marvelous caramel cake?"

"Ruby knows how much I appreciate her cake," Beth said, moving toward the living room. "She's off the hook. The rest of you owe me presents." The family laughed and patted her and playfully poked at her as they all crowded through the dining room door. Beth went to where she knew the big armchair would have been set like a throne in front of the fireplace.

The slight warmth of a slim body came close to her arm. "Can I sit by you?" Steve said under his breath. "It still makes me nervous to be around everybody when they're not eating or something. You don't scare me so much."

"Sure you can, baby," she whispered back. "I'm glad I don't scare you." She felt him settle at her feet, leaning against her legs.

"You're soft," he said. "It's nice. I never saw a girl while I was with Bert, so sometimes I feel like girls are weird. But I'm getting over it. Celia's a little bossy, but she was really nice to me the other day, and she helped me with those guys in the playground, too. And you weren't mad when I left that box out and tripped you, and after that I started noticing you were pretty easy to be around."

"Because I can't see?"

"Maybe. But it's more like you don't want me to change or be anything different. I mean, I know Mom and everybody are helping me, but around you I feel like I can just rest."

Beth reached down and stroked his cheek. "What about Joy? Are you getting used to her, too?"

"Joy's different. I was never scared around Joy. She's just a kid, like me."

"Hey," Robbie called. "Let's get this show on the road. Whatever you two are whispering about can wait till after Beth flips over the fabulously cool present I got her."

Someone started playing "Happy Birthday" on the baby grand piano in the corner. *A little heavy on the left hand—it's Celia.*

Steve said, "Can everybody in this family play something?"

"Pretty much. Mom and Dad had us all take lessons in grade school, just so we could learn about music. Some of us kept up with it more than others. Like Laurie, he took violin but after two years it still sounded like he was strangling a cat."

"Hey, I heard that," Laurie said. Beth, who'd known he was sitting in earshot, stuck her tongue out at him.

"Yeah," Joy said from the other side of Beth. "The poor violin was so goofed up by the experience, by the time I got to it, it sounded like strangling *two* cats."

"Just remember, Jo-Jo, I can run like the wind," Laurie retorted. "Don't think you can get away from me if I get mad."

"Ooh, I'm so scared, big man track star. But if you want to see everyone else run, just let the two of us play a duet." They both snickered.

"I wish I could make music," Steve said softly. "I hear it in my head, but I don't know how to make it come out."

Before Beth could respond, someone put a package into her lap; she smelled Mom's Tweed perfume.

"Here you are, angel girl," Mom said. "For your party with your friends this weekend, from Dad and me. God bless you."

Beth tore off the paper and opened the long, flat box. Her fingers met silk, soft and light as cobwebs. "A neck scarf," she said happily.

"There's more," Dad said. She felt along the box to a hard, cool circlet the size of a napkin ring.

"A slide for the scarf?" she guessed, fingering its carved whorls and a smoothly rounded bump in the middle.

"Yes," Mom said. "It's silver with a pink opal, and the scarf is rose-colored—they'll go with the french-cuff blouse you said you wanted to wear to the concert, along with the cuff links we gave you last Christmas and your taffeta skirt."

"Thank you, Mama, Daddy," she said, kissing them as they leaned over her.

Half an hour later, the little party had broken up. Celia and Robbie were playing "Heart and Soul" on the piano and giggling, Ruby was corralling Laurie and Joy to clear the table and help her with the dishes, Jamie had gone away to do homework and Mom and Dad to watch *Kraft Theater* on TV. Steve was wadding up the wrapping paper around her feet and stacking her gifts into a pile.

"Stevie," Beth said, "Thank you again for the record. I love Ella Fitzgerald. You know, I've been thinking about what you were saying, that you didn't enjoy reading. And also that you like music so much. Do you ever read poetry?"

"You mean like, 'Roses are red, violets are blue'? What does that have to do with music?"

"Well, there are more musical poems than that." *What can I give him? Oh, I know.* "Let's see if you like this one." Beth thought over the lines for a minute, then started to recite:

"'In Xanadu did Kubla Khan
A stately pleasure dome decree:
Where Alph, the sacred river, ran
Through caverns measureless to man
Down to a sunless sea...'"

As she pulled the poem out of her memory, Celia and Rob stopped playing to listen and Steve stopped rustling the paper. By the time she got to

"'A savage place! As holy and enchanted
As e'er beneath a waning moon was haunted
By woman wailing for her demon-lover!'"

the people clearing up had swung open the dining room door so they could hear.

When she finished with,

    "'For he on honey-dew hath fed,
And drunk the milk of Paradise,'" there was a
deep silence.

After a minute Steve took a breath. "I didn't know
it could be like that," he said. "I don't get what it's
really about, I don't know a lot of those words. But I
could hear the music."

Chapter 12.

Wednesday, December 25, 1957: 8:30 p.m.

Steve

Steve couldn't believe how much noise and light and confusion there was in the living room. He looked around from where he sat, on a small chair that was hardly ever used, by the opening to the front hall.

There was the tall tree in front of one bay window. Steve had heard of Christmas trees, but he'd never seen one. *Do they always have cookies and apples and other things to eat hanging from them, or is that just here?*

I know most people don't also have that candle thing in front of the other window. That's about Jamie's religion. Jamie's holiday had been going on all week, and now there were eight candles burning in the brass holder, plus a higher one in the middle.

The big room seemed even bigger than usual, somehow, with the decorations and the plates of goodies and unwrapped presents and empty red felt

Christmas stockings on every surface, even on the polished top of the baby grand piano. The air was warm and smelled of spices and pine. There seemed to be people everywhere he looked.

Robbie was sitting by the fireplace, the firelight making his blond hair shine as his head moved, playing Christmas songs on the guitar. *Wish I could do that.* Beth sat next to him, singing. Her hair was the same as Rob's except it flowed in waves down her back; her sightless eyes seemed to see something far away. *She looks like that doll thing on top of the tree, only she doesn't have wings.*

Laurie and Jamie were playing chess at a side table. As Steve looked, Laurie moved the tallest white piece, strong dark face intent on the board. Jamie was leaning back, away from the lamplight, looking at Laurie, his hawk nose raised and his black eyes narrowed behind his glasses, slight smile on his narrow lips. *They'll both be gone to college next year. I don't want things to change.*

Joy was sitting in Dad's lap on the other side of the fireplace, her long legs draped over the arm of the deep, soft chair. *Just like a little kid. But she's thirteen, like me. Wonder what he'd do if I—* Steve pushed the thought out of his head; it scared him.

Dad was reading out loud, a story with lots of words Steve didn't know but it seemed to be about Christmas and snow and kids and toys and food. "and still the dazzling sky-blue sheep are grazing in the red field under the rainbow-billed and pea-green birds," he read. *I can hear the music, but that's not enough right now,* he thought, trying and failing to make sense of it.

Mom and Celia sat on the floor near them. *You can see how alike they look, with their faces so close together.* They were listening to Dad's story while they wound up ribbons and put them in a box to save for next year's presents.

Steve had gotten one of those new pocket-sized transistor radios this morning. He wished he could take it up to the attic cabinet now and listen to it all by himself. *I don't know how to make music or play chess, I don't get that story, they don't need me to help with the ribbons.* But he'd promised Mom he'd stay with the family for the evening.

Someone came down the front stairs behind him and stepped into the room, standing next to Steve. It was that man they called Uncle Kevin, who'd arrived from Chicago a few days ago. He was dressed in black pants and a black sweater with a high neck, like a beatnik. It looked good with his blond hair, which was kind of long. *He looks like Dad, only smaller and younger. He's always laughing and joking and clowning around, though. Dad doesn't do that much. This afternoon when he started dancing in the middle of the living room, it was like he was in a movie or something. But when he stops, like now, he looks sad.*

Uncle Kevin looked at the room for a minute and then down at Steve. "Christmas around here can get to be a little much, can't it? And Hanukkah on top of it, this year. You look like you could use a break. Want to help me with the dishes?"

"Sure." *Finally, something I know how to do.*

He followed Uncle Kevin around the edge of the living room, through the empty dining room into the kitchen. The place was a wreck, with platters of leftover food all over the table and stacks of dirty dishes and glasses on the counter.

Steve started filling the sink with hot soapy water. Uncle Kevin pulled open a high cupboard and hauled down a big metal bowl. He piled leftover turkey and stuffing into it. Then he opened a drawer and took out a soft plastic thing with elastic around it that looked like a shower cap and put it over the bowl.

Uncle Kevin slid the turkey onto a refrigerator shelf and got out some smaller bowls from a lower cupboard to put the other leftovers in. "You know where everything is," Steve said, washing glasses and putting them in the rack to drain.

Uncle Kevin nodded at Steve. "I should. Ruby hasn't changed the way this kitchen is organized since I was a kid."

"Oh." Steve felt stupid. *Of course, he grew up here. He's Dad's brother.* "How come Ruby's not here, anyway? Doesn't she want to be with us at Christmas?"

"Sure she does. But she wants to be with her sister Pearl, too. She'll be back tomorrow."

"I never thought about her having family— besides, uh, us."

Uncle Kevin smiled like he knew Steve wasn't used to thinking of himself as part of a family. "I know what you mean. When I was little I thought she was my mother. Mama was sick for years, and she finally died, but Ruby was always there for Sean and me." He picked up a towel and started drying glasses. "Then when Sean ran off—"

What? "Dad ran away from home?"

Uncle Kevin's mouth pressed into a line and he kept polishing a glass that was already dry. "Yes, he did," he said. "He went away and joined the navy when he was seventeen."

"Why?"

"Our father beat him once too often."

Steve's head was spinning. *Dad knows how that feels?* "Did he beat you, too?"

93

Uncle Kevin finally put the glass away and picked up another one. Steve started in on the silverware, leaving the big carving knife untouched on the drain board. "Yes, he did," Uncle Kevin said, "but not as much as Sean. He never expected as much from me, it was Sean who was supposed to be the star athlete, the top student, the best in everything as long as it was something Father thought was worthwhile. After Sean left, though, and there was only me… Well, if I hadn't had Ruby to go to, I don't know what would have happened."

"What did happen?"

"Father dropped dead in front of me in the middle of a fight about whether I was going to go to art school. Turns out he had a brain tumor. Maybe that was part of why he couldn't control his temper." Uncle Kevin reached across Steve for the carving knife and washed and dried it himself without comment.

Steve lost track of his voice for a minute, then tuned in again. "I guess Father wasn't completely insensitive," Uncle Kevin was saying. "He at least had enough decency to leave Ruby some money. He must have realized how important she'd been to all of us. It wasn't enough to make her rich, but it did mean she didn't have to keep doing this kind of work if she didn't want to."

Steve slid a pile of dishes into the water and waited for them to soak a little, resting his wrists on the edge of the sink, thinking. Uncle Kevin stood by patiently. Steve asked, "What did you do?"

"I took my share of the inheritance and went to the Art Institute in Chicago. When I was finished studying there, I went to work in a studio and eventually opened my own gallery."

"I don't know what that means."

"Sorry. It means I paint pictures and put them and other people's artworks up for the public to see and buy if they want. The big still life in the dining room is mine—"

"The picture of the celery and cheese?"

"That's right, and the abstract over your parents' bed. I don't know if she's asked you in there yet, but Ruby has one in her sitting room, too."

"So Ruby just stayed here in the house by herself?"

"No, the house was closed up. Then Sean met Martha while he was stationed at the naval base in Philadelphia and she was a grad student in psychology at Penn. They got married and came back here. Ruby had gotten married, too, meanwhile, but her husband was killed in the attack on Pearl Harbor a couple of years later. He was a steward in the navy. So she moved back to help Martha—and Sean when he came back from overseas—raise Laurie and Celia and eventually the rest of you."

"What about Robbie? He's the same age as Celia."

"Yes, but he wasn't adopted till he was older. After the war, I think. You should really ask your folks about the details of your family history. I wasn't around during those years, so I'm not clear on all of it."

Steve started scrubbing the dishes and handing them to Uncle Kevin to rinse and dry. "What do you mean, you weren't around? Didn't you, like, come for Christmas every year?"

"No. This is only my third Christmas here since I left when I was eighteen. I thought I'd never set foot in this house again. Sean and I didn't speak for years. I was filled with anger and resentment, and as for Sean, he was..." Uncle Kevin paused, searching for a word.

"Sean was scared," said Dad from behind them. He had come into the kitchen while they were talking. Now he stepped over and put his arm around Uncle Kevin and kissed him on the side of the head. Uncle Kevin closed his eyes and leaned into him. "I was afraid to face the fact that I'd abandoned my little brother to that angry, violent man," Dad said to Steve. "I was afraid he'd hate me, or, worse—that he wouldn't care one way or the other any more." He looked down at Uncle Kevin, who met his eyes, smiling. "When I met Martha, I started being able to look at what I was afraid of."

Dad took his eyes off Uncle Kevin and turned them to Steve. "Remember this, Stevie. Your mother had been telling me almost from the day we met that I needed to find Kevin and make my peace with him. She grew up in foster homes; she knew how precious family connections are. And her studies in psychology taught her that pain can't be just left to fester. But I wouldn't listen, I felt like I couldn't. Finally she was the one who found out where he was living. Laurie went to see him without my knowing about it, and Kevin was brave enough to come here and let me talk with him, and generous enough to forgive me. But I lost over twenty-five years of having a brother because your mother's advice seemed too hard to follow."

Dad gave Uncle Kevin a squeeze, then let go and started scraping the roasting pan. "You guys shouldn't have to deal with this disaster area all by yourselves. At this rate, it would take you till tomorrow and when Ruby came home she'd turn on her heel and walk right back out again. She did that once, back when we were kids, remember, Kev?"

He handed the pan to Uncle Kevin, who scooped some soapy water out of the sink with it and started sloshing it around, saying, "I sure do. I was scared to death she wouldn't come back. We always made sure we pulled our weight around here after that, didn't we?"

Dad took the other end of the big roaster to steady it. "Yes, we did. Seems like old times, cleaning the kitchen with you," Dad said. "I think to complete the effect, though, we need to argue about something."

Uncle Kevin laughed. "Remember that Thanksgiving when we were doing the dishes and you stabbed me in the arm with the meat fork?"

Steve cringed, but Dad was laughing. "I stabbed you in the arm? I stabbed you? You mean you attacked me without provocation and I tried to defend myself..."

They both started giggling and bumping into each other like kids. Steve looked out the window over the sink. He could see his own reflection, and theirs, in the glass. *Out there it's dark and cold. In here it's bright and warm.*

Chapter 13.

Rob

Robbie was sick of winter. Once the Christmas break was past, there didn't seem to be any point to it. And now, in late January, there still hadn't been any decent snow. Just fog and cold rain, icy sleet and frozen mud.

And it was all worse when you had to spend the day in an overheated classroom, especially when the teacher was that idiot Hoke. *I'd like to smack that smug grin off his face,* he thought. *"Mr. McAlister, I realize you don't have the brains of—hmm, how shall I put this?—others who share your name, but if you had done your homework you would know that the rule is* 'ad *with the accusative except with verbs of coming and going.'"*

Robbie slammed the front door behind him, piled his books on the floor, then shucked off his parka and dumped it on top of them. *I suppose it wasn't smart to come back at him, but cripes, what a jerk.* "If you mean *my* brother *Laurie* and *my* sister *Celia, I guess the difference is they actually think there's some use to learning Latin. With Sputnik in the sky, I don't really see the point.*"

So now he had detention every night for a week, even though they needed him at basketball practice. *The one scene that was really mine,* he reflected as he used the downstairs toilet. *I know Dad says not to worry about making sports a big deal, the way his father wanted him to, but I like having something I'm the best in the family at.* Washing his hands, he shook his head discontentedly at his own reflection in the medicine cabinet mirror and came back out into the hall.

Robbie could hear voices of the others upstairs. He went into the living room instead of going up and threw himself onto one of the settees by the fireplace. He lay back at full length and only then noticed that Steve was sitting in the matching settee on the other side of the coffee table, drumming his fingers on the seat beside him the way he always did. *Shit. I really wanted to be by myself. Great plan to dump yourself down in the living room, then, Einstein. Too lazy to get up and go upstairs now. If I don't say anything, he won't either.*

He lay there in silence with his eyes closed for a few minutes. *So what am I going to do with my life?* he wondered. *I don't like cracking the books the way Laurie and*

Celia do. I'm sure not some kind of egghead like Jamie. Beth doesn't need me to take care of her any more. Joy and Steve are just kids being kids. Nobody needs me, there's no place for me. He opened his eyes and stared at the ceiling. His stomach clenched and the air seemed to scratch his lungs.

Laurie came in through the door to the dining room carrying a dish of green olives in one big hand. "Hi, you two. Want an olive?" he said.

Steve shook his head, then nodded, then shrugged.

Probably doesn't even know what they taste like. Lucky him. Robbie craned his head around the arm of the settee and snapped, "I hate olives. You know that. Course, Ruby knows it too, but that didn't stop her from putting them out for our snack, did it?"

"She put out apples and walnuts, actually. I felt like something salty, so I got out the olives myself."

"Pin a medal on you."

Laurie came around, bent to put the dish on the coffee table where Steve could reach it, then said mildly to Rob, "You might want to take your shoes off the couch."

"You might want to mind your own beeswax. I already have a mother, thanks a lot."

"It's our mutual mother I was thinking about, just trying to save you from getting on her bad side. I hung up your parka for you, by the way."

"Ooh, Laurence McAlister, big Daddy-o. Just leave me the hell alone, will you? Isn't there anyplace in this damn house where I can get five minutes' peace and quiet?" *Is this really making me feel better, being snotty to him? Uh, oh, here he comes.*

Laurie crowded onto the settee near Robbie's hip and gave him a long look. "Ok, I don't know what's going on here, Robin, but this isn't the way we talk to each other. If I did something to make you mad, I'm sorry. Tell me what it is and I'll try to make it up to you."

Robbie grabbed his own hair in both hands and pulled. "God, I hate it when you do that," he said.

"Do what?"

"That whole more-in-sorrow-than-in-anger thing. You know as well as I do that you didn't foul up. I'm just acting pissy."

"So—what, you'd rather I just clout you on the head?" He gave Robbie a gentle cuff that turned into a caress.

Robbie sat up and buried his face on Laurie's broad shoulder. "I had such a crappy day." They held each other for a minute and Rob felt the tight, scratchy feeling draining away. "Love you a lot, Laddie." He raised his head.

"I love you, too, sweetheart," Laurie said, ruffling his hair. He sighed. "I've got a ton of homework, I better get going. And take your damn shoes off the couch," he said, getting to his feet and picking up the olive dish. "See you two later."

Rob had forgotten Steve was there. He turned toward him as Laurie left the room. *Hope that didn't make him flip his lid.* But the kid didn't look wigged out, he looked puzzled.

"Are you queer?" Steve asked, as though he was asking whether Robbie liked fish.

Robbie swung his feet to the floor. "Nope. I dig chicks. How about you?"

Steve did a little sort of flinch and flutter. "I don't know who I like. But when Laurie got that award the other night, and Dad kissed him in front of everybody, the whole school was talking about it. I heard somebody say they were both queer."

Robbie gave a short bark of laughter. *Jesus, people are stupid.* "Yeah, well, it's true most guys don't do that. At least not in America. So what? If you feel like kissing somebody, do it. If you love them, tell them. It makes them feel good, and you, too. Nothing to get shook up about."

Steve pondered that, then it seemed another thought struck him. "You called him Laddie."

"Yeah, we all do sometimes. We picked that up from Mom. She calls him that after a character in some soppy book she liked when she was a kid. She got 'Laurie' from a book, too. She asked him a couple years ago whether he wanted to change it, but he said it would be a shame to waste all the effort he spent learning not to mind when people made fun of it."

"And he called you Robin. I thought your name was Robert?"

"It is. Robin's a special name he has for me. Now that you mention it, I don't think he's ever used it in front of anybody else before."

"I called him—something bad, once."

Oh, Lordie. Rob blew a breath out. "Did it start with 'n'?"

Steve nodded.

Am I really going to tell him this? Look at his face, poor puppy. I guess I am. "I called him that once, too."

Steve's jaw dropped. "You did? I said it sort of by accident. Is that what happened to you?"

"No, I said it trying to hurt him. It did, too. We were just little kids then; it wasn't long after Bethie and I were adopted, and I was mad about a lot of things, and I took it out on him. Kind of like I just did today."

"But you l-love him?"

"When Beth and I first came here, and Dad was still at sea most of the time, Laurie was the one who made me feel safe, who made this home for me. There's nobody in the world I love more than Laurie. People who love each other forgive each other, even when they hurt them." *Man, could I conceivably sound any more rectangular?*

"I don't get that."

"I know you don't. You'll get with it, don't worry. Look, I'm going up to the music room to get rid of the last of my funk. You want to come along? I'll show you some chords on the guitar, like I promised the other day. Let's split, we'll make some sounds."

Chapter 14.

Saturday, February 27, 1958: 3:30 p.m.

Laurie

Laurie lunged for the ping-pong ball as it bounced off the old table, ricocheted from one of the floor joists ribbing the low basement ceiling, and flew into the laundry area to lodge behind the washing machine. His momentum carried him past the furnace and toward the workbench, hopping on one foot and flailing for balance. He banged his head against an asbestos-wrapped overhead hot water pipe, teetered, dropped the paddle, and caught himself by thrusting a hand against the tool rack. He banged against the edge of the wood chisel, which cut a nice slice into the base of his thumb. *Shit on a stick.*

"I win!" Celia crowed behind him. "Anyway, leaving the field of play before the game is over constitutes a default, so I win double!"

"You can call it whatever you want to, you play like a complete klutz," he growled, looking for a rag clean enough to press against his wound. *My hand's too dirty to suck it. Damn, it stings.* "Get that ball out from behind the machine and put the paddles away in the cabinet," he ordered Celia. *If she hadn't hit the ball so wild, this wouldn't have happened.* "Then you can throw our Coke bottles out."

"Who died and made you—" she started, then stopped short as he turned and she saw the blood running down his wrist. "Laurie, what happened, are you ok?"

"I'll live, no thanks to you." *Boy, I hate it when she gets that mulish expression.*

"I don't see how it's my fault."

"You never do. Just put everything back, I have to take care of this."

"You're not the boss of me," she said childishly.

"I am, actually, when Mom and Dad and Ruby aren't here, smarty pants." *Laundry sink is full of something soaking, can't wash the cut there.* Laurie kept turning his wrist so the blood wouldn't drip on the floor as he went up the cellar stairs.

At the kitchen sink, he hissed when the cold water hit the open cut. Celia came up from the basement and crossed behind him, tossing their empty bottles in the trash and leaving the kitchen without saying anything. *Fine, never mind about me, I'm just bleeding to death here.*

The flow of blood had slowed almost to a stop and the coldness of the water had numbed the pain when Celia reappeared, carrying gauze, tape, and a bottle of Mercurochrome. *I should have known. Little Miss Fix-It.*

"Here," she said coldly. "Let me see that hand."

"I can do it myself."

"Don't be an idiot."

"Idiot yourself." *What's the matter with me? It really wasn't her fault.*

"Double idiot."

"Triple idiot with spots on it." *We're a couple of idiots.* They both started giggling. As they sniped, Celia had blotted his hand dry with some of the gauze. Now she withdrew the cap from the Mercurochrome bottle and started gently dabbing its attached glass rod along the line of Laurie's cut. "Ow, ow, ow," Laurie said.

"Don't be such a baby." But she raised his hand to her mouth and softly blew across the orange stain to dry the antiseptic and stop the stinging. She wound gauze around his hand, then tore off a piece of tape with her teeth and secured it. "Better?"

"Much. Thanks, Cissy."

"So I guess I'm good for something?"

"When you're asleep, maybe." He hooked an arm around her neck and kissed her forehead. She still had the gauze and tape in her hands; he snagged the Mercurochrome off the side of the sink and started waltzing her out of the room, singing, "'Does your *moth*-er know you're out, Cccccecilia?'"

They spun and snickered their way through the dining room. Halfway across the living room, Celia stopped dancing and pulled on his arm with a level look. "You're in trouble at school, aren't you?"

Laurie sighed. "Good old rumor mill. What have you heard?"

"Dean Dunkelman is giving you a hard time about going to the prom with Linda?"

"Not me, just Linda. She's threatening not to write Linda a college recommendation if she goes with me."

"What? She can't do that!"

"That's what you think."

"Anyway, what are you supposed to do? There aren't any Negro girls in our school, are you just supposed to have no social life?"

Laurie shrugged. "Not the dean's problem, evidently. Linda says she just kept talking about 'the good of the community.'"

"What are you going to do?"

"Don't know. Talk to the parents, for openers."

While they spoke they had moved through the hall to the downstairs bathroom, where they returned the first aid things to the medicine cabinet. As they came back out into the hall, the front door opened and cold, damp air flowed in like water. *Not as cold as last week, though,* Laurie thought. *Maybe spring really will get here some day. Spring. The dance. Damn, what will I do?*

Mom, Dad, and Steve came in and started hanging up their coats. Dad was in his blues, Mom was wearing her good red wool suit. Steve had on a white oxford button-down shirt under a blue sweater vest, and pressed gray slacks over polished loafers. *The adoption hearing!* "How did it go? Everything all right?"

Mom turned from the closet, beaming. Dad put a hand on Steve's head and announced, "Lady and gentleman, allow me to introduce Mr. Steven McAlister. It's official, he's ours for keeps." Steve gave a shy smile.

"Yay!" Celia ran up and threw her arms around Steve's thin shoulders, rocking him back and forth. Steve stiffened a little, but stood still for it.

"Now that he's safely ours," Mom said to Laurie, "I can really get busy on system reform. I don't want any other orphaned kid to just get passed off to the nearest blood relative without proper review." Steve looked up at her with his eyes wide.

That's my Mom. Always saving the world. Laurie skirted around the others to peck her on the cheek, then turned back to Steve.

As Laurie came over, Steve's eyelids fluttered with uncertainty but his mouth firmed when he looked up. *He's still nervous around me, but he's trying not to be.*

Celia let go and stepped away from Steve, leaving him and Laurie face to face. "I can't shake hands with you, sweetheart," Laurie said, showing him the bandage. "Can I give you just a quick hug, please?"

Steve nodded. *Easy, don't push it.* Laurie leaned down and gathered the slight body into his arms. *Just let him hear my heart for a minute.* Then Laurie felt Dad's hand on his own shoulder, pressing gently. *Time's up.* Laurie let go. "Thank you," he said gravely.

"You're welcome," Steve said equally formally.

Mom came up behind Steve and put her hands on his upper arms. "Let's go get our good clothes off, and then we can round everyone up and do something together to celebrate, what do you say?"

She and Steve started upstairs with Celia trailing behind. Dad still had his arm around Laurie. "What happened to your hand, son?" he asked.

"Oh, nothing, really. Cissy and I were playing ping-pong and I managed to cut myself on a chisel. I gave her a hard time about it, like it was her fault, but she helped me fix it up anyway. No big deal."

Dad ran his thumb along Laurie's cheekbone. "But you are upset about something," Dad said. "I hear it in your voice. Is it the way Steve reacted to you? He's really trying, you know."

Laurie leaned his face into Dad's hand. "No, I know, that was pretty nice, all in all," he said. "It's about something else."

"Want to talk about it?"

"Yes, sir, I would. But maybe now isn't the best time. It's nothing urgent, though it is important. Tonight before bed? I don't want to derail Steve's celebration."

"Tonight it is, then," Dad said, but he didn't let go of Laurie right away. "Do you have any idea how much I love you?"

Laurie straightened up and grinned at him. "Not a clue. Why don't you tell me about it later, when you're out of uniform and your chest isn't covered with scratchy ribbons so I can snivel onto it properly?"

Dad laughed. "That's a date, Laddie."

"Mom, too, please."

"You bet, I'll tell her."

They both turned as Steve came tripping down the stairs, now in t-shirt and jeans. He skidded to a stop when he saw them.

"Hey, little brother," Laurie said. "I spotted a carrot cake with your name on it on the sideboard when I came through the dining room. Ruby's still out shopping—want to go filch some frosting before she gets back?"

Steve looked uncertainly at Dad. "I didn't hear that," Dad said, waving his hands and starting up the stairs.

Laurie moved toward the dining room. *He's tagging after me all right.*

"Can I have a corner piece tonight?" Steve asked. "I decided that's what I like most."

"It's your cake, sweetheart. You get first pick."

"Corner piece, then," Steve said firmly.

Chapter 15.

Thursday, March 13, 1958: 7:30 p.m.

Joy

A bright fire countered the gray icy fog outside, and the living room was warm. Mom was thanking everyone for her gifts from the "birthday throne" in front of the fireplace. Joy smiled back automatically, but she was a little worried about Steve. He was the only one who hadn't given Mom a birthday present, and he was looking uncomfortable, head down, fingers tapping on the arm of his chair in a way he hadn't been lately. *I should have helped him pick out something.*

Joy had been finding eighth grade a little hard to deal with. The problem wasn't the schoolwork, it was the socializing. She'd been one of the last girls in her class to start menstruating, but now she suddenly needed a bra and was feeling uncertain about how to cope. Her girlfriends only wanted to talk about boys, and the boys didn't want to talk at all. *But at home I'm still a little girl— safe, but boring.* Joy wondered whether Steve had any of the same confusions. *Maybe I can talk to him later. He seems to spend all his time with Robbie these days, though.*

Now Beth went to the baby grand and started playing "Mostly Martha"; they all joined in singing, shouting and laughing at the last line, "She's got the most!" Rob ducked out of the room as the others started to chat.

Steve was sitting by one of the front bay windows, huddled up as though he felt cold. He hadn't joined in the song. *I can't go sit by him there,* Joy thought. *It would draw attention to him and make him self-conscious. Something's off, though, he's not happy. He's nervous about something.* She shifted from the long couch to the ottoman, just to get a little closer.

Rob came back into the room carrying Mom's old Spanish guitar, the one he'd been teaching Steve to play. He brought it over to Steve and said in a low voice, "It's all tuned." Robbie turned to the rest of the room, holding his hands out in front of him in a quelling gesture. "Cool it, guys. Steve's going to give Mom her present from him."

The room quieted down. "Dad told me this was Mom's favorite song, back when he was away in the war," Steve said in a quavering voice. "Robbie taught it to me." He bent his head to the guitar and started to play.

He opened with a plaintive, longing chord strummed slowly across the strings and began to sing in a pure, tremulous tenor:

> ""There'll be bluebirds over the white cliffs of
> Dover
> Tomorrow, just you wait and see;
> There'll be love and laughter and peace ever after
> Tomorrow when the world is free.""

Mom gave a deep sigh, looking across to Dad, as Steve shifted to a brighter tone:

> ""The shepherd will tend his sheep,
> The valley will bloom again,
> And Jimmy will go to sleep
> In his own little room again.""

On the last line, his eyes shot up to meet Mom's, then down again as he went into the refrain:

> ""There'll be bluebirds over the white cliffs of
> Dover
> Tomorrow, just you wait and see.""

He repeated the last two lines and ended on a gentle chord.

How did he do that? Joy wondered. His playing had been simple, just strumming without the fancy picking Robbie sometimes tried, but the combination of the basic chords and the deep emotion in his voice with the lilting tune and longing words gave the song an eerie, skin-prickling force.

Steve drew a deep breath, visibly relaxing. Mom's eyes were bright as she came to kiss him. "Thank you so much, my darling. That was a wonderful gift."

As she leaned over him, the silver filigree pendant Joy had just given her swung forward toward his face. Steve cried out and covered his eyes, twisting over the arm of the chair and struggling to disentangle himself from the guitar without touching Mom. People made noises of alarm and concern; Dad got up but then stood hesitating by the fireplace.

Mom pulled back from Steve and made a calming gesture at the others. "Give him a minute," she said in a low voice, tucking the pendant into the neck of her dress. Then, to Steve, "Take a breath, darling. It's all right. You're all right. You're safe. It's all over, you're safe with us now." She kept talking in a steady, soothing tone as though he were a spooked horse, or a squirrel in a trap.

Steve quieted down and reached out a hand. "Joy," he said in a muffled voice.

Me! He wants me! Joy got up from the ottoman and hurried to Steve. She settled on the floor next to him and took his hand.

"Can you tell us what happened?" Mom asked. "What did you see?"

"It was his belt," Steve said, taking his other arm away from his face but keeping his head down. "The buckle, I saw the buckle coming at me." He took a long, hitching breath.

Joy reached up and smoothed his soft blond hair. *It's getting longer. Looks good on him, less like a scalped rabbit than when he first came.*

At a cock of the head from Mom, everyone else got up and silently left the room. The three of them sat quietly for a few minutes.

Finally Steve raised his head and took another long breath, looking around as though he'd just woken up. "I'm ok now," he said shakily. Mom leaned forward again from her perch on the arm of his chair, putting her arm along the chair's back. Steve leaned his head against it, looking up at her. "I'm sorry I wrecked your birthday."

"You didn't wreck it at all," Mom said. "I had a fine party, and your present was perfect. I'm sorry that bad experience came back to upset you, but you know we talked about how those things will keep happening for a while. It should get better over time. Would you like another piece of my cake? A little sugar and chocolate might help you feel calmer, oddly enough, since you've had a kind of shock."

Joy jumped up. "I'll get him one," she said. "Do you want more, too, Mom?"

"I'd better not, thank you," Mom said. "I shouldn't have had the first one, really, but it is my birthday."

"Why shouldn't you?" Steve asked as Joy went toward the dining room.

"Because I'm at least thirty pounds overweight, Stevie," Mom said.

"You are?" Steve said.

"Isn't it obvious?"

"I never thought about it. You just look like Mom to me. Nice and soft."

Way to go, Steve, Joy grinned to herself. *Make her feel better.* Mom had been looking worried lately; her trying to get some of the child custody rules changed wasn't making her any friends at work. The last thing she needed was to be worrying about her weight right now.

In the dining room, Joy cut a piece of cake for Steve, dodging around Jamie and Celia as they cleared the table, nodding and smiling to show things were going all right in the living room.

She brought the cake out and Steve started nibbling at it.

"Do I have a birthday?" Steve asked.

"Of course you have a birthday," Mom said. "It's July second. Rolling Meadow got a copy of your birth certificate when you first arrived there. So when that day comes, we'll have a party for you, too. Carrot cake again, like when we celebrated your adoption, if that's what you want. You get to pick."

He doesn't look happy. "Don't you like the idea?" Joy asked.

Steve tapped his fingers on the edge of his plate for a few seconds, then said reluctantly, "Do I have to sit in that chair in front of everybody?"

"Of course not, darling," Mom said. "Not if you don't want to. The idea is to have fun on your birthday; it's your day, we can celebrate it however you want within reason."

Steve's shoulders loosened. "But I can still get presents, right?"

Mom and Joy both laughed. "You can still get presents," Mom assured him.

"Well, that's ok then," Steve said.

Chapter 16.

Saturday, April 19, 1958: 4:00 p.m.

Beth

Beth's fingers moved over the piano keys, softly teasing out the opening notes of Mozart's piano concerto 19. On such a fine day, she preferred this little practice spinet in the music room to the big baby grand downstairs. The long broad keys slicked against her finger pads, the shorter narrow ones pressed down with a satisfying feeling as her hands arched over them. The sun shone warm on her forehead and the scents of spring came through the music room window: lilac and cut grass, and the tender new needles on the larch trees by the back door.

Just barely audible on the edge of her hearing, the whisper of Steve's radio fell silent. She immediately went into a series of arpeggio exercises, using the pedal to produce a cascade of sound. *He doesn't know I can hear him in there. Don't let him find out or he won't have a safe place any more.*

Under the noise she was making, she felt a disturbance in the air as much as hearing the low door behind her opening and closing again. After his quiet footsteps moved past and down the stairs, she started noodling, improvising softly as she thought about Steve. *He's letting us touch him once in a while, he's talking more, and the music—it's like Robbie's set something free in him, showing him how to play.*

Footsteps coming up the stairs now—not Steve, though. Robbie. He came up into the room.

"Hey, angel." Slight twang as he bumped his Gibson a little against his knee, picking it up.

"Hey, big brother." She kept noodling while he tuned up, then joined him as he went into "Heartbreak Hotel."

Before long, Beth heard footsteps on the stairs again, hesitant, tentative. *Is it that he's not sure of his welcome, or is he not sure he wants to come up with both of us here?*

Still, the music drew him into the room, and soon the second guitar joined in. Rob started doing Elvis, deepening his voice and slurring syllables for comic effect, but there was nothing funny about the way Steve sang, "I get so lonely I could die."

The song came to an end and there was a pause. Then, "Is that guy going to off himself?"

Oof. Let Robbie handle that one. Silence. *Ok, up to me.* "I think that is one way to read the words," Beth said carefully. "Because he's alone. Because he thinks no one loves him."

Steve said, "I feel like that sometimes. But not so much when I play."

"Me, too," Beth said.

"But how can you play when you can't see?"

"I can feel."

"Oh. Oh, yeah."

"And that's you, too, Stevie," Robbie said. "You've got it made in the shade. You're in the groove when you play, and that comes through. That's why you're better than I am."

My Robbie. Biggest heart in the world. His voice was coming from somewhere around her knee; he must be leaning against the piano bench. She dropped her hand to feather her fingers through his hair.

But Steve sounded insulted, the rage that always lay banked just under his timidity seeping out. "What are you talking about? I'm just learning, you play way better than I do."

"I know more technical stuff, fingering techniques and all that jazz, so someone listening to us without a clue about music might think I was better. But you have the heat, Steve. Nancy heard that, when she listened to us the other day. She wants us to play at this party she's having next month."

Now Steve sounded scared. "I can't do that, play in front of people."

"Sure you can. It'll just be a few kids like us, no big deal. And you're good, Steve. When you play, and even more when you sing, something happens that has nothing to do with how many chords you know, or how well you pick. Am I right, Beth?"

"He's right, Steve. What comes through in your voice and your playing is powerful in a way I've never heard before."

There was a clang as Steve dumped his guitar on the wooden floor, then his rapid footsteps receded down the stairs. Next came a thud that resounded through the house as he slammed his bedroom door. Robbie's head fell forward onto his arms; Beth could feel her fingers sliding back along his neck till they caught in his collar. They both sighed.

"Now what?" he asked.

"I'm going to talk to him," she said.

"I'm going to hang out here and play some more."

"Ok." She leaned forward to drop a kiss on his ear, then swung her feet over the piano bench the other way and stood up with a rustle of crinoline.

"His guitar's on the floor," Rob said, "about two

feet in front of you and one to the right."

She stepped around the obstacle, found the head of the narrow staircase, and went down to the second floor hall. Turning right, she let her hand trail along the wall, feeling the door to Rob and Laurie's room on her right, the long blank stretch where their bathroom was, and next along to the door of Steve and Jamie's room. There was a whiff of Tweed in the air. She knocked and decided to assume the sound she heard from inside was an invitation to come in.

Inside the door, which she left open behind her, Beth stood and oriented herself. *Window in front of me, about six steps. Dresser on the right, Jamie's bed on my left. Steve's bed on the other side of Jamie's.* "Steve, are you here?"

"What do you want?"

He sounds sulky, she thought, *but there's a little fear there, too.* "Are you all right, baby?"

"No."

He's on his bed. She walked forward to the window seat and settled herself in the corner of it, feeling the sun on her back. "Why did it upset you that Rob and I think you have a gift for music?"

"I just get mad sometimes. I don't really know why. I guess it made me feel like you want me to do something I don't know how to do. And the song made me nervous, what you were saying about him

125

thinking he was alone and wanting to die. I was alone a long time, but I didn't want to die."

"I'm glad you didn't want to die. I'm glad you stayed alive, Steve."

"Do you ever feel like dying? Does it feel like too much?"

His voice is coming closer. "You mean because I'm blind?"

"Yeah, that must be tough."

"I don't know what it's like to see, though. I've been blind since I was a tiny baby. Mom thinks they gave me too much oxygen when I was born; they did that sometimes then, without knowing it would harm the babies' eyes." She felt a slight sag in the cushion as he sat on the other end of the window seat.

"So you have, like, super hearing?"

She laughed. "No, I know people think that, but it's just that I listen more. I can hear that you're scratching your knee right now, for instance; the sound fingernails make on jeans is different from the sound they make on skin."

"But you can never hurt anybody, can you?"

"Sure I can. I can say hurtful things, and if I know where somebody is I'm just as able to hit out at them as anyone else. I almost never want to do anything like that, though, and even if I do, I don't act on it."

"But what if somebody hurt you?"

Careful, now. "I don't believe in hurting back, even then. I'm a Friend, you know, what some people call a Quaker."

"That church you go to, when everybody else but Jamie goes to Mass?"

"That's right. We call it Meeting, though."

"And if somebody tries to kill you, you think you shouldn't kill them?"

Beth reached out and found his skittering fingers and folded them softly in hers. "Oh, baby, I've never been tested the way you have. Robbie used to fight to protect me when we were little, and since we've been in this family no one tries to hurt us."

Now his breath, harsh and a little sour, gusted against her cheek. She reached out with both arms and gathered his thin body to her till he was leaning on her breast, half in her lap.

"You know I killed him, Bert?" he whispered.

"I know," she whispered back.

"He was going to kill me that night. He had a knife, and he told me."

"I know." She rocked him a little, feeling his hot, silent tears soak through the shoulder of her blouse.

"Am I bad?"

"No."

"How do you know?"

"Nobody could have a bad heart and make music the way you do."

He gave a long, shuddering breath and pushed away from her.

"Do you need to be alone now?" she asked.

"Yeah."

"Ok, baby. I love you."

Beth stood up and walked back out into the hall, closing the door behind her. She turned to her right, where she knew Mom was standing, and fell into her waiting arms.

Chapter 17.

Monday, April 28, 1958: 2:30 a.m.

Jamie

Jamie lay on his bed in the soft spring night, thinking. *It's not ratting him out. Ridiculous phrase, anyway. I'm seventeen years old; I'm not a child. He is. Something serious is wrong. It's not my business, though. Yes it is, he's my brother. So how can I rat him out?* His thoughts circled around for the dozenth time that night.

With an impatient jerk, he tossed back the covers. He groped for his glasses on the night table and put them on, slid his feet into slippers, shrugged on his robe, and padded out into the dark, silent hallway. He passed Rob and Laurie's room on his left, the girls' rooms on his right, then moved past the stairs that went up to the music room and down to the kitchen, and fetched up outside Mom and Dad's room. He hesitated. *It's so quiet, I'll wake everyone up if I knock. They've been asleep for hours, maybe they'll be annoyed... Stop stalling, Hymie.* He gave two subdued but firm raps on the door.

There was no response for long enough to make him wonder whether he should knock again or just forget about it and go back to bed, then the door opened. Dad was there, his ash blond hair tousled, looking strangely young in his pajamas and bare feet. Without a word, he stepped back and pulled the door wider so Jamie could come in. Mom was sitting up in bed, looking poised to jump up, her long dark hair tumbled around her shoulders. Their bathroom door was open, spilling light into the bedroom; the room was filled with shadows.

Dad put on his dressing gown and sat down on the bed, his back to his pillows. Jamie sat on the foot of the bed looking at him and Mom. The big painting by Uncle Kevin that hung over their bed glowed where the light hit it, glinting mysterious jewel tones. So far, no one had spoken.

Jump, Hymie. "It's Steve," he said. They both kept looking at him, but their hands reached to each other across the patchwork quilt on their bed. "There's something wrong. I know he had a conversation with Beth the other day that upset him. Since then he's been sneaking out at night."

"Out of the house, you mean?" Mom asked.

"I don't think so. I think he goes to—to our secret place."

"Hmmm," Dad said. "Is it safe there, for him to sleep? Enough air and so forth?"

"Yeah, I think so. Maybe I'm making too much out of it—"

"No," Mom said, "you were right to come to us. This is not a good development. Do you know anything about how he's feeling?"

Jamie shook his head. *Come on, Hymie, spit it out.* "Actually, I think that's part of the problem. He sounded like he was trying to keep from crying the other night. I, uh, I'd said something nasty to him a long time ago about him crying all the time, and since then he tries not to show when he's feeling bad around me. But that's when he started sneaking out, after that night. I think it started with him not wanting me to hear him cry." Jamie swallowed. "There's something else, too. There's a… smell. I think he's wetting the bed, and stuffing towels in there to hide it."

Mom sprang out of bed as though he'd said the house was on fire. She grabbed her robe, already moving toward the door. "Show us, son," she said in a voice that allowed for no argument.

He almost tried anyway. *I knew this would happen.* "But—" Then he looked at her face as she stood over

131

him. "Yes, ma'am," he said in a small voice, getting up. Dad got up, too, and squeezed his shoulder.

Jamie led the way up the music room stairs and through into the attic. He pointed at the cabinet door and stood back. Dad put his hand on Jamie's shoulder again. Mom crouched down by the cubbyhole and said softly, "Stevie? Steve, sweetie, we need you to open the door. Please let us talk to you."

Almost at once the door banged open, nearly hitting Mom in the face as it slammed back. The light from the battery lantern threw shadows into the hollows of Steve's face. *He looks like a skull, like an inmate at the camp.* But his eyes were burning in their sockets, glaring straight at Jamie. *Oh, God.*

Steve pushed past Mom and darted toward the attic door. Dad let go of Jamie and caught Steve in one arm, pressing him against his side. Steve suddenly went limp and started to cry. They all moved out of the gloomy attic and into the music room. It was silvery and dreamy in the moonlight; Jamie was sorry when Mom flipped on the light and the windows went black and opaque against the yellow glare.

Mom sat on the piano bench and Dad moved Steve to stand between her and himself, almost touching Mom's knees. Jamie stood by the stairway, watching. He really didn't want to be there, but it felt cowardly to leave. *Just stand here and take it, whatever it is,* he told himself.

"Steve," Mom was saying, "can you tell us what's wrong?" He shook his head miserably. "Then, can you tell us why you can't tell us? Remember, we've talked about this in our sessions: just say what you feel able to say, and we'll go from there."

Steve didn't answer. He stopped trembling and his eyelids drooped. His hands fell loosely at his sides and his head hung down. Mom reached forward and gripped his arm above the elbow, hard. "Steve," she said sharply. "Steven O'Riordan McAlister, stop that this instant. Come back, do you hear me?" She gave his arm a shake.

Dad put his hands on either side of Steve's head and leaned forward beside his ear. "It's all right, honey," he said in a low voice. "No one is going to be mad at you. No one is going to hurt you. Come back to us, son."

Steve started trembling again, and shaking his head violently back and forth, so that Dad had to let go. "I can't, I can't," he wailed. "It's too bad. I'm too bad. You'll hate me."

Mom's eyes met Dad's and she gave a little nod. Dad grasped Steve's upper arms and spun him around to face him. He lowered his head till their noses were

133

almost touching and said fiercely, "That is not going to happen. I have never lied to you, Steve, and I never will, and I am telling you we are not going to hate you. No matter what it is, we love you."

Steve twisted his face away. "You'll kill me," he whispered.

Jamie sank down onto the first step, suddenly too shaky to stand. *My God, he means that literally. He really thinks they're going to kill him.*

Dad dropped to his knees in front of Steve, still holding his arms. "No, we will not," he whispered back.

Mom stood up and wrapped her arms around Steve from behind. "No, we will not," she repeated.

Steve put his hands over his face. "I didn't mean to, I didn't mean to, I couldn't help it," he coughed, sobbing. "I just wake up and it's already there, it's all sticky and disgusting. I know I'm disgusting, I know I'm bad, but don't kill me, 'cause I can't kill *you*. I got the knife away from Bert that night because he was drunk, and I killed him so he couldn't kill me, but I don't want to kill you and I don't want to die and I don't want to be bad any more." He was crying so hard he was practically barking, and he sank down into a ball on the floor.

Mom moved down with him, folding her arms around him as though to keep him from flying into pieces. Dad, though—Dad stood up, picked up the metal music stand next to the piano, and swung it with all his force against the shelf of knickknacks on the wall. Bits of glass and china sprayed everywhere. Dad threw the music stand to the floor and stood there shaking and red-faced, tears on his cheeks.

There was a shocked silence except for Steve's breath as he scraped air into his heaving chest. His eyes were huge in his thin face; he shrank back against Mom as though trying to disappear into her.

"Sean, speak to Steve," Mom said quietly.

Dad turned toward him and spoke in an even tone as though this were an ordinary conversation. "I served in two wars, Steve," he said. "I've had to fight for my life in a lot of tough places. But I have never before wanted to kill someone the way I want to kill your cousin right now. If he weren't already dead, if you hadn't already done the job for me... even so, I'd like to drag Bert out of the grave and kill him all over again for what he's done to you."

Steve stared for a minute, trying to catch his breath. He pulled away from Mom a little, never taking his eyes off Dad. "You'd do that for me?" he said wonderingly.

"I'd fight the devil himself for you, Stevie."

Steve scrambled to his feet and looked at Dad, at Mom, at Jamie in turn as though he'd never seen them before. "You're on my side," he whispered.

"Yes, we are," Jamie said.

Mom got up and brushed shards of glass from the skirt of her nightgown. "Let's go down and see about that bed," she said briskly. "We'll worry about this mess in the morning, and we'll talk about all this in the morning, too."

Back in the bedroom, Mom and Dad swung into action. Mom had Steve help her strip the sodden sheets and towels off his bed, bundling them into a big lump with the wettest parts inside, then thrust them at Jamie. "Put these into the machine, please, sweetie."

As he took them and headed down the hall for the back stairs, Dad stuck his head out the door and said to Rob and Laurie, awakened by the commotion, "Boys, go and get the top mattress from the smaller spare-room bed, will you, and bring it here?"

Celia and Joy were standing in their doorway, wide-eyed, with their arms around each other's waists. When Celia saw the bundle Jamie was carrying, she pulled away and started for the linen closet.

Jamie got downstairs into the cellar and stuffed the smelly sheets and towels into the washing machine. He was standing there trying to decide which settings to use when Ruby came down from her apartment off the kitchen. She took in the situation with a glance and a sniff. "I'll do that, child," she said. "Just run up and fetch me the jug of vinegar like a good boy. Then tell your parents I'm awake if they need me." Jamie nodded and ran to do as she said.

When he got back upstairs, Celia was wrestling the stained mattress out the bedroom window; it fell to the yard below as he walked into the room and gave Mom Ruby's message. Joy was helping Mom put clean sheets on the mattress Rob and Laurie had just carried in. Jamie could hear the sound of the shower, and Dad's soft murmur coming from the bathroom. The water turned off, the bathroom door opened, and Dad came in without his pajama top, carrying Steve in his arms like a baby, wrapped in a big towel.

He set Steve onto the clean bed and finished drying him. The others all left, saying quiet goodnights, while Mom got out clean pajamas and helped Steve get into them and Jamie climbed back into his own tousled bed. Then they turned out the lights and she and Dad each kissed Steve and Jamie goodnight and left the room.

Silence settled over the house once more.

Jamie lay still for a few minutes, thinking again. *He's not asleep. He's not crying. He's just lying there.* Suddenly Jamie knew what to do. He got out of bed in the moonlight and rummaged through the boxes on the closet shelves. *Here it is.* He brought the tattered old bear over to Steve's bed. Keeping his eyes on Steve, he kissed the bear—the plush fur at once soft and prickly against his lips—and thrust it at him.

"Where did this come from?"

"It was mine. They got it for me when I first came here. You can have it."

"What's it for?"

"It's to hug."

Steve turned the bear in his hands for a minute. He kissed it on the same spot Jamie had, then tucked it into the crook of his arm, curling around it. "Ok," he said. "Thanks."

"You're welcome," Jamie said, and went back to bed as the window turned pink with the dawn, wavering through his tears.

Chapter 18.

Friday, May 30, 1958: 3:45 p.m.

Steve

Steve trudged up the driveway, happy that at least school was over for another week and would soon be over for the year. Tomorrow night he and Robbie were supposed to play and sing at that party Nancy was giving at her house. The idea made Steve nervous, but part of him was also eager to try it, to see what it was like to make music for other people.

Now Joy and Rob were playing Horse at the basketball hoop over the garage door, dodging puddles from the day's rain, sweating in the late spring heat. Robbie held the ball out toward Steve, inviting him to join them, but he shook his head and went on up the walk. *Something else I'm no good at,* he thought.

Since that night when he'd fallen apart, Steve felt stronger in some ways and weaker in others. It felt like part of him had been peeled away. More light and air was getting in, and that felt good, but it hurt, too.

Things were coming to the surface that had been buried for a long time. He felt safer about being a real part of the family, but more scared about what was in his past, whether he was good enough, just how he would fit in. *I don't want to think about this again,* he thought, shaking his head.

Inside the house, he slid his books onto the hall table. He could hear voices in the living room—Celia and that guy she was dating, Ray. Steve stiffened at the sound of Ray's laugh. *I don't like the way he looks at us when she's not watching. Like we're all freaks. Not curious, like Nancy. Mean. At least Beth's boyfriend can't look at us funny, since he can't see. And Jamie and Rima are always just making out in corners like nobody else is here.*

Steve didn't like having all these outside people hanging around the house. It didn't feel safe. Of course, things inside the house didn't feel quite as safe since that night, either. Steve was never sure what Dad was going to do if he got mad. Dad hadn't been mad again, though—instead, he was too quiet and his lips were pressed hard together a lot; Mom seemed to be getting a permanent worry line in her forehead. *Grown up stuff, it could be, probably nothing about me,* Steve thought, but he wasn't convincing himself.

Steve went under the wide front staircase and out the hall door that led into the screened porch, figuring he'd go around to the kitchen that way and see what Ruby had out for their after-school snack without having to pass Celia and Ray. Skirting the big table taking up most of the porch space brought him close under the window to Ruby's sitting room. He could hear her voice inside. *Who's she talking to? She sounds so— colored.*

He peered over the sill. Ruby was sitting on her sofa, under the big painting Uncle Kevin had told him was there, squares of brown and tan with soft orange strips, sort of like melon, running through them at different angles. It gave Steve a feeling that was solid but somehow exciting at the same time. Ruby was looking at someone in the chair in front of her, with its back to the window.

"I can't tell you what to do, child," she was saying, her words blurring into the soft accents Celia had told him were Southern. *She doesn't usually sound like that,* Steve thought. "But I can tell you this. You're all fired up for some big crusade, takin that gal to the dance no matter what, and a little part a you even thinks it's goin to be a little bit fun. You know I grew up in Georgia," the way she said it sounded like "Jo-jah," "I've seen a thing or two in my life. I'm sayin it's not goin to be fun. Not one *tiny* smidge a fun."

141

There was a silence, then Laurie's voice said, "Maybe you're right. Maybe I am being naïve about what this will really be like. But how can we knuckle under to these people, Ruby? Not just the school bureaucrats, but whoever egged Dad's car last week, and the kids who leave anonymous threatening notes on my locker and Linda's? Mom and Dad say not to worry about them, just do what I think is right, but how can I not worry about what this will do to them? To the whole family? And to Linda?"

"What does she think about it all?"

"She wants to go to the dance. Her mother's hysterical about the college rec thing, but Linda doesn't care. I care, though. If she can't get into college because of this, she'll be sorry she knew me, and I don't ever want her to be sorry she knew me. But if I say I'll take her, she'll go to that dance if they have to bring her in on a stretcher, I think."

Ruby gave a little laugh. *It doesn't sound like she really thinks it's funny, though.* "This is hard, Laddie," she said, sounding more like her usual self again. "Things are changin from the way they been all my life, and thank God for that. But it's a rocky road. I'm scared for you, and for your folks. Still an' all, I know you can't just Uncle Tom your way through life. You have to find your road and set your own feet on it. Just know I'll walk it with you, and Sean and Martha will too, and everyone in this house down to that blessed child listenin outside my window right now."

It took a minute for that to sink in. *She's talking about me!* Steve scrambled on into the kitchen. Two shiny brown loaves of braided bread rested on a cooling rack on the work table, giving out a rich, yeasty smell. There were fresh strawberries and oatmeal cookies on the breakfast nook table beyond. But Steve's appetite was gone. *They'll be mad.*

The door to Ruby's rooms opened and she and Laurie came out. They were between Steve and the back stairs; Celia and Ray were in the living room. There was no getting away except to run out the porch door again, and Steve figured that would just be putting off whatever would happen.

"I did something bad, didn't I?" he mumbled, looking at the linoleum.

"Well, it's not polite to listen at windows," Ruby said, "but no harm done."

"It's ok, buddy," Laurie said. "If you want to talk some more about it, we can."

Steve looked up then. "You're not mad?"

"Nah," Laurie said. "What we were talking about is no secret, anyway. Do you have an opinion, sweetheart?"

"I don't know what you should do," Steve said. "I just don't want anybody to get hurt, and I don't want anything to change. But it seems like that could happen no matter what you do."

Laurie sighed. "Yes, it does," he said. "I'm going to go up and get on the horn to Linda, hash this over some more." He picked up a cookie and crossed toward the back stairs. Ruby had gone to the stove and was bent over the open oven door, poking at the two big chickens roasting in there. Laurie rubbed his hand on her back as he passed. "Thanks for listening," he said.

"What I'm here for," she said.

"I knew it was for something," he said, pulling open the knot in her apron ties.

"Devil's spawn," she said, yanking a dishtowel off the oven door handle and snapping it at his backside as he dodged out of the way and ran upstairs, laughing.

Everybody here jokes around, even when they're worried. Then a new thought struck Steve. *Maybe it's* because *they're worried. How does that work?* He reached for a cookie, thinking about it.

The back door opened and Dad came in, home from the office. He drew in a deep sniff of the air. "Ah, the Sabbath smell," he said. "Roast chicken, fresh bread, and mildew."

"I been telling you for years those larches are too close to the house," Ruby said. "But nobody listens to me." She'd closed the oven and now was feeling the bottoms of the bread loaves, sliding her pink palms under them.

"If we got rid of everything around here that's a little inconvenient or doesn't work quite right, what would be left?" Dad said, winking at Steve. He joined him standing at the breakfast table. "The first strawberries of the season!" he said. "Did Jamie say the first-fruits blessing over them?"

Dad's so tall. Steve edged away from him. Dad's eyes narrowed a little, and his lips opened as though he was about to say something, but Ruby said, "I don't know, I've been in my room talking to Laurie about the dance." That distracted him.

Steve, vaguely relieved, popped a strawberry into his mouth and headed for the dining room while Dad and Ruby went on talking. Celia was in there, smoothing the white Friday night cloth onto the table. "I wondered when you'd show up," she said. "Did you forget it's our night to help?"

"No, I was just waiting for that guy to go away," he said.

She turned to him with her eyebrows drawn down. "Why the tone?" she said. "You don't like Ray, do you?"

Steve went to the sideboard and got out the cloth napkins, counting ten from the drawer onto the table and folding one at each place. "He doesn't like us," he said. "I guess he likes you ok, but he talks to me like I'm a moron and he looks at Laurie like he thinks he's going to steal his wallet."

"He does?" Celia said, following Steve around the table with the fancy stemmed glasses they only used on Fridays and holidays. But she didn't sound surprised, she sounded thoughtful. Steve felt good that he'd found the courage to tell her what he thought about Ray. *Maybe I can help people here, too. Maybe I could even help Laurie.*

Celia was still talking about Ray. "He was ticked that I wouldn't go out with him tonight to see that new Hitchcock film, *Vertigo*. I told him we could go tomorrow so I wouldn't have to miss Shabbat with the family tonight, but he didn't get it." She glanced around the table, then turned back to the sideboard, pulling out the special silver bread tray. "That's it," she said suddenly, slapping it into the middle of the table near Jamie's seat. "I'll dump him."

"You like Jamie's Friday night thing that much?" Steve was setting out the good china plates.

"I do," Celia said. "Don't you? I don't think of it as Jamie's thing. We all like it. Bad enough Robbie has to miss Fridays in basketball season, and Joy when the swim team meets. I actually invited Ray to stay tonight, and he acted like it would be some kind of detention. If he doesn't like my family or what we do, the heck with him." She nodded sharply and clanged the brass candlesticks together as she lifted them off their shelf and swung back toward the table.

"Whoa, Nellie," Dad said, coming in from the kitchen and going to the liquor cabinet in the bottom of the sideboard. Steve slid around the corner of the table away from him and started arranging silverware the way Ruby had showed him, suddenly feeling powerless again. *I'll never be like him.*

"On your high horse about something, Cissy?" Dad said, pouring whisky into the glass of ice he'd brought from the kitchen. Steve's nose twitched at the smell. *Crashing. Lights. Bert.* He closed his eyes for a minute. Celia was talking to Dad about Ray, far away like a voice on the radio.

"Steve?" Celia's voice was close now, real. "Are you in there?" She rapped a knuckle on his forehead. "It's almost time for everyone to sit down."

Dad was watching them from the sideboard, his drink in his hand. When he saw Steve looking, he took a swig from his glass and said, "I'll call the others." He went the long way out of the room, around the table on the side opposite Steve.

"Bring the challahs, ok?" Celia said to Steve. "I'll get out the bread cover for them."

In the kitchen, Ruby had set the golden, crispy chickens on the big china platter next to a bowl of potatoes and onions and mushrooms that had cooked in the bottom of the roasting pan. She had made the salad herself tonight instead of asking them to cut up the ingredients. Now she turned from the drain board with the huge wooden bowl in both hands. "You can take this on out," she said.

Steve did. By the time he'd gone back to the kitchen and come out a second time with the two challah loaves, people were settling into their places. He slid into his chair and waited.

Jamie sang the blessing on the wine and passed the big silver goblet around the table. They each took a sip. When it got to Steve, he took an extra swallow and relaxed as the liquid warmed his throat. *That's good,* he thought.

Chapter 19.

Sunday, June 1, 1958: 9:15 a.m.

Celia

Celia stood at the front hall mirror, adjusting the hat she'd gotten for Easter with the money from her after-school cashier job. It was a dramatic hat, navy blue straw with a big curvy brim. *Glamorous. I hope.* She picked her white gloves up off the table and turned into the living room, where Laurie and Steve were waiting for Mom and Dad to come down and drive the three of them to Mass. *Good a time as any,* she thought.

"Hey, Warrie," she said to the back of Laurie's head where he half lay on the long couch.

He sat up and looked at her, surprised. "Wow, that's the second time lately you've called me that. Are you regressing—Ceecee," he said.

"Speaking of prehistoric times," she laughed. "What can I say? I'm feeling sort of soggy and sisterish."

Laurie cocked his head to one side. "Just what form will this excess of feeling take, I wonder? And what will it cost me?"

Steve, who had peered up at them over the piano, where he was picking out a tune, ducked back down behind the music rack again.

"So suspicious," Celia gibed. "You cut me to the quick." *He's really looking wary now, better cut to the chase.* She came over and sat next to him on the couch, sobering. "Have you decided what to do about the prom?"

"We're still going back and forth on it," he said. "We have to make up our minds pretty soon, since it's next week. Why?"

"Well, I had an idea. You know Rima's going to be out of town? Her family's going to Cape Ann for the week. So Jamie doesn't have a date."

"This helps me how?"

"Hang on, I'm getting there. The other thing is that Ray and I broke up. So I don't have a date either." *It's starting to dawn on him.* She nodded encouragingly. "That's right. Jamie takes Linda, you take me, then you and Linda spend the evening together. Nobody could come down on you for going with your own sister, and Dunkelman sure couldn't threaten Linda if she goes with Jamie. So everybody's happy."

"Kind of a boring evening for you and Jamie."

Celia shrugged. "We'll manage." *He doesn't look exactly thrilled.*

Laurie took her hands in both of his. "Cissy, don't think I'm not grateful. I can't tell you how much I appreciate your coming up with this idea. You and Jamie, both. But I have to think about it. It's not only about going to the dance, you know."

"I know. You want to make a statement about the race thing. But you'll be there, and you'll be dancing with Linda, and everyone will know you outsmarted Dunkelman."

"Not much of an achievement, that last. Woman's an idiot. Let me mull this over, sweetheart —I'll think about it at Mass, and later I'll call Linda and see what she thinks. And thank you, really." He leaned forward and ducked under her hat brim to kiss her cheek.

Beth came through the dining room door, wearing a pale blue shirtwaist dress and white flats. Her golden hair flowed loose down her back under her little white hat. *She looks like a china doll,* Celia thought.

"What's that you're playing, Steve?" Beth asked.

"That new thing, 'Volare,'" Steve said. "It's a dumb song, but it's easy. I'm trying to figure out how the piano works."

"I think you're off by a third, baby," Beth said, moving to stand beside him. Her fingers skimmed the keyboard, then she struck a note. "Here's your G, like the third string on your guitar."

"Oh, I see," Steve said, starting the song again. "Thanks."

Beth drifted over to the armchair by the window. "Who else is here?" she said.

"Me and Laurie," Celia said. "Your outfit looks nice, Bethie."

"Does it? Thank you."

"We're just talking about a plot to get Laurie and Linda to the dance without starting World War Three. Are you and Peter going?"

"I don't think so. He isn't comfortable around large groups of sighted people." She turned toward Steve. "I just had a thought. Our own school is having a dance in a couple of weeks, but we won't have any live music. Maybe you and Robbie could play?"

"We're not ready to play at a school dance yet," Steve said. "Even a small school like yours. Not after just a couple of birthday parties and that sock hop in Nancy's basement."

"And the school assembly last week, don't forget," Celia said.

"Even so," Steve said.

"Well, let me know when you think you are ready," Beth said.

Mom came down the stairs. "Ready to go?" she said, pulling on her gloves. "Joy and Rob are going with Ruby, so you three are with us."

Steve got up from the piano reluctantly. "Why do I have to go to Mass?" he said. "Jamie and Beth don't." He came forward toward the hallway, but stopped short when he saw Dad coming down the stairs, hat in hand.

"Jamie goes to services in Lancaster on Saturday morning, and Beth will be leaving in a few minutes to go to Quaker Meeting with the Johnstons, as you know perfectly well," Dad said. Steve shrugged impatiently, but Celia noticed he avoided meeting Dad's eyes. *Something's wrong there*, she thought, as Dad stepped back out of Steve's space.

Mom was putting on her raincoat. "Why don't you want to go, Steve?" she asked.

"It's boring—it's not even in English. And I don't like all those strangers, and the big room makes me nervous, and all those statues are creepy."

There was a crack of thunder outside. Celia laughed. "You're making God mad, Stevie," she teased.

153

Steve shot her a look. "I think you're the one God's mad at," he said. "I don't know much about hats, but that one doesn't look like an umbrella to me."

Gah, he's right! Even under an umbrella, the dampness will make this hat wilt like a dead cabbage. Celia clutched at the broad brim, then pulled her hat off with a sigh and went for a headscarf.

"Could Steve come to Meeting with me?" Beth asked. "It's not so big, and there's no Latin, of course. I don't think the Johnstons would mind if he rode along; I'll take one of their boys on my lap."

"How come you have a different religion, anyway?" Steve asked. "Robbie's your real brother, and he's Catholic like everybody but Jamie."

"It was my choice," Beth said. "I got interested in the Friends when I met one at my school, and the more I learned the more it seemed like the place for me."

"So why can't I pick what I do?"

"You can, when you know a little more," Dad said.

"I'll be fourteen next month," Steve said, still not looking at Dad.

"And Joy turns fourteen tomorrow, but she doesn't get to pick whether she goes to church or not, either."

"How old was Beth?"

"That's different, she had seriously thought about what she believed, and looked into her choice. When you've done that, you can make your own decision, too."

"What if I pick nothing?"

"You need to have some connection to God," Mom said. "Even if you don't feel like it. I think just being there is good for you. It's what the Church calls actual grace: you put yourself in the right place and let it come to you. You can go with Beth if you'd rather, though."

"Yeah, I'll try it," Steve said.

"Well, whoever's going with us better get moving," Dad said. "We're going to be late."

As Celia followed Laurie out the door, she thought, *I wonder if Mom and Dad realize what a big deal it is that Steve felt able to argue with them.* She looked at their faces out of the corner of her eye. *Yeah, they do.*

Chapter 20.

Saturday, July 12, 1958: 3:00 p.m.

Joy

Steve and Joy dumped their bikes in the garage and walked around to the front door. "Dibs on the first shower," Joy said as they came in.

"Shower?" Steve said. "We just spent an hour in the water, what do you need to shower for?"

"It's not good to leave chlorine on your skin and hair." *He doesn't know what I'm talking about.* "That smell you were complaining about, that's a chemical that kills germs in the pool," she explained. "You know, like in the cleanser we use on the bathroom sinks. And riding home we got dusty and sweaty, anyway. You did really well on Laurie's old bike, by the way, for somebody who just learned to ride. And in your swimming lesson, too."

Steve shrugged. "You're the good swimmer. You looked like you were just as easy in the water as out of it."

"I should, I've been on the swim team for a couple of years now. But it's fun, once you get over being scared."

"I wasn't too scared. A little, but going into the water wasn't as hard as going to school. I'm glad for summer vacation. I don't have to be around so many people all the time."

"But I thought you liked it when you and Robbie play at birthday parties and stuff—isn't that being around strangers, too?"

"That's different. I don't have to talk to them. I sort of talk to them with the songs, with the music. And Robbie's right there with me."

Look at his face when he talks about making music, Joy thought. *It's the only time he looks really happy.* "Do you know that on Wednesday it will be a year since you came here?"

He gave her an exasperated grimace. "Of course I know it." *Oh.*

They were upstairs by now, in front of their bedroom doors. "See you in a few minutes," Joy said. "I was kidding about the first shower, by the way. We don't need that much hot water on a day like this, go ahead and take yours at the same time. I'll meet you downstairs after. I think there's watermelon."

Twenty minutes later they were sitting on wicker chairs in the screened porch, slurping watermelon and spitting the seeds into a wooden bowl between them. Steve had swallowed the first few of his, but he watched Joy and quickly copied her. *He's getting better at figuring things out. He's not so afraid all the time now. Except—*

"Steve?"

"Yeah?"

"Ever since that night when you, uh, got so upset..."

Steve hunched his shoulders up. "What about it?"

"Just, I noticed you kind of shy away from Dad. Even on your birthday last week, when he handed you your present from him and Mom it looked like you were afraid to take it."

Steve looked nervous, but he answered her. "He scared me that night. I mean, he was really nice to me, but he smashed that stuff upstairs. It was because he was mad at Bert, but afterwards I started thinking, what if he gets mad at me like that?"

"He never would, Steve. He'd never do anything bad to you."

"I don't know. Uncle Kevin said their father used to beat Dad. And I know Dad killed people in the war.

Can you tell me he's never hit anybody here, even once?"

"Well, actually…" Joy shifted uncomfortably in her seat. "Oh, don't look at me like that, Steve, it was a spanking, it wasn't the Spanish Inquisition." *He doesn't get that. Make him understand.* "Listen, I really deserved it. I was mad that Beth got a new outfit and I didn't, so I switched all her clothes around so she wouldn't know which was which, and she got dressed for school in a madras plaid skirt and a striped shirt and I made fun of her. She cried, and then Dad smacked me and I cried, and then Dad cried—it was a mess. And he slapped Laurie once, but that was—" She stopped talking with a gulp. *Oh, God, look at him, he's terrified.* "He would never do anything like that to you, Steve."

Steve dropped his watermelon rind on the floor and lurched out of his chair. Joy headed him off as he ran for the door into the kitchen. "Wait, Steve, please wait." She put her arms around him. He was vibrating like there was a motor inside him, a steady small thrum against her.

"Dad being mad was just the start. There more, that night," he whispered. "Bad stuff I remembered. Jamie gave me this old bear thing, and when I held it I could see in my mind that I used to have a bear when I was little. And then, holding it, I

159

heard the glass in the music room smashing again, and I remembered the crash."

"The crash?"

"When my parents were killed."

"You were in the car?"

"I must of been. I was in the back holding my bear. Then there were bright lights, and the crash. I don't remember anything else, just the smashing glass and the bear. The only other thing I know is Bert, and being in The Room like I'd always been there." He was crying in soft little hitches of breath. "And the hitting, and the—" he brought one hand up and bit down hard on his knuckle. "Crashing and smashing and hitting," he said around it. "I can't take it, I can't, not again."

Joy squeezed him harder and buried her head in his shoulder. "Oh, Stevie."

Steve put his hands on her shoulders and pried her off him. "I have to be alone a little, Joy. I know you all know where I go now, but please don't follow me."

Joy sat in the living room waiting for Dad to get home. As the others came in, they'd asked her what was wrong, but she just said she was waiting for Dad. Then when he did come home, she didn't say anything. She let him go on upstairs to change out of his uniform into soft Saturday clothes. Somebody up there must have said something to him, though, because when he came back down he went straight to her, sat down beside her on the long couch by the door, and put his arm around her. "What's the story, Joy-of-my-life?"

She told him about her conversation with Steve. "I'm really sorry if I messed things up, Daddy. I wanted to tell him the truth, and I thought I could make him understand—"

"You didn't do anything wrong, precious." She sagged against him in relief. "In fact," he went on, "I think this is a good thing. Your mother and I have talked about the way he's acted around me since that night, and what to do about it. This gives me an opening. He's not in the cubbyhole any more; when I was changing I heard him playing above with Rob. Would you go up and bring him below to me in the study, please?"

Joy got up to the music room just as Steve and Rob finished playing "That'll Be the Day." The room was hot, and there was an old print of some guy in a big feathered hat hanging where the knickknack shelf used to be.

"I think the Kiwanis Club will go ape for that one," Robbie was saying. "Oh, hi, Jo-Jo, come to listen to us practice for next Friday?"

Joy was too tense to react to the hated nickname. "No, actually, Dad wants to see Steve downstairs for a few minutes. Sorry to butt in."

Robbie looked over at Steve's clenched right hand resting against his guitar strings, and the way his left hand was bent around the neck of the instrument and up to his eyes. "It's ok," Robbie said gently, tugging the guitar away and setting it down. "Go on, honey. I'll work on that bit I've been goofing up. You cut out and see what gives with Dad."

Joy took Steve's hand and pulled. He got up, unresisting, and followed her with his head down. All the way down both sets of stairs, he walked with his hand limp in hers, not looking at her. *Anything I say would probably be the wrong thing,* she thought. *Better just keep quiet.*

Dad was waiting for them in the study, standing behind his desk. He had the big red family Bible and a typewritten piece of paper in front of him. Joy could see the note Steve wrote him as a birthday present last year pressed under the glass on top of the desk.

"Uh, I guess I'll let you two talk," Joy said, dropping Steve's hand and starting to back away.

Steve shot her a look of appeal and Dad shook his head. "No, please stay, Joy," he said. "I want you to be a witness."

"A witness?"

"To a formal document I've just drawn up. Look at me, please, Steve." Steve looked up. Dad put his right hand on the Bible and picked up the paper in the other hand. He started to read: "I, Sean Patrick McAlister, do hereby solemnly swear that I will never, under any circumstances, strike or physically assault Steven O'Riordan McAlister for any reason. I make this pledge on my honor as an officer and on my love for him as a father, so help me God." He put the paper down, signed and dated it, and turned it toward Joy, handing her the pen.

Joy signed it on the line marked "Witness" and, at a gesture from Dad, handed it to Steve. Steve's mouth was open and his lips were trembling. He tried a couple of times to say something, but nothing came out. He took the paper and read it through, and then again. Then he carefully folded it into a tiny square and put it in his shirt pocket. Dad came around the desk and held his hand out to Steve and they shook hands as though they were two grown men making a deal.

That seemed to break something open in Steve. He fell against Dad's chest, sobbing. Dad scooped him up in his arms and carried him to the big rocking chair by the fireplace, sitting down with Steve in his lap. He petted Steve's hair and held him and rocked him and crooned a little hum to him.

The room was warm in the summer afternoon, but Steve was shivering. Joy picked up the afghan from the sofa and gently laid it over him, tucking it around his shoulders and closing him in with Dad. Then she left them alone together.

Chapter 21.

Sunday, August 17, 1958: 6:15 p.m.

Steve

Steve rattled down the back stairs into the kitchen, where Jamie and Beth were helping Ruby get dinner ready. It was Mom and Dad's anniversary; a huge sheet cake lay ready on the breakfast table, ready to be carried out later. Jamie was chopping peppers and onions *knife don't look at the knife* and Beth was tearing chicken meat from a cold carcass with her clever fingers. Ruby pulled fresh hot biscuits out of the oven to go with the salad. Steve liked salad nights: the big bowl of greens and cold vegetables, with chicken in it tonight—he'd never eaten anything like that before he came here. And having it on the screened porch in the warm summer evening was nice. *Outside, but still safe.*

"Anybody know where Robbie is?" he asked. "He isn't in his room or the music room."

"I think he's watching TV," Jamie said.

"Tell him it's just about time to sit down; everybody should wash up," Ruby called after Steve as he crashed through the swinging door to the dining room. He went on through the living room, jerking his chin to Laurie, who was reading by the window, and on into the front hall toward the narrow room behind the stairs they called the TV room. Steve was feeling good. *Wait till he hears.*

Rob was watching the news with Dad and Mom, the three of them squashed onto the shabby little couch together, talking about the quiz show scandals. Joy was at the end of the room in an old wicker chair reading a movie magazine. They all looked at Steve.

"Ruby says it's time to wash up for dinner," he said. They started to move; Dad reached over and turned off the television. But Steve still stood there in front of them. "I just got a phone call from Mr. Masland," he said.

"The high school principal?" said Mom in surprise. "Didn't he want to talk to your father or me?"

Steve shook his head. "He wanted to talk to me or Rob." He turned to Robbie. "His wife heard us play at that bar thing."

"Bar—oh, you mean the Feldman kid's bar mitzvah," Robbie said.

"Yeah, that. He said she liked it so much, he wants us to play at the homecoming dance!"

"He does?"

"And we're going to get paid: fifty dollars! Each!"

Mom and Dad gasped. That was serious money. Robbie looked like someone had hit him over the head with a guitar. Joy ran forward and hugged Steve around the middle, squealing. "Ooh, I'm going to have a famous brother! Uh, two famous brothers!" Steve picked her up and swung her around.

Dad hugged Robbie and clapped Steve on the shoulder. "I'm happy for you, boys. All the hard work you've put in practicing, and playing at those private parties—you really deserve this."

"You sure do," Mom said, kissing them both. "Let's go tell the others. We have to get to the table, anyway, before Ruby disowns us."

"I'll call Celia, she's upstairs. Can I tell her about this?" Joy said, and raced off at Steve's nod.

The family gathered around the table on the big shady porch. Since it had been Jamie and Beth's turn to help with dinner, they got to say the grace. Beth's grace wasn't anything said, though, it was just silence. Steve liked that, just sitting quietly together; he didn't even mind the holding hands so much any more. And then after a while Jamie put on his little black prayer hat, picked up a biscuit and quietly started in with his grace, half singing it in that language—Hebrew—like what Steve had heard at the bar thing. *That's nice too. Like a coda on Beth's prayer and a prelude to dinner, both together.*

Jamie said amen and ate a piece of the biscuit, and everyone but he, Beth, and Steve crossed themselves. Then the chatter started as the basket of biscuits went around the table and Ruby dished up salad to everyone at one end while Mom poured punch and iced tea at the other. A little silence fell once everyone was served and people started eating. Rob, next to Steve, gave him a nudge and motioned with his head to the others. *He's going to let me tell them.*

"Um," Steve said. Everyone looked at him. *Don't get scared. It's just the family. No, pretend they're an audience. You're on the stage and they're not.* Reassured, he cleared his throat and told them about Mr. Masland's call.

The ones who'd already heard about it nodded as he spoke and smiled to hear it again. Joy, on his other side, squeezed his hand under the table. Laurie thumped a happy tattoo on the table with his fists, making the silverware jump. Beth said, "Oh, Stevie, I knew it was only a matter of time till you and Robbie got discovered."

Rob laughed. "It's not exactly *Ed Sullivan,* you know, Bethie."

"Maybe not," Ruby put in, "but it's a start. Hey, should all us old folks show up at the dance and embarrass you two?"

"Don't you dare," Rob said as Mom and Dad joined Ruby in thinking up ancient dance styles they could resurrect.

The conversation broke up into teasing and bantering. Steve didn't know how to do that. He was just starting to feel bad about it when he looked across the table at Jamie. Jamie was watching him and smiling, just a little crook at the sides of his lips that lifted his cheeks a little without showing his teeth, but it made Steve feel warm all over.

After dinner, he and Robbie went up to the music room to start working out their program. Joy came with them and perched on the piano bench while they ran through their repertoire.

"What about that Platters song, 'Great Pretender'?" Robbie said.

"Ok, I guess so."

"You don't like it?"

"I like it ok, it just seems kind of—I don't know, like, tired."

"Hmm. I guess that means 'Heartbreak Hotel' is out."

"Nah, that's like our whaddayacallit, our signature song. Besides, with Elvis in the army, somebody has to step up," Steve laughed.

"That Ritchie Valens kid's stuff is boss."

"True. And good to dance to."

"I wish we could manage 'Bye, Bye Love.'"

"Me too."

"Why can't you?" Joy demanded. "That's a great song."

"I know," Steve explained, "but when we tried that sort of close harmony the Everly Brothers use, our voices didn't go together right in those parallel thirds."

"Oh." Joy subsided, looking a little mystified.

"The way it usually ends up," Robbie said, "is that Steve takes the melody in the verses and I back him up in the choruses."

Steve looked down uncomfortably. *I didn't know he'd noticed that; we've never talked about it. He doesn't seem upset, though.*

The boys noodled around for a while and scrabbled through some sheet music. Rob made notes on what they came up with.

After a bit Robbie went into Buddy Holly's "Peggy Sue" while Steve listened. *Funny, it's a cool song, but it's just not my song. Rob sounds good with it, though.*

Then Steve did "Tom Dooly." *And that's not his song. Look at his face, he's being polite. He doesn't like the Kingston Trio at all. But Joy does. She never smiles unless she means it. She smiles a lot, though.*

Steve tried a few bars of "Guitar Boogie Shuffle," but as usual it was too much for him. "Did you hear Big Bill Broonzy died last week?" he said.

"Yeah, a real drag," Rob said.

"Who's that?" Joy asked.

"Best blues man ever," Steve said. "Listen."

He slid onto the piano bench next to her and started a honkytonk beat. "'I just keep on drinkin, till good liquor carry me down,'" he sang as Joy giggled.

Rob chuckled. "We can't sing that at the homecoming dance," he said. "Big Bill himself couldn't make that scene."

"I didn't know you liked music like that," Joy said.

"I like all kinds of music," Steve said. "Besides, without the blues, there's no rock 'n' roll."

"And without a program, there's no McAlister Brothers at the homecoming dance," Robbie reminded him. "Come back from your little trip down musical memory lane and get with it."

"Well, what about Woody Guthrie?" Steve said, sliding into "This Land Is Your Land."

"Uh, uh. Mr. Masland thinks Woody's a Commie. Anyway, I don't think the crowd at the high school will dig that folky bit."

Steve swung around to look at Rob. "There should be a way to do the folk sort of storytelling, real storytelling about real people, and do it with a rock 'n' roll beat."

Robbie tilted his head to one side, considering. "Cool idea," he said. "Maybe you should invent it. But right now we have to get with the program. Come on, how about some ballads—'Kisses Sweeter than Wine' almost sounds like folk music."

Steve looked down and put his mind back on the program. *Don't push it. Don't make anybody mad,* he thought.

"Well, I think Steve's right," Joy said.

Chapter 22.

Tuesday, September 2, 1958: 11:00 a.m.

Laurie

Laurie was on the phone in the upstairs hall. "I know, Linda," he was saying, "but Haverford's not that far away, and you'll have a great time at Dickinson. We'll see each other at Thanksgiving, or I might even sneak back here for a weekend in October. I'll miss you like hell, I told you that last night, but we've talked about this. You're going to concentrate on your writing and I've got to get ready for law school; that's why we're going to different colleges."

On the other end of the line, Linda said, "Laurie, be honest. You could do pre-law perfectly well at Dickinson, and go to law school here, too. I understand why you picked Haverford, but it's not just about our taking different career paths. It's about cooling down what's been between us. You're going to meet someone, I just know it."

Laurie put his back against the wall and slid down it, ending up on the floor next to the telephone table. *How can I make this better?* "Babe, we've talked about this. We're both going to meet people. I love you a lot, we'll always be close, but you know we never thought this was forever, at our age."

Linda started to cry. *Guess that wasn't the way,* Laurie thought resignedly. "Sweetheart—"

But she was talking again. "I know what's going to happen. You're going to meet somebody… somebody more like you, who knows—stuff. Somebody who understands things the way your little white high school girlfriend can't."

"So I'm going to dump you because you're white? After all that crap we went through to go to the prom? You really think that if only there'd been a black girl in our school I would rather have gone with her? Jesus, Linda, what do you take me for?"

Still sniffling a little, she said, "Of course I don't mean that. But pretending to be your brother's prom date made me feel like there was something wrong with me. We talked about that; how afraid it made me. Then there's all this stuff happening, those kids in Oklahoma sitting-in to integrate lunch counters and that awful business last year in Arkansas—it just seems like every time we hear about something like that, you get a little farther away from me."

She's right. I do. Laurie propped an elbow on his upraised knee and rested his forehead against his fist. "At least you won't have to be afraid any more."

"That's not it, either!" she protested. "Do you think I'll stop caring what happens to you? And I've been—I don't know, getting used to it, to living with that edge, wondering when someone's going to attack us just for being together. But now that you're going away I realize I don't want to lose you; I want to stay part of your life."

"I don't know what to say, Linda. What we've been through together is important to me, too. I can't imagine what my life would have been like without you, these past four years. But I don't like the idea of you being in trouble or danger because you're with me. And it's true that all the civil rights uproar makes me think more about being black, about what people who don't live in my safe little world go through every day. But I can't do anything about that, I can't promise not to care about it. How can I?"

"You can't. That's why I'm upset. Once you leave here, nothing will ever be the same." She blew her nose. "I'm sorry, Laurie. I didn't mean to do this. Have a great time and I'll see you in October." Before he could speak again she had hung up.

Laurie reached up to put the receiver back on the hook, then crossed his arms on his knees and lowered his head to them. *Nothing will ever be the same.* After a minute he heard a creak and a rustle. When he looked up, Steve was peering out of the open doorway to his bedroom.

"Did you and Linda break up?" Steve asked.

"Good question. Maybe."

Steve sat cross-legged on the floor in the doorway. "Because you're black and she's white?"

"That makes it sound too simple, but yeah, it does complicate everything. Things are changing, especially in the South. They've formed this group in Atlanta, the Southern Christian Leadership Conference—SCLC, they call it. After the Montgomery bus boycott, they realized they had to get more organized. Jim Crow is on the way out."

"Who's Jim Crow?"

"It's not a who, it's a what. It's the name for the way colored and white are segregated in some places. People are starting to say they're not going to put up with it any more."

"You mean like that lady who wouldn't sit in the back of the bus?"

"Rosa Parks? Yes, that's what I'm talking about. Buses and lunch counters and railroad waiting rooms and public restrooms and even water fountains—the days when people who look like you and people who look like me have to use separate ones are coming to an end."

Steve picked at the carpet between his feet a little, then said, "You know, I never saw anybody who looked like you before I got to that place, to Rolling Meadow."

"Well, you never saw much of anybody but Bert before then, did you?"

"No, nobody I could remember. But those kids scared me. Like you scared me." He bent his head lower. "You still scare me, sometimes," he said softly, "when I just see you all of a sudden, before I remember who you are."

Laurie dropped his head back onto his arms.

"I'm sorry," Steve said. "I shouldn't have said that."

Laurie looked up again. "No, I want you to say what you're feeling. It's the only way to make things better, Steve."

"But now you're going away. I won't get a chance to get used to you more."

"I'm not going forever, you know."

177

"It feels like you are. It doesn't feel safe. Here in this house, here we're all safe. I need to have everybody inside it. When I k-killed Bert, I couldn't leave The Room. I just sat there next to his body till they found me. It was a couple of days, I think."

"Oh, God, sweetheart, I didn't know that. You were scared to leave?"

Steve nodded, gulping. "Then they took me away to Rolling Meadow and there were all these kids and grownups and colored people and women and noises and weird food and I didn't know what to do. Then Mom brought me here and it was quieter and it was safe. Going to school was hard, but I knew I was coming home at night. Singing, too—but Robbie's always there to get me back safe. Now you're going out there where maybe people hate you. How can you do that?"

"I have to go out and face the world some time; now's the time. I'm nervous about it, but I'm ready to go."

Mom appeared at the top of the stairs. Her lips were pressed together and her hair was coming out of its usual neat French twist. "'Ready to go'?" she repeated. "Ready to go is exactly what you're not, young man." She came forward to tower over Laurie where he sat on the floor. "I just looked at the car to see how much room there was left. You know what I saw? Plenty of room, because you haven't loaded anything into it yet." Her voice was rising. "Nothing is loaded—are you even packed yet? Have you done anything at all this morning? Jamie's suitcases are there, but nothing of yours. No suitcases, no boxes, no typewriter—have you forgotten we're supposed to leave in an hour and a half? You are nowhere near ready to go. And I find you here lounging around and chatting as though you had all the time in the world, as though—"

Laurie had pushed himself to his feet and stood looking down at her. Suddenly he overrode her with a high, swooping noise: "Whoop, whoop, whoop! Dive! Dive! This is not a drill! This is not a drill! Whoop, whoop, whoop!"

She gaped at him for a second, then collapsed onto the telephone chair in helpless laughter. *That did it,* Laurie thought with satisfaction. *I still have the touch.*

Mom got hold of herself and stood up, shaking her head. "Get back to work, you lunatic," she said. "We really do have to leave soon, and we have to eat lunch first." She gave him a playful smack on the arm and went on to rummage in the linen closet, repeating under her breath, "Whoop, whoop," and chuckling.

Steve peered around the edge of his doorway from where he'd retreated during Mom's tirade. "What just happened?"

Laurie shook his head, smiling. "Mom gets a little carried away when she's nervous or upset. The idea of Jamie and me leaving is making her crazy. But when she gets like that, if you can make her laugh, you can usually jolly her out of it." He cast the last few words at Mom's back where she was getting linens out. She snorted.

Better get moving, he thought, slapping the wall lightly and starting toward his room. *Don't push your luck.*

Steve followed him. "What was that you were saying, and that noise you were making?"

"I was imitating what they say on submarines when they're being attacked. And there's a horn that makes that whooping sound." Laurie turned toward him. "Hey, how about giving me a hand with this stuff before she really gets after me?"

Steve hauled a box of books off Laurie's dresser. Laurie shouldered a garment bag, grabbed one suitcase handle and slid another case under that arm, and picked up the case of his portable Smith-Corona typewriter in his other hand.

"I never think of Mom getting upset about things," Steve said as they started down the front stairs with their burdens. "Dad, yeah, I've seen that, but Mom always seems so—together."

"I know," Laurie said. "But she's human, too, believe me. The two of us leaving is hard on her. She hates change as much as you do, for kind of the opposite reason. Things changed too much for her for too long. When she was growing up, she was always getting dragged from one foster home to another. Some of them were pretty bad, too. So she never knew what the next one would bring." He put down his typewriter to open the front door and they went through.

Steve slung the box against his hip to free a hand and closed the door behind them. "Did she get beaten up, like Dad did?" he asked as they dropped their loads behind the shabby old Pontiac station wagon.

"Not so much that," Laurie said, opening the back flap with its scarlet and black Haverford decal next to the MIT one in gray and crimson. They started to stash things in the tail compartment next to Jamie's two suitcases. "Though she did tell me that in one of the places she stayed, they used to punish her by making her kneel on raw rice. But she was never abused the way you were, or even Dad. It was more that she never felt like anybody really cared about her. Some of those people were just in it for the government check."

Ruby had come around the house with a grocery bag that she handed to Laurie to put in the car. "That's one reason she got her law degree on top of the one in psychology," she said. "She wanted to work to tighten up the regulations on fosterage, like she's doing at Rolling Meadow. It's hard to buck a system like that, though. But that's why she brought you home in the first place, Laurie. She told me she couldn't stand the idea of you getting shunted around in the foster system, especially as a black child who wouldn't get much consideration."

She stood back and considered him appraisingly. "And you were such a cute little guy before you got big and mean and ugly. There's a tin of cookies and another one of brownies in that bag. Maybe you can buy yourself some friends."

Laurie chuckled and made a face at her as Mom came out the front door carrying Laurie's sheets and towels in a plastic storage box. "I'm sorry I yapped at you, Laddie," she said as he took it from her and loaded it in.

"It was worth it to see the look on your face when I did the 'dive' routine," he said, bending to kiss her cheek. *God, in a minute I'm going to bust out crying.* "Hey, what does a guy have to do to get a little lunch around this place before being cast into the outer darkness?"

"Well, you could find yourself a cheaper hotel," Ruby said. "Or I might be able to scare up a little something—say, your favorite tuna casserole, that nasty thing with the potato chips in it, that just happens to be in the oven right now?"

They went into the house laughing, and Steve followed them in and closed the door behind him.

Chapter 23.

Tuesday, September 2, 1958: 12:15 p.m.

Jamie

Jamie smiled when Ruby brought out dessert after their hurried lunch. *Tapioca: my favorite.* "Thanks, Ruby."

Laurie looked at the creamy, lumpy mass in the bowl and said, "Are you going to eat that, or have you already?"

"Funny as a crutch, big brother. Did you notice me heroically refraining from commenting on your ghastly casserole?"

"Yeah, you're one of nature's gentlemen, Hymeleh."

He can joke, but he only calls me that when he's feeling sentimental. I will not, will not, have another big emotional scene today. Saying goodbye to the other kids was bad enough. "Did you finally get your stuff in the car, smart guy? I don't want to miss my train just because you had to have one

184

last bill and coo with the lovely Linda." *Guess that was pretty transparent—he's still smiling at me.*

"All packed and loaded, thank you for your concern. How about you?" Laurie said. "Have you and Rima had your dramatic farewell?"

"Rima and I were over at the beginning of summer, I thought you knew. I had enough dramatic farewells this morning before the others left for school, didn't you?"

"Ah, you know me. I can never get enough adulation from our younger siblings." Laurie turned to Steve. "I'm glad the folks let you stay home today to see us off, Steve, so at least there'll be one of you to wave a hankie out the window."

"Hankie?" Steve asked from the other end of the table.

"A handkerchief," Laurie told him. "Like a Kleenex, but made out of cloth. You know, like Dad uses."

Steve nodded and poked at his tapioca. "Do I have to eat this? It tastes like snot."

"Hey, you little ingrate," Ruby said, coming in from the kitchen with a handled shopping bag. "Children starving in China would give anything for a nice bowl of snot." Steve looked uncertain and Ruby's tone gentled. "No, you don't have to eat it. But please don't say rude things about the food I fix you. Jamie, I put your brownie and cookie tins in this bag in case you want to carry it with you. If not, we can mail it."

"No, I'll carry it, thanks, Ruby. I might get hungry on the train." *And it will be nice to have a taste of home.*

Mom poked her head in the door to the living room. "Let's get a move on, boys. Your father's already in the car, worrying that we can't get Laurie settled at Haverford and still get Jamie to Philly in time for the Boston train." She came a step farther in and said in a stage whisper, "He's looking at the map for shortcuts."

"Oh, God," Laurie said, leaping to his feet.

"Ruby, quick, give me that bag," Jamie said.

He and Laurie hurriedly kissed Ruby goodbye and pushed into the living room, followed by Steve. Laurie hugged Steve and moved on out the front door, but Jamie stopped to look around the room, sliding his hand along the edge of the chess table.

He and Laurie had stood here last night, heads bowed, while Dad held his hands over them and said the priestly blessing: "The Lord bless you and keep you, the Lord make his face to shine upon you and be gracious unto you, the Lord lift His countenance upon you and give you peace." *Like Tati used to say, only he said it in Hebrew. Now I'm at home in this House of Rimmon, with their alien faith. But they are my family too, they are.*

Mom stepped back from the front hall. "Ok, son?" she said softly.

"Suddenly, skipping ninth grade isn't looking like it was such a hot idea any more. I could have had another year before doing this."

She came close and rubbed her fingers lightly over his. "You could change your mind," she said. "Stay home for the year. Go to Dickinson and keep living here, or just get a job and take some time to think about what you want to do."

Jamie gave a little laugh. "You're a fiend, you know? You go and give me carte blanche for what I say I want, forcing me to acknowledge that I don't really want it."

Mom smiled. "Just call me Dr. Machiavelli," she said. "Seriously, Jamie, I think you're going to love it at MIT. There'll be people like you there that you can make friends with."

"People like me? Jews, you mean, or—?"

"Intellectuals, mathematicians, people with brains who aren't intimidated by other people with brains, that's what I meant. Though yes, there'll also be Jews and—" she glanced at Steve, looking woebegone by the window, "—and all kinds of people like you."

But how many of them will be dragging the dead after them, all six million, and the other ten thousand, and my own particular two?

Mom was looking at him keenly. "Leave the dead behind you, my darling. It's time for you to start living."

"Are you a mind reader?"

"No, but I happen to be an absolutely brilliant psychologist." They smiled at each other. She held his eye for a minute, then turned to rummage in her big purse. "Here, I was going to wait till we got to the 30th Street Station to give you this, but—" She pulled out a wool muffler in MIT gray and crimson and wrapped it around his neck. "It's too warm for today, of course, but I wanted you to have something of home in those cold Boston winters. I've been knitting it in Ruby's room so you wouldn't see."

Jamie rubbed his cheek on the back of her hand as she fussed and patted at the scarf. Her hands stilled and she dropped her forehead lightly to his upper arm.

The front door opened and Laurie called, "You guys, he's saying Route 30 would be faster than the Turnpike. Get out here!"

"Coming!" Mom hustled out.

Jamie turned to Steve. "Enjoy having our room to yourself, monster." Steve just looked at him. *I can't touch him, I can't, I'll fall apart,* Jamie thought. "Good luck playing at the homecoming dance," he said. Still no response. "I'll be back, I promise." Steve nodded.

Jamie went into the hall and out the door without pausing again. He piled into the back seat of the station wagon next to Laurie, hunching against the door to keep a space between them. Laurie didn't notice; he was mopping his eyes and gazing at the house. In the front seat, Mom and Dad were arguing about which route to take.

The car backed out of the driveway. As they turned and pulled onto the road, Jamie leaned forward to see across Laurie. Steve was standing in the living room window, waving a Kleenex.

Chapter 24.

Sunday, October 26, 1958: 1:30 p.m.

Cecilia

Celia was on one of the short settees in the living room, cuddled up to Mom, sniffling onto her breast. "And then Bill comes out with, 'I think of you like more of a sister,'" she said. Mom's arms tightened around her. "I'm everybody's sister," Celia complained. "My nickname even sounds like 'sister.' But my own boyfriend? Ex-boyfriend, I should say. That's two exes in less than a year. What am I doing wrong, Mommy?"

Mom kissed the top of Celia's head. "You're not doing anything wrong, my darling," she said. "I think the only problem is that you're more mature than most of the boys you know. When you get to the age where you're meeting older boys, and especially when you start dating grown men, you'll find they prize that sweetness and seriousness in you."

Oh, great. Celia sighed and pushed away a little. "I'm sure you're right, Mom, but—sorry—it's not much comfort. I'm seventeen, not thirty-seven. I want to have fun, too, and I want to have it now, and I want to have it with a real boyfriend, not a guy who thinks it's a great date to spend the whole homecoming dance telling me about his problems with his father. I mean, I know it's flattering that he thinks I might be helpful, but I would have liked to have a few dances, too, and maybe make out behind the bandstand like everybody else."

Mom nodded, making a little sympathetic sound, and kept stroking Celia's hair. After a minute she said, "Steve, did you want something?"

Celia craned around to see behind her. Steve was hovering in the doorway, looking as though he might bolt any minute. "Come on in," Celia said. "I'm just about done feeling sorry for myself for the moment." Then, when he still hesitated, "I mean it, Stevie. There's room for one more here."

He came forward and squeezed onto the settee on the other side of Mom, who disentangled one arm from Celia to put it around him. "Everything all right, sweetie?" she asked. Steve nodded.

"You guys were really great last night," Celia said. "Everybody was saying it was the best music we've had at a dance since anyone can remember. Not just the kids, the teachers were saying it, too."

"We were good, weren't we?" Steve said, brightening. "I was so scared before we went on; I've never been in front of so many people before. I threw up—I always throw up before we go on. But once the music started it, like, took over, you know?"

"I think that's one reason you were so good, it seemed like you weren't even aware of anything but what you were playing and singing."

"I wasn't. Except when we rested between sets, then I had to look around and see everybody. I saw that guy."

"What guy?"

"The one who gave me a hard time that day in the playground, with his friends."

"You're talking about Tom Varner," Celia said. "He didn't have any business there, even if he did flunk last year. I saw him, too, he was flashing a flask around at those bully sidekicks of his like a big man."

"Flask?"

"Liquor—you know, alcohol, booze."

"I thought it was something like that. They were talking too loud and pushing people, like they did with me, but they seemed sort of looser and like they didn't care. They reminded me of Bert." Steve started drumming on the upholstery with his free hand. "I wasn't close enough to know what they smelled like, though. I don't like that smell."

"The smell of the liquor?" Mom asked.

"Bert used to smell like that. Usually the way you smell reminds me of my mother. I can't really remember her, just sometimes the way she smelled, and the way she said... you know, *lovey*. And I don't remember my father at all. But that other smell reminds me of the night they died. They were fighting, and they smelled like Bert did later when he—and he'd make me drink it sometimes, too." Steve pulled away and went to stand looking into the fireplace, pushing against a half-burned log with his foot.

Mom nodded sadly. "That was probably a way to control you, to make you weaker."

"I guess. I didn't care as much about what he was doing when he made me drink first. Sometimes I wish I had that feeling again."

Mom's brow was furrowed and she was gripping Celia's hand hard. "Maybe you should mention that to Mrs. French, if you haven't already," she said. "You don't have to tell me whether you have or not," she said quickly as Steve turned farther away and started fiddling with the fireplace tools. "Remember, I told you, that was part of the reason for finding you a different therapist, so you would have someone to talk to apart from us. I'm not any more thrilled with Mrs. French than you are, but she can help you while we're looking for someone for the long term. Meanwhile, what you talk about with her is between you and her. I'm not trying to intrude on that. It's just a suggestion, since this seems to be bothering you."

Steve nodded and relaxed a little. *It's still too easy to throw him off,* Celia thought.

But Mom seemed troubled, too. "I hope it wasn't a mistake for you to go to that dance, Steve," she said. "It's really for high school kids, after all, and you're just in eighth grade—"

"But I wasn't *at* the dance," Steve protested. "Playing there is different. It's not like I was dancing or had a date there or something. Besides, Robbie was with me the whole time."

"I know," Mom said. "But—"

Steve had come back to the settee opposite Celia and Mom, leaning forward to talk to her. "Please, Mom, please don't say I can't do this stuff. I love it, I need to do it."

"I understand," she said. "But you've only been with us for a year and a half. You're still under a lot of strain. Maybe we're moving too fast—"

She was interrupted by Joy, damp and smelling of woodsmoke. "Hey, you guys," she said. "Come out and see the neat-o corn-shock-and-pumpkin decoration Dad and I put up. Mom and Celia, haven't you gotten out of your church clothes yet? Come on, Steve. You can help hang the ghost sheets. I can hardly wait for that eclipse of the moon tomorrow night. This is going to be the spookiest Halloween yet. Come on, before it starts raining again."

Mom laughed and got up. Celia rubbed her arms, suddenly feeling cold with the removal of Mom's body beside her.

"You two go on out," Mom said. "I have to help Ruby put up this year's applesauce. Steve, your father and I will talk about this, but I do understand it's important to you."

Steve bit his lip and nodded reluctantly. He started outside. Joy reached out and they brushed fingertips as he passed her.

Celia got up, too. "I'll be out as soon as I change," she said.

Joy looked impish. "You might not want to change, actually," she said. "You look awfully nice in that coat dress."

She's up to something. "What are you talking about, pipsqueak?"

"Well, it's just that there's somebody else out there with Dad right now."

"Who?"

"That college guy, Rick."

"Rick Hartzell?"

"That's the one. He's cute, you were right."

"Joy, if you said anything to him about me, I swear I'll—"

Joy giggled, backing away. "I didn't need to say anything, I promise. He's out there helping with everything and calling Dad 'sir' every third word and looking at the front door like if he stares hard enough you'll suddenly appear, like a vision of the Virgin Mary."

"Brat," Celia laughed, throwing a couch cushion at her. *Suddenly I feel so much better.* She started for the front door after Steve.

Chapter 25.

Rob

Rob came out of the TV room groaning. *The Lions won again. That's seven out of the past eight Thanksgivings—do the Packers just like losing?* He went through to the kitchen and into Ruby's sitting room, where Steve and Joy were watching *American Bandstand* on Ruby's TV. He looked around the pleasant room with its blonde furniture and bright upholstery, so different from the more traditional dark wood and pastel colors Mom favored. "Where's Ruby?"

"Lying down in there," Joy said, nodding toward Ruby's bedroom. "Worn out from Thanksgiving dinner. She said if we want anything else to eat today we're on our own, don't bother her unless the Russians land."

"God, I don't think I'm going to eat again till Christmas. Is this almost over?"

"Yeah," Steve said. "Is the game over?"

"Close enough. The others are torturing themselves to the bitter end, except for Celia, the

197

traitor, who's gloating. I couldn't stand it any more, so I decided to split."

Steve stretched and yawned, then got to his feet. "I'm tired of watching kids dance to other people's music anyway," he said, pulling Joy up after him. "Come on, let's do something."

"Want to go upstairs and make some sounds?" Rob said, turning off the TV.

"Hey, what a brilliant idea. What made you think of it?"

Crazy, he's actually teasing me. Rob grinned. "Just a genius, I guess," he said.

Steve started out of the room but Joy grabbed the back of his shirt. "If we leave Ruby's room like this she'll have our heads."

He turned back and helped her straighten Ruby's couch cushions. "You're a lot more careful here than you are in the living room or the TV room."

Joy refolded the afghan on the back of the couch. "That's because those are our rooms, too. Mom might get after us about making a mess, but she's not going to keep us out of them. If we leave Ruby's place a disaster area, she won't ask us back in."

They carried their soda bottles out to the shadowy kitchen, setting them next to the dark shapes of the upturned pots and pans on the drain board. Rob followed, closing the sitting room door behind them. As they went up the back stairs, Steve took Joy's hand.

They had settled in to the music room and tuned their guitars—Robbie the cheap Gibson he bought last year from his allowance and Steve the battered but better quality Spanish one that once belonged to Mom. They were warming up with "Heartbreak Hotel," Joy singing along, when Dad's head poked up from the stairwell.

"Hey," he complained, "are you swabbies going the whole vacation weekend holed up here? Anyway, the Field Marshall wants you to come below. She wants us to call Jamie in Boston soon." Robbie flipped open his guitar case, but Dad said, "Why don't you bring your instruments? It's been a long time since we've had a family sing."

Three hours later, with the family gathered around the fire in the living room, Steve was singing,

"'Young Jimmy was buried in one churchyard,
Barb'ra Allen in another;
A rose grew on young Jimmy's grave,
Barb'ra Allen's grew a green briar.'"

They had started it all together, as they had most of the repertoire of old favorites that night, but on this one the other voices had dropped out as they listened to Steve's pure, clear tenor with his slight vibrato winding around the old song like a vine.

"'They grew, they grew to the steeple tall
Till they could grow no higher,
And there they tied a true lover's knot:
The red rose 'round the green briar.'"

The guitars repeated the refrain and then there was quiet.

Radical, Robbie thought. *He really is better than me.* "Stevie, you know I'm no big fan of folk music," he said, "but you're radioactive when you sing that." *So where does that leave me? Behind?*

Joy, on the floor next to Steve, rested her head against his leg, saying nothing. *But she looks like she's praying.*

Head down, still in the thoughtful mode of the song, Steve spoke as though he'd plucked Rob's thought out of the air. "Today when we said the prayer before dinner, and we went around the table and everybody said what they were thankful for—who were we thanking? I mean, that sounds like a stupid question, but I really want to know. Everybody here prays all the time. Do you really think there's some God taking care of us? If there is, why didn't he take care of me?"

"He did take care of you, child," Ruby said, sitting with Mom on the long couch in her robe and slippers. "Because here you are."

He doesn't look convinced, Robbie thought.

Mom started passing around the plate of cocktail wieners and pineapple chunks she'd brought out for people who'd recovered from their mammoth afternoon dinner. "There's another way to think about it, maybe," she said. "Steve, when you go into yourself the way you do when you're really upset—is there anyone there?"

What on earth is she talking about?

But Steve seemed to understand; a look of wonder came over his face. "That's God?"

"That's the way I think about God: that sense of peace and clarity you can find inside yourself. You can sense it outside yourself, in the world around you, too, but it's the one inside that makes my life possible."

"But I thought that was bad, when I... you know, go away like that. That it was good if I stopped doing that crazy stuff."

"Steve, you 'going away' as you call it, isn't crazy; what happened to you is crazy. You found a way to deal with the craziness around you. Now that those terrible things aren't happening to you any more, maybe you can use what you've learned to go into yourself in a good way, to find the God in you."

"Mom," Rob said, "I don't think that's what they taught us in Catechism. Of course, you always were a troublemaker." He handed the snack plate back to her with a fond smile. "I remember you yelling at Sister Frances George for telling us only Catholics went to heaven."

"I don't believe the priests know everything," Mom said. "Or the sisters, either. We're the Church, too."

"I agree," Dad said. "How could I not? I have a Jewish son—do any of you think Jamie's going to hell because he's not a Catholic? To say nothing of our Bethie, here."

Beth gave a sad little laugh. "I'm afraid there are people in my church who think Catholics can't think for themselves, though."

Celia said, "Fascinating as this theological conversation is, if we're finished singing I'm going to go call Rick. We're supposed to go out tomorrow night, to that mixer at the community center. You guys are playing at that, right?"

"Right," Rob said. "In fact, Steve and I need to run through 'I Walk the Line,' that new Johnny Cash song." *And I need to get over being jealous. He's better, but he still needs me. Like Beth did when we were little. I can take care of him.*

Steve moved Joy's head off his knee, brushing his fingers through her hair, and picked up his guitar again as the others started to scatter.

"Can I go to the dance, too?" Joy asked as Dad got out of the armchair.

He looked over at Mom and some silent communication passed between them.

"There'll be other eighth graders there, and this is Thanksgiving weekend, so the answer is yes, this time. But we don't want you to think you'll be going to a dance every weekend. That goes for you, too, Steve."

Rob's stomach dropped. "But Dad," he said. "We're just really getting going. We can't turn down gigs and expect to be successful."

"We're less concerned with your being successful musicians than we are with your laying down a good solid base for your lives. It's bad enough that you've quit the basketball team, Robbie, and Steve's not doing any other extracurricular activities—"

"Music is my life," Steve said. "It's all I need, I don't care about anything else." Robbie groaned inwardly. *Exactly the wrong thing to say.*

But Dad smiled sympathetically. "I really do understand that it's important to you, son—to both of you. And we're not trying to stop you from doing it. We just want you to keep it in perspective, and develop some of those other parts of life that you haven't had a chance to explore yet."

"I don't want to explore anything," Steve said stubbornly. Joy was holding his ankle again. "I want to make music, and do something important with my music, mine and Robbie's."

"There's plenty of time for that," Mom said. "You've got your whole life ahead of you."

Chapter 26.

Monday, December 1, 1958: 7:30 a.m.

Steve

Steve woke up feeling pretty happy. The phone ringing in the hall had jolted him awake before his new clock radio went off, but he didn't mind. *Probably a call for Mom, some kid's in trouble at Rolling Meadow.* He liked the idea that she was helping other kids, but he liked the idea that he was special—part of the family and not just a patient at the institution—even better.

Life is copacetic, he thought, using a word he'd heard Robbie say lately. Thanksgiving had been great, and this Saturday would be the first night of Hanukkah this year, when they'd light the first candle and sing the songs while someone held the phone in the hall so Jamie could hear them all the way in Boston. It made Steve feel safe to think they would keep doing that even with Jamie out of the house. Jamie and Laurie would be home in less than two weeks, school would be out for almost a month, and he and Rob had three gigs lined up at private Christmas parties and another one at the Knights of Columbus Hall—and Mom and Dad were letting them go. *Copacetic.*

He took longer than he had to in the shower—he never got tired of being able to stand there in the hot water as long as he wanted. Today he sang "Love Like This"; he usually didn't think his voice suited to Buddy Holly's material, but the rollicking tune and happy lyrics seemed to match his mood. That made him a little late, so he wasn't surprised that the upstairs hall was empty and quiet as he made for the back stairs into the kitchen. *They're probably about ready to go. Better hurry if I don't want to walk to school.*

But when he got into the kitchen they were all there except Beth, crammed in around the breakfast nook table. Even Ruby was sitting down instead of bopping around frying eggs and popping toast the way she usually did on a school morning. "Do we have a snow day?" he asked, looking doubtfully out the window at the thin layer of white coating the lawn.

Then he saw that Joy had been crying, and Mom and Dad were holding hands so hard their knuckles were white. "Sit down, son," Dad said.

Steve's stomach churned and his knees got weak. *What happened? Did I do something? I should have known it was too good to last....* He squeezed in next to Rob, who put an arm around his shoulders without asking. *It must be bad.*

Mom was watching his face. "Yes, it's something serious," she said before he had a chance to ask. "But I want you to try not to be too upset. We're here with you, and we're all going to be with you—supporting you—no matter what."

"Just tell me," he said.

Mom took her hand from Dad's and rubbed her forehead. Then she dropped her hands into her lap, pressed her lips together, and looked straight at Steve. "I've stirred up a hornets' nest, criticizing the fosterage policy that sent you into your cousin's custody without oversight just because he was a relative," she said. "I've made one of my supervisors mad—Marty Henderson—and now he's trying to get back at me through you."

"How?"

Mom's mouth opened and closed, but no sound came out. Dad reached forward and put his hand on Steve's arm. "He's pushing to make you stand trial for killing Bert," he said.

Steve pulled away from Dad's hand and Rob's arm and went to the sink. He picked up a scouring pad and started scrubbing the top of the stove.

Behind him, Dad said heavily, "All right, kids, let's get going. I'll drive you all to school."

"No, Dad!" Joy cried. "We can't go to school."

"She's right," Rob said. "How could we think about school when something like this is going on?"

Joy nodded vigorously. "Don't we need to stick by Stevie, sir?"

It was Celia who said quietly, "We're going to stick by Stevie, of course we are. But I think we probably need to give him and Mom some space right now. I'm not going to be able to think much about schoolwork today either, but remember that nothing has actually happened yet. Us staying home from school would be like saying they've wrecked our family. If… something bad does happen, I bet Mom and Dad will let us be with Steve as much as we can."

Steve was scrubbing so hard, little metal bits from the scouring pad were getting wedged under his fingernails. He welcomed the pain as Dad said, "Thank you, Cecilia. Come now, all of you."

Steve heard the swishing sound of people sliding out of the breakfast nook benches and the scrape of Mom's chair as she pushed it back. But he kept his focus on the scrubbing as Rob, Celia, and Joy came up behind him and kissed or stroked whatever part of him they could reach. Last came Dad's broad, warm hand on the back of his head. "I'll be home soon, son," he said. "Try not to be too afraid. We're with you."

Cold, dry air washed into the kitchen as the back door opened and they all went to the garage through the porch. Steve stopped scrubbing and let his shoulders sag. He tried to sink down into his safe, secret place, but he couldn't find it. *Think of a song, some music to take me down,* he thought frantically.

Mom's hand came into view, dropping lightly onto his. "Steve," she said softly.

A humming filled Steve's head, but it wasn't music, it was like a siren or an alarm clock, a maddening high-pitched screeching. He pulled his hand out from under hers and wheeled around, slapping her on the arm. "Don't touch me! I hate you!"

He raised his hand again, but this time she caught it. "I love you," she said. "You can hate me if you want to, but you're not going to stop me—or any of us—from loving you. I will not allow you to strike me, though."

Chest heaving, he let his arm go limp and she dropped his hand. "Talk to me, Steve," she said. "Why do you say you hate me?"

"I'm so mad at you. Why did you have to worry about saving other kids, making trouble so your boss would want to get even with you? Didn't you care about me?"

She took a long breath. "Of course I care about you, Steve. Looking after other kids is my job, and it's also my calling. But if you're asking me to choose between all the children in the world outside this family and you, then I choose you. Is that really what you want, though? For me not to care what happens to any other child?" She held his eyes till his dropped, then she said, "I'll be in the study when you're ready to talk."

She turned and left the room, the swinging door flapping after her and stirring the warm air in the kitchen.

Steve went back to scrubbing the stove. *I've scratched the white stuff off, here. Maybe I better just go upstairs to the cabinet—*

He'd forgotten he wasn't alone in the room yet. From behind him, Ruby clamped her hands on his shoulders, gripping hard enough to bruise, and swung him to face her. "I heard your father signed a promise to never hit you," she said in a low, trembling voice. "I don't know if he was right or wrong to do that, but I made no such promise. And I am telling you, child, if I hear you speak to your mother that way again, I will smack your mouth." She gave him a shake.

The tears that Steve had been fighting came spilling out of his eyes and down his face. Ruby pulled him to her in a fierce hug, then pushed him toward the door. "Go find her," she said.

Steve stumbled through the dining room and living room and into the hall, tears flowing down his cheeks like there was a faucet behind his eyes. He stood outside the study door with his hand raised to knock, but he couldn't make his hand fall to the wooden panel.

Instead he turned around and went up the stairs to the second floor, then down the hall and up the other stairs into the music room. He'd been thinking about the attic cabinet, but he stopped when he saw Mom's Spanish guitar, the one Rob taught him to make music on, lying on the spinet by the window. The music stand Dad had smashed the shelf with stood next to it.

Steve picked up the pretty brown guitar with the little bits of green and pearly inlay around the hole. He took it by the neck and brought it down hard on the music stand. There was a twanging sound from the strings and a crunch as the top of the metal stand went through the back of the guitar. He had to wrench it to get it free again, holding the music stand down with his foot. Then he smashed the guitar down again and again, grunting and sobbing as the pieces came apart and finally all that held them to the neck was a mass of sprung and twisted strings.

He dropped the neck on the floor and turned from the wreckage to see Mom standing in the stairwell. They looked at each other for a long minute, then he turned again and pushed through into the attic. She made no move to stop him as he crawled into the cabinet and closed the door behind him.

It was freezing under the eaves. Steve wrapped himself in his blue blanket and wriggled around till he could drag Jamie's sleeping bag over that. He took the old bear Jamie gave him out of the corner and jammed it in beside him. He pushed the battery lantern aside without lighting it up, but he turned on his transistor radio, tuned to WHYL. He closed his eyes and let the music take him down.

Steve came to the surface again when the noon news came on. His face was freezing, his legs were cramping, and his bladder was screaming. Reluctantly, he turned off the radio and unlatched the cabinet door. Mom was sitting on a storage trunk there in the attic, bundled against the cold in an old coat.

She didn't speak as he clumsily dragged himself free of the covers and out of the cabinet and staggered stiffly out of the attic, but she followed him down the stairs and into his room and when he came out of the bathroom she was there on the window seat. A glass of milk sat on the table by his bed, and a peanut butter and jelly sandwich wrapped in waxed paper the way Ruby always did it.

Steve edged past Mom's knees, not touching her, and got over to his bed. He took a drink of the milk, then picked up the waxed paper package, unfolded it, and started stuffing the sandwich into his mouth, cramming it in the way he used to gobble food Bert gave him.

Mom cleared her throat. Her eyes were red and puffy. When she started to talk, her voice sounded rusty. "You and I are going to leave for Rolling Meadow in half an hour," she said. "I have some arrangements to make about this hearing they're going to have next Monday, and I've set up an appointment for you with a new therapist."

Steve stopped eating at that. *She doesn't want me any more.*

Mom shook her head as though he'd said it aloud. "Ever since that night you had the breakthrough—" *Is that what you call it,* he thought. "—I've been looking for someone new for you, as you know. It's too hard on both of us for me to be your doctor and your mother

213

both. I don't think Mrs. French was the answer, though."

"She doesn't like me," Steve said.

Mom sighed. "Unfortunately, I think you're right. I also think she doesn't have the qualifications you need; she's a counselor, not a trained psychologist. I think highly of Dr. Benson, though. He was going to have an opening for you next month, but under the circumstances he's agreed to start seeing you right away."

Steve jammed the last of the sandwich into his mouth and washed it down with the rest of the milk. "What's going to happen?" he demanded.

She sighed. "It's hard to say, exactly." Steve made an impatient movement. "Really, Steve," she said. "Juvenile court is hard to predict. There's an idea that it's better for kids to keep things relatively informal and not stick to the strict regimen of the adult legal system. The problem with that is it leaves you without the protections of adult law. A lot depends on the judge: whether you're formally charged at all, or remanded for treatment of some kind, or adjudicated to the juvenile criminal system—that's really up to the judge's opinion of what's best for you."

Steve was shaking. "What's the worst?"

Mom came over and sat beside him, drawing one knee up onto the bed and propping herself on one arm so she was leaning over him. "You could be sent to the criminal facility at Rolling Meadow for six years." She said it in a rush, as though she had to force the words out all at once.

Steve curled over onto himself and pulled his pillow over his head. Mom bent down to speak to him under the edge of it. "If that happened, I would be there every day to see you. Every day, Steve. And the rest of the family as often as they are allowed. We would still be a family. We will still be a family, I promise you, no matter what happens. But I don't think that will happen, I really, truly don't." She was talking softly, almost crooning. "When the judge hears the circumstances—Steve, my darling, darling boy, I honestly think it will be all right. But if there is a bad outcome we will still be there, I swear it on my soul. If that juvenile judge won't listen, you'll still be our beloved son."

"Sweetest baby," he said, voice muffled in the pillow.

"What's that?"

Steve pulled his head out. "Sweetest baby—in the world? Something like that. She used to sing it to me. A song about buying stuff."

215

Mom's lips moved silently for a minute as she thought about it, then a small smile came over her face. "'Sweetest little baby in town'? Was that it?"

"Maybe."

She lay down next to Steve and drew his head against her chest and started to sing softly, "Hush, little baby, don't say a word...."

Steve shivered and snuggled in.

Chapter 27.

Beth

Beth leaned her head against the back of the bathtub, letting herself relax in the warm water, feeling the scintillation of the bubbles against her chin and toes. *God is here; I am in God.* She silently held her brother Steve in the Light.

She had not gone back to school for the week last night, but stayed home to be with Steve during this trouble. She'd wanted to be there with him at the hearing in Harrisburg, but after an hour had left in despair, pulling away from the rest of her family and stumbling and groping, tapping her cane, till she found her way out of the courtroom, down the stairs, and out of the building. She'd stood in the freezing wind off the river that tore down the tunnel of Chestnut Street into her face.

She'd taken the wind into herself and let it calm her and focused on the words of George Fox: "Then, oh then I heard a voice which said, 'There is one, even Jesus

Christ, that can speak to thy condition': and when I heard it, my heart did leap for joy."

Then she'd heard the door behind her, and felt the warmth of Robbie's body sheltering her. "It's going to be ok," he'd said.

"I know," she'd said, "I know it is."

And it was. The judge had declared Bert's killing self-defense. But the whole experience had been harrowing, and she was sure Steve would be set back by it. *But it will be all right.*

On the ride home from Harrisburg, she and Rob had been in Mom's Dodge with Steve and Mom and Dad. Joy and Celia and Laurie rode with Ruby in the station wagon. They were taking Laurie to the train station so he could get back to Haverford, carrying his birthday presents to open when he got there. Then they would call Jamie in Boston from a pay phone to let him know what had happened. Beth would go back to Paoli in the morning.

In the Dodge, Rob drove so Mom and Dad could sit on either side of Steve in the back seat. "December eighth," Dad had said as they sped along Front Street. "Laurie's birthday. What a celebration for him. Pearl Harbor Day yesterday and now this."

"Two days that ended in victory, Sean," Mom said quietly. Then the only sound inside the car had been

Mom's voice softly singing "Hush, Little Baby" to Steve, then a long silence.

When their tires had finally crunched onto their gravel drive, Mom had whispered, "He's asleep." Dad carried him in as Steve murmured sleepily, and Beth had made her way to the tub to get warm again.

Now she let go of the day's turmoil to sink back into the quiet sense of communion, surrounded by warmth, floating in warmth, free of strife, free of fear, adrift on the breast of the Holy, brimming with peace, breath and the Spirit one—

The bathroom door opened, the light switch clicked, and a cold draft washed over Beth, pulling her abruptly out of her calm meditation. "Celia? Joy? Who's there? Is something wrong?"

She heard a gasp. "Sorry, sorry, I didn't know anybody was in here." The door banged shut again.

"Steve!" she called, sloshing water as she sat up. "Stevie, don't go away, baby, I'll be right out. Stay there in my room, please, please, Stevie." She pulled herself out of the tub and bundled on her thick terrycloth bathrobe, twisting the damp ends of her hair out of the way but not bothering to dry herself properly.

She hurried into her bedroom. She could hear him breathing hard, over on her bed. She sat down next to him, tucking her wet feet up under her robe and drawing him to her till they were huddled together with their shins pressed against each other's and their arms around each other's waists.

"I was going to clean the bathroom," Steve said. "The light was off and the door wasn't locked, I didn't know you'd be there. I didn't mean to—"

"I never lock the door; I can easily hurt myself in a bathroom so I want people to be able to get to me if something goes wrong," Beth said. "And I don't need the light."

"I'm sorry. I didn't really see you. I mean, I saw you, but I didn't look. I mean—"

"It's all right, baby, it doesn't matter even one tiny bit. What matters is you, and how you're feeling. I thought you were asleep?"

"I was. I just woke up, and felt like I needed to clean something, and Rob was in our bathroom." He took a shuddering breath. "Why did you leave, in that courtroom place? It's not like you could see the pictures they were showing."

"No, but I could hear what they were saying about them. It made me feel like evilness and filth was seeping into me, I needed to get away from it. I was still with you, though, keeping you in my heart. I'm sorry if it felt like I was leaving you."

Steve clutched her harder for a second, then moved away. "Evilness and filth?" he whispered.

"Not from you, baby. What was done to you. When that doctor was testifying, describing the injuries they'd found on you. I knew Bert had hurt you, of course, but hearing the details, the descriptions of your wounds and scars—oh, baby, it was so hard to hear. I can't imagine how you lived through it."

Steve shifted to sit next to Beth with his head on her shoulder. "I felt like I was living it over again, listening to that and looking at the pictures," he said. "And knowing that the others were seeing them, Joy and everybody, looking at what he did to me." His voice got very low. "And seeing what I did to him. Bethie, he looked so small when he was dead. I thought he was so big."

Beth twined her fingers around his where they twisted in his lap. *There is one, even Jesus Christ, that can speak to thy condition.* "Stevie, he's in God's hands now. Like you, like me. Just rest in them, sweet brother. Just rest."

Steve was partly sitting on the skirt of Beth's robe. She pulled it out from under him and cuddled up to him again. His wet lashes moved against her cheek and his breath was warm on her throat.

They stayed like that for a long time, till the sound of the phone in the hall startled them upright. Beth felt the pulse in Steve's neck thrumming under her fingers. *The phone frightens him now.* She patted him reassuringly as they listened to the murmur of Mom's voice.

Then it stopped, and they heard a door across the hall open and Mom calling Steve's name. Then she called it again, closer and louder.

"We're in here, Mama," Beth called back.

The door opened, the bedroom light clicked on, then Beth felt the mattress sag as Mom sat down on the other side of Steve.

"Sweetie, Marty Henderson is on the phone."

Steve stiffened. "The guy who caused all this? Who wanted me in jail just because he was mad at you?"

"He's very sorry, Steve. That's why he called. He says that seeing those pictures in juvenile court today, and seeing you looking at them, made him realize that you were a real child, not just a pawn in some game he was playing with me. A child who had suffered. He was crying just now."

Steve drew in a sharp breath. Beth could feel that Mom was rocking Steve against her a little. "He wants to talk to you," Mom went on. "You don't have to if you don't want to, darling, but I think it might help you to hear what he has to say."

Beth reached forward to pat Steve's back, then felt the mattress heave as he and Mom got up. Mom dropped a kiss on Beth's head as she went out of the room behind Steve. Steve's voice shakily said, "Hello?" and then was silent. Beth closed the door and got dressed.

When she came out into the hall she could feel there was no one there. She went downstairs to find the family gathered in the living room. Steve was talking as Beth dropped onto the ottoman by the long couch.

"... that kid they were talking about today," he said. "David, was it?"

Mom breathed out sharply through her nose. "They were trying to show that we were not adequate guardians for you, since we lost another boy, David, a few years ago."

"What do you mean, 'lost'?"

"He'd seen his father stab his mother to death. Then he was sent to a custodial institution—it's closed now, partly because of what happened to David—where he was regularly beaten and generally neglected. Then he was put in a foster home, but he attacked his foster father and broke his nose."

Mom sounds so tired, Beth thought, remembering the bright, skittish, angry boy who'd visited them for days at a time when Beth was—*what, it must be over five years ago now, I was eleven.*

Dad took up the story. "Your mother got to know him when he was sent to Rolling Meadow. We started having him here when we could, hoping we could bring him into the family."

"You just brought me here," Steve said. "There weren't any visits or, like, trial period."

"No," Mom said. "we were afraid they were going to foster you out or move you into the closed facility and we'd miss our chance. And I was so sure with you, that we could make you part of the family. Dad and I argued bitterly over David, though."

Beth remembered that, the stiff silences and the sharp words behind closed doors. *I never heard them go at each other like that before.*

Now Dad said, "There was something about him— a sort of undercurrent of violence, a crazy heedlessness to consequences—something was permanently out of kilter there, and it frightened me."

"Thank God I finally listened to you," Mom said.

"Really?" Dad breathed. "Christ, Lass, I always thought you resented me for that, blamed me for what happened."

Beth heard the soft sounds of her parents coming together.

"But how did you lose him?" Steve persisted.

When Mom's voice came again, it was muffled as though her face was partly hidden. "He attacked another boy at Rolling Meadow and beat him almost to death," she said. "They put him in the lockdown ward but he got hold of a bobby pin out of someone's hair. He sharpened it on the grout in the bathroom and cut his own throat with it."

"But," Steve said, "didn't he know you would love him, you would take care of him?"

"He couldn't believe it, Stevie," Mom said, more clearly now, and bleak. "He never could believe us. Not like you."

"And he didn't have your strength," Dad said. "He could never have listened to Marty Henderson the way you did tonight."

"I didn't say anything except hello," Steve said. "When he stopped talking, I just hung up."

"But you listened," Mom said. "You were able to hear him, and that will make all the difference for you. Now I think it's time to light the Hanukkah candles. We missed last night, we were all so upset, but I think it's important to get back to normal. Besides, it's a good time to celebrate freedom, and lights in the darkness."

They called Jamie in Boston for the second time that day. Dad led the blessings and songs. Beth could hear Steve's voice joining, thin and thready at first, then gaining power till the last line, "And Thy word/Broke their sword/When our own strength failed us," was carried by his voice above all the others.

Celia's voice came from the dining room door. "Time to sit down, everybody," she said.

Rob caught Beth's arm and hooked it through his as they went to their places.

"Oh, this smells scrumptious, Ruby," Beth said, settling into her chair and inhaling the rich, meaty aroma wafting out of the plate before her. "What is it?"

"It's lamb and barley stew," Ruby said. "I put it in the oven on low this morning. I figured, whatever happened, we'd need something comforting and easy to digest tonight."

"You're a genius, Ruby," Celia said. "Joy and I should have set the table this morning, too. We were so happy, we were a little spacy tonight. Jo-Jo, you want to take the grace?"

Beth reached her hands out and felt Rob's join hers on the left and Joy's on the right. They were all quiet for a while, then Joy said, "Thank you, God, for—" Her voice wobbled. "Thank you—" She made a little choking sound and stopped.

Dad said firmly, "Amen."

Chapter 28.

Monday, January 12, 1959: 9:25 p.m.

Celia

C elia came out of the study and crossed over to the TV room. *Yes, she's in here.* "Mom? Can I talk to you or are you watching this especially?"

"No, I'm just waiting for the next show," Mom said from the couch where she was sitting with Steve. *Since the hearing he's been practically glued to Mom.* Celia dropped into the wicker chair nearby. "This one's almost over," Mom said, picking up a coffee mug from the table in front of her and taking a swallow. "What is it, darling?"

"D'you want me to leave?" Steve asked.

"No, it's not private," Celia said quickly. "You can stay, Steve. I just wanted to talk about my visiting Rick at Duke over spring break. You know he had set it up for me to stay with that girl he's made friends with, but tonight he told me they had a fight and she doesn't want to do it any more. So what do you think about if I just sneak into his dorm? He'd sleep on the floor, and his roommate won't tell. What difference would it make?" Celia held her breath.

Mom put her mug down and thought it over for a minute, running her thumb over Steve's knuckles where his hand lay on her arm. "Well, I can think of two objections," she said slowly. "First, it's always good to have your own space, a place you can retreat to if things get at all tense or uncomfortable between you. The second point is, you want him to date other girls there; we all agreed it wasn't wise for you to go steady with a boy who's already in college. If you stay in his room, even though *we* know nothing's—ah," she bit her lip, "—going to *happen,* it will create assumptions that will make it harder for him to have a social life."

I knew she'd come up with something, Celia thought, sitting back with a grin. "Gee, Mom," she said. *"Those* are *good* reasons. I asked Daddy and all that happened was, steam came out of his ears!"

Mom gave a yelp of laughter as the driving theme music on the TV signaled the end of *Peter Gunn.* "You rascal," she said, and pitched a magazine at Celia.

They settled back to watch the next program. Celia's mind kept wandering, though. *It's amazing that Steve was able to do those music gigs with Robbie after the scare*

228

about the murder charge, she thought, keeping half an eye on him as the drama on the screen unfolded.

Christmas had been a little tense; Steve had been nervous and out of sorts. Uncle Kevin had tried to keep them all entertained, but it was an uphill battle. *In a way it's made it better for Steve, though. It's like the bad thing he was waiting for finally happened, but it came out all right.* He couldn't seem to settle, though. His moods swung back and forth, and only music could really calm him. *It's as though he's not quite sure who we are any more. And finding out about David upset him, too.*

Celia stretched and looked at the clock as the commercial for Alcoa aluminum came on. *Quarter to ten. Good thing I did that essay before dinner.* She turned to Mom and Steve. "Think the Jack Carson character is going to let his foster son keep those puppies?" she said. Steve shrugged; Mom didn't respond. "Mom?" *She's watching that commercial like she's planning to buy stock in the company.* "Mom?"

Now Steve was looking worried. "Mom?" he said. His fingers started drumming on his knee.

Mom shook her head a little and came out of her trance. "I was thinking about David," she said.

"I think about him, too," Steve said.

"What do you think about him?" Celia wondered.

229

"Dad said he was broken," Steve said. "And then he went crazy and did bad things. How do you know I'm not, that I won't do things like that?" His hands were stuffed deep in his pockets as he sprawled on the couch, and his shoulders were up around his ears.

Mom scrubbed her hands over her face and sat with one over her mouth for a minute before answering. "The only way I can describe it is to say that I can see you hearing us when we speak to you. With David, he would smile or he would cry—he was great at producing big sad tears—but it somehow didn't get below the surface. There was a hardness there, an emptiness. I kept hoping we could get through, but maybe there wasn't anybody to get through to any more."

She took a last sip of her coffee, then set the empty mug back on the table. "And you remember a little of your life before; that makes a difference, too. David was three when he saw his mother murdered and his father went to prison, but if there was anything left of his memories before that, they were buried too deep."

"But I still don't get why you couldn't help him, when you could help me? Why couldn't you and Dad caring about him be enough?" Steve said.

"I don't know for sure, darling," Mom said. "But you were evidently able to keep an idea in your head about a better life for yourself, a safer place, even when you were trapped in that room."

Steve was trembling, staring at the TV screen. "Could we just watch the program?" he said. Mom put a hand on his arm but he pulled away and she let him be as they all pretended to watch the end of *Alcoa Theater*.

Arthur Murray came on. *It's really* Bandstand *for old people,* Celia thought, twisting the knob to turn the TV off. The door opened. "Oh, hi, Dad, did you want to watch TV? We were just...." Celia's voice trailed off. *He can't be that mad over me asking Mom about staying with Rick after he said no... No, he wouldn't even know about that yet. So—?*

But Dad wasn't looking at Celia. He was looking at Steve, and he had what Celia thought of as his "Commander McAlister" face on, the one that could make you feel not only like you were in big trouble but like you were a bug speck on the windshield of the universe.

Steve had been standing next to Mom, ready to leave the room. Now he stepped back so she was between him and Dad, half hiding behind her. Mom, though, looked at Dad's face and stepped aside, turning to face Steve so they were both looking at him.

"Ruby tells me you refused to help her with dinner tonight, and that you were rude to her when she reminded you it was your turn; you left it all for Celia to do. Is that so, son?" Dad said.

Steve set his jaw and stared at Dad defiantly, not speaking.

"Cissy, is it true?"

"Oh, Dad, he's been through so much with the hearing and everything, I didn't really mind—"

"Answer me, Cecilia."

Oh, God. "Yes, sir."

"Steven, you will apologize to Ruby first thing in the morning, and you will spend all day next Saturday helping her with whatever chores she assigns you, is that clear? And you are grounded for two weeks."

Steve broke his silence. "Rob and I are supposed to play at that confirmation party Saturday night."

"You may play at the party, since that is a commitment you have made, but you will come home immediately after your performance." Dad's voice softened. "I know this has been a difficult time for you, Steve."

Mom nodded. "I think you're testing us, Steve, seeing how far you can go. We've been lenient with you

232

because you've been under so much strain. But that stops now. You will follow the rules or pay the consequences."

Celia held her breath. *Are they pushing him too hard?*

Sure enough, Steve's next move was to swing around to the coffee table. With a sweep of his arm he pushed the magazines and newspapers and Mom's empty mug to the floor.

Mom caught his arm on the backswing and pulled him around to face her. "You can misbehave all you want, Steve," she said as Celia crouched to pick up the mess. "We still love you, you are still a member of this family, and the rules still apply to you."

"Why?" Steve shouted. "It doesn't matter what I do. I'm just bad. You try to tell me I'm not like David, but all I do is make trouble for you. Why don't you just get rid of me, too?"

"You are not bad," Dad said. "You are a good boy who's behaving badly. You are ours, in a way David never got to be. And we will take care of you, no matter what."

Steve ran from the room with the others hard behind him and charged for the stairs. Halfway up he crumpled, collapsing across four steps. He lowered his forehead to his hands and lay there trembling. Celia made to go to him but Mom silently put a hand out and held her back.

Dad moved past them and up to Steve, bending down and speaking softly into his hair. Then Dad put his arms around Steve and hoisted him up as though he were four instead of fourteen. Steve wrapped his legs around Dad's waist and buried his face in his shoulder.

Celia and Mom followed them upstairs, where Celia went toward her room as the parents brought Steve into his. Joy darted out of the room past her and stood in the hall, watching anxiously. Just before Dad turned in to the other bedroom, Steve's eyes opened and he gave Joy a long look.

"Get ready for bed, sweetie, it's getting late," Mom said to Joy as she closed Steve's door.

Celia stopped in her bedroom door, thinking. *He was pushing them tonight—and so was I. But he was really pushing his boundaries; I was just pushing their buttons. Hmm, maybe I'm actually growing up.*

"Come on, Jo-Jo," Celia said to her little sister. "Steve will be fine."

Chapter 29.

Tuesday, February 3, 1959: 4:00 p.m.

Joy

Joy and Steve sat at the dining room table doing their homework. Steve had brought his transistor radio down; the music seemed to hang a cozy curtain of sound between them and the steady drizzle falling outside the long windows in the gray afternoon.

As the swinging beat of "Come On, Let's Go" gave way to an announcer's voice, Joy stopped listening. She read over the page in front of her again.

"Hey, Steve, listen to this—did you ever see this poem? Listen: 'Margaret, are you grieving/Over Goldengrove unleaving…' Steve?" *What's the matter with him? He looks like he used to look at the beginning, all scared and panicky.* Then she registered what he was listening to.

"…songwriter and singer Ritchie Valens, dead at seventeen. Again, Valens, along with singers Buddy

Holly and J. P. 'Big Bopper' Richardson, was killed early this morning in a plane crash near Clear Lake, Iowa. Valens was the first Latin American performer to…" Steve lunged at the radio and turned it off. He slumped down at the table again and buried his head in his arms.

"Oh, my God," Joy said. "Oh, Steve. Oh, God. It's awful, it's just awful. I can't believe it. Oh, God." She couldn't seem to stop talking. *There's nothing to say, stupid. Just go to him.* She moved around the table and dragged a chair close to him, leaning forward to rest her head awkwardly on the back of his shoulder. Tears ran sideways across her face and into her ear. *This is really uncomfortable,* she thought after a minute. She raised her head and tugged at his elbow till he looked up. *He's not crying, but he's whiter than his shirt.*

Steve stared at her as though he didn't know who she was or what she was doing there. Then his eyes snapped into focus and he seemed to see her again. "What are you crying about," he said roughly. "It's not like you knew them."

"No, but—I don't know, it's hard to explain, but it's like I did know them, you know? Because we heard their voices so much, and saw their faces. And their songs were important to us."

"Their songs are still important."

"I know that. I'm not saying this very well. Geez, Steve, I know you're upset, but I'm upset too. Don't take it out on me." She tried to stop her lips from trembling. *Why is he staring at me?*

Without warning, Steve leaned forward and kissed her on the mouth. His hand cupped the back of her head and his tongue found its way between her lips. She stiffened in surprise, then relaxed into the kiss. *Is this all right? We're not related by blood, but—*

Joy had kissed a few boys before, but never with this intensity. She felt heat rushing up through her body, and a lightness in her head. Suddenly his mouth was gone. She blinked and looked at Steve, but he had turned his head away. His arms fell away from around her, leaving her feeling chilly and not sure where she should put her hands.

Robbie came in carrying a stack of plates, tablecloth over his arm. "Hey, pipsqueaks, I need to set the table, could you make like a hoop and roll away?" He looked at their faces. "Oh, I see you got the news about those poor cats on the plane. Listen—"

But Steve dove through the door to the living room and disappeared. Joy numbly gathered her books and his.

Robbie put down what he was carrying and put an arm around her shoulder, squeezing her up against

237

his side. *That's what a brother's supposed to feel like.* She nuzzled his ribs.

"Yeah, it's awful, but it's not like we knew them or anything," she said. "Would you put Steve's radio on top of this stack so I can carry it up to him?"

That night Joy couldn't get to sleep.

Steve hadn't opened his bedroom door or answered her when she brought his books and radio up. With Jamie off at college, he had the room to himself and lately he seemed to be shutting himself into it more. She was glad he was supposed to see his therapist tomorrow—not that awful Mrs. French, but the new one, the one as qualified as Mom but who wasn't also trying to be his mother. *Just a few weeks ago he was acting like a little kid, now he's kissing me like that?* Joy didn't know what to make of it.

At dinner he'd been subdued even for Steve, avoiding her eye; afterwards he'd gone up to the music room with Robbie and she'd somehow not felt welcome to join them as she'd been doing since last summer. *Or maybe I was just scared.* She'd ended up watching Westerns all evening.

When she'd gone to get a glass of water before bed, he'd come into the kitchen from the dining room, headed for the back stairs. "Stevie, listen," she'd said, but he'd brushed past her without speaking, a whiff of liquor on his breath.

Now she couldn't seem to get warm, shuffling her feet in her chilly sheets and thinking about the young musicians strewn across the snowy Iowa landscape, and about Steve's tongue in her mouth, and about him sneaking that drink tonight. She'd mentioned all three things in her prayers, which usually left her feeling calm, but not tonight.

"Cissy?"

"Hmmm?"

"Can I come over?"

"'K."

She hopped across from the braided rug by her bed to the one by Celia's, avoiding the frigid floor. *Eliza crossing the ice,* she thought.

Celia had opened her covers so Joy could slide in. "Hurry," she whispered. "All the heat's escaping."

But it was still cozy in the narrow bed. Joy spooned up against Celia, whose arms went around her from behind and drew her close as she settled in. Joy breathed in the comforting smell of her sister's shampoo and her warm flesh and her slight sleep fug.

"Yikes," Celia squeaked, "your feet are like ice cubes."

"Sorry."

"'S ok. What's up? You want to talk?"

"Not really. I just want to be close to somebody."

"Thinking about those poor boys?"

"Mmm." *Can't talk to her about the other thing. Don't know what I think about it yet.*

"I love you, Joy May."

"Me, too, Cecilia Anne." *What would she say if she knew? What would any of them say? But it's never wrong to show you love someone, is it? Those boys on the plane, out there in the cold—no one's ever going to kiss them again.*

Joy gave an involuntary whimper. Celia kissed her on the back of the head and pulled her closer.

Joy thought about the end of the poem she'd read earlier. *"It is the blight man was born for/It is Margaret you mourn for."* Within minutes the rhythm of the poem in her head and Celia's slow, even breathing behind her soothed Joy to sleep.

Chapter 30.

Beth

Beth reached for the door handle as she felt the Johnstons' car pull to the curb. "Thanks so much, as usual, for the ride," she said.

"It's no trouble, dear," Mrs. Johnston said. "Are you sure you don't want Sherm to walk you to the door?"

"No, thank you, I'm fine."

"All right. Happy Easter. Tell that new brother of yours that he's welcome to come to Meeting with us again any time."

"I will. Good-bye, boys. Bye, Dr. Johnston. Happy Easter." She closed the car door behind her, found the flagstones with her cane, and started up the familiar front walk. The Johnstons were nice people, the only neighbors who didn't act like the McAlister family came from another planet, and Dr. Johnston was the only dentist in the county who would treat Negroes.

241

Fifteen steps. I should be at the front stoop. She tapped. *There it is.* Beth stepped up and opened the front door. The Johnstons' car pulled away. "Hello?" she called.

No answer. She closed the door behind her, slipped her cane into the umbrella stand, hung her jacket in the closet, and walked to the right, into the living room. "Steve? Are you here?" A faint clink from the dining room, then a click.

"Here I am," Steve said from the dining room door.

"The others still at Mass?"

"Yeah."

"The Johnstons say if you want to come to Meeting with us again you'd be welcome."

"Maybe. I liked the quiet but sitting with all those strangers felt creepy. They kept staring at us."

"Did they?"

"A couple of them. That woman with the curly white hair, for instance."

"I can't see what they look like, Steve."

"Oh, yeah."

Something's wrong. His voice is off somehow. Beth moved toward him, touching the edges of the furniture as she passed through the living room. "Are you all right, Steve?"

"Why wouldn't I be?"

He's backing away from me. "I don't know, you just sounded a little funny. I wonder if it's a good idea for you to be all by yourself here on Sundays. I know you've been missing Laurie and Jamie, we all have, but—"

"Just quit nagging at me, will you? I told you I'm fine."

There goes the door to the kitchen. He's gone upstairs. Beth sighed and turned back to go up the front stairs so Steve wouldn't think she was following him.

In her own room, she opened her window a crack and sat at her reading stand, feeling the cool March breeze on her face and running her fingers over the Braille edition of the new Leon Uris book, *Exodus.*

After a few minutes she stopped. "I know you're standing in my doorway, Stevie. Did you want something?"

"I'm sorry I talked to you like that. I know you were just trying to help, but really, you don't need to."

"Ok." She let her fingers move along the page a little.

"Can you really read that stuff?"

"Yes, they taught me how at my school, remember? It's about Israel after the war. This is just the first volume—a group of Jewish women volunteers are working on putting it into Braille. Want to come and touch it, see how it feels?"

"Uh—no thanks."

Enough of this. Beth turned her swivel chair so she was fully facing him, breeze on the back of her head. "Steve, I'm blind, but I'm not stupid. I know you were drinking while everyone was out. I heard you putting the bottle back into the liquor cabinet. So you don't have to stay away from me to keep me from smelling it."

"Oh." He came into the room. "It's just, I didn't want you to worry. I know you can tell a lot about what's going on even if you can't see. And you get around everywhere with that cane. How come you don't have one of those dogs?"

"A guide dog is a big responsibility. I don't need one here at home, where I have my own room and know where everything is. When I go to Perkins year after next, I might think about getting trained with one. But I want to be a teacher, and having a dog might complicate that. I'll just have to take it one step at a time. With my cane." Beth chuckled, then sobered. "Don't think I haven't noticed that you changed the subject about your drinking, though."

"What is there to say about it? It was just one drink."

"This time. And this wasn't the first time, was it?" *He's not saying anything. If it were his first drink, he'd say so.* "Steve, you've got to stop it, you know."

"I know. I will. It's just, it helps sometimes."

Beth rolled her chair closer to where he was sitting on her bed. "What is it that drinking helps, baby?"

"Feeling scared. I'm scared so much. Not as much as when I first came here, but a different way. It was a little better after the hearing, when that judge said I didn't have to get locked up because of what I did to Bert. I liked it that Mom and Dad stuck by me, even when I acted like a jerk for a while afterwards."

He shifted on the bed with a soft metallic creaking of the springs. "I tell myself I'm fifteen years old, I've been here almost two years, it's about time I stopped being such a baby. But it doesn't really help. All the singing and playing with Rob, it's great, but I'm not sure where it's going or whether I'll be good enough, and when those guys got killed in the plane crash, I thought how they were only a little older than me and it's already all over for them. I just get scared. I know you don't get what I mean."

"What makes you say that? Do you think I'm never scared?"

"Are you? What do you have to be scared of?"

Beth pushed her chair back away from him in exasperation. "Steve, Steve, for heaven's sakes! I've lived all my life not being able to see. Can you imagine what that's like? When we were little and homeless, I used to spend whole days crouched in a box, afraid to move or make a sound, while Robbie was off finding food for us. Every sound, every draft of air, made me jump and shiver, not knowing who might be standing behind me or... or reaching for me. Here I've been safe, surrounded by familiar things and the people I love. Even boarding at Bolotin during the week, I've known I'd be home on the weekends and when anything special was happening. But when I think about going to Perkins, going to a strange city and living among strangers, sometimes I get so frightened I don't know what to do."

Steve's finger brushed her cheek, wiping off a tear she'd let fall. "Don't go, then," he said. "Why do you have to go?"

"Oh, I want to go, Steve, really I do. I need to make my own life, and most of the time it's exciting to think about starting to get myself ready for that. And Jamie will be nearby at MIT for my first year, anyway, so that'll help. But I got a little sidetracked there. I'm afraid of things that have nothing to do with my sight. I'm afraid I won't do well in school, I'm afraid I won't find the right person to love, I'm even afraid of the same thing you are—that the success you and Robbie are having with your music is going to make things change too much. I'm afraid I'll lose the special bond I have with him, and the different one I have with you. "

He was quiet for a minute. "I never thought about you having problems except, you know, the blind thing. You always look so—when I first came here, I thought you looked like the angel on the Christmas tree."

This again. Be patient. "It's because I have long blonde hair, evidently, Steve, though I don't really know what 'blonde' means. And they tell me I'm pretty. And partly because I can't see how people move when they talk and partly because I guess I'm naturally just a quiet kind of person, I don't make a lot of fuss and I sit pretty still. So people tend to think nothing bothers me. *That* bothers me, to tell you the truth. I'm just a person, Steve."

"Robbie calls you 'angel'."

"That actually started as a joke, because he knows better. Then it got to be a habit. But I'm no angel. I'm your sister, and I know you've been feeling bad lately."

"It's like you said, things keep changing. I thought I'd like having a room to myself again. I was so mad at the beginning when Mom and Dad made me share with Jamie when there were two perfectly good spare rooms. But it's lonely without him. I just get used to things and they change. Laurie and Jamie going to college, now you're talking about leaving, and things are changing for Robbie and me, too." His voice was muffled now, and a little farther away.

He must be lying back with his arm over his face. "What's changing for Robbie and you? Do you mean because you're getting so successful?"

"There was a guy at the talent show last week talking to us about making a record."

"Wasn't that exciting?"

"It was, yeah, but scary, too. I don't know what to do, I don't know what will happen. Music is the only thing I'm good at. If I can't do anything with my music, what good am I?"

Beth sighed. "You're the only one who can answer that, Steve. The answer is inside you. I know you can find it. Mom and Dad will help you, and so will Robbie. But drinking won't help, Steve."

"Yeah, ok."

Car doors slamming. The others are back from Mass. "I mean it, Steve. We'll all help you through the changes. God will help you."

No answer. He's gone.

Chapter 31.

Wednesday, April 22, 1959: 5:00 p.m.

Steve

Steve's pulse was hammering in his forehead and he felt like there was a fire under his skin. He lay on his bed with his eyes closed, pretending to be asleep when Jamie came in. *This would happen right when he's home for the week.*

Jamie had come down from Boston for the civil rights rally in Washington on Friday and stayed for Passover. Last night they'd had that meal that lasted for almost three hours because of all the praying and singing. Steve had thought he was going to keel over before it was finished. The weird food he remembered from last year wasn't any different—the stuff with apples and nuts still looked revolting and tasted great, the stuff made of ground up fish still looked innocent and tasted gross, and the stuff that looked like big white radish slices still made it feel like the back of your head was about to blow off if you took too big a bite.

The four cups of wine: that had been the best part, though drinking them hadn't done Steve's throbbing head any good.

It took forever to get through the first half of the special Passover prayer books with the Maxwell House ads on them before they finally got to eat the real dinner. That food was good, but Steve hadn't had much appetite for it. Then when they finished eating they still had to do the second half of the prayers. For once, Steve didn't even enjoy the singing; all he'd wanted to do was get to bed before somebody noticed how bad he was feeling. *And later tonight they'll do the whole business over again.*

Jamie had been messing with some stuff in the closet. Now Steve heard him cross the room and sit on his bed. *Is he looking at me?* Steve kept his eyes closed and tried to make his breathing slow down, but his heart was racing so hard he thought it must show.

"Are you sick?" Jamie demanded. "You are, aren't you?" He reached forward to put his hand on Steve's forehead, but Steve flinched away. "Did you tell Mom or Dad or Ruby? What did they say?"

"No," Steve pleaded, opening his eyes, "don't tell them, please don't tell!"

Jamie's eyes narrowed. "Don't tell? Why not? They're going to figure it out anyway, you know, especially when I move into one of the spare rooms." He shook his head at Steve's betrayed look. "I can't stay in here and catch whatever you've got. I need to get back to school next week. Look, whatever you're worried about, just stop, ok?"

Steve groaned as Jamie left the room. *Easy for him to say, he's not the one who's sick.*

Sure enough, before ten minutes had passed, Dad came in, carrying a thermometer. He put it in Steve's mouth and stood beside him, holding Steve's wrist and looking at his watch. After a while he took the thermometer out and held it under the bedside lamp to see better.

Dad shook his head. "You're burning up," he said. "I'm going to call your mother so she can pick up some children's aspirin on her way home from work."

He went out into the hall and Steve could hear his voice rumbling. He'd left the door open behind him, though, which surprised Steve. *Isn't he going to shut me in?*

No, here he came again. He sat down on the bed next to Steve and picked up his hand, holding it between both of his. "Jamie says you didn't want us to know you were sick," he said. "Why not, son?"

"How come you're touching me?" Steve said. "Aren't you scared you'll get it? I don't want you to get it. My breath, there could be germs on it, right?" He was furious to feel that his voice was shaking a little, and tears were prickling behind his eyes. *What's the matter with me?*

Dad got up but he didn't go away. "If you're worried about that, I'll sit behind you," he said. He put an arm behind Steve's shoulders and propped him up so he could sit against the headboard, then let Steve lie back so he was leaning against Dad's chest with Dad's arms around him, basically in Dad's lap. "Now, is that all that's bothering you? You didn't want anyone to catch whatever you have?"

"I didn't want to be locked up," he said, and started to cry. *Damn.*

Steve gulped back his sobs for a while, then Dad said, "Is that what happened when you were sick with Bert? But he locked you up all the time, didn't he? Not just when you were sick."

"But if I was sick, he wouldn't come in for days. He said I had germs, so he didn't even open the door to give me food or let me use the bathroom or anything. I had a bucket, and a bowl of water, that's all. Then when I said I felt ok again he'd be so mad at how disgusting the room was and he'd beat me and beat me and then I'd have to clean everything with Lysol, and take a bath with Lysol, and sometimes I was so t-t-tired—" Steve gave up on trying to hold himself in and just wailed.

Dad pulled a box of tissues off the nightstand and put it where Steve could reach it, then put his arms back over Steve's chest. "But the other kids have been sick once in a while since you've been here, and nothing like that went on. Surely you didn't think we would do that to you?"

"Not really, but I didn't know what would happen."

"What's going to happen is that we're going to take care of you, as we always do, as we always will. Whatever you need, you're going to get, Steve."

Steve fought to get himself under control. When he thought he could speak again, he said in a small voice, "Why do I cry so much? I'm like a baby, I just fall apart. I was starting to feel stronger, but after the hearing I started going to pieces again. What's wrong with me? Bert said I was just a weakling."

"Nothing is wrong with you. And you are most certainly not a weakling. You have years of suffering and mistreatment to get out of your system, that's all. And you had a bad scare over the hearing, we all did. Over time, that will even out. But there's nothing weak about needing comfort, Steve, or crying when you feel sad or scared. Everybody needs to let go once in a while."

Steve craned his head back to look at Dad's face. "Do you?"

"Of course I do." Dad shifted so Steve could see him better, and looked at him seriously. "Listen to me, Steve. I've known men in the navy who never let their feelings out, who keep rigid control at all times. In my experience, one of two things happens to them. Either they get dried out and brittle and eventually fly to pieces under pressure, usually at the worst possible time, or they harden up till they gradually turn to stone and are no use to God or man. I don't want to get like either kind."

"So who holds you?"

"Who do you think?"

"Mom?"

"Right. I can't sit in her lap, poor girl, but I've cried in her arms more times than I can count. Do you think I'm a baby, or a weakling?"

Steve snuggled against Dad's neck. "No. But I bet you're not scared all the time like I am."

"You'd be surprised how often I'm scared. I was really, really scared when it looked like you might be tried for murder, for instance. But watching how brave you were helped me be strong."

"I wasn't brave, I was a mess. When I thought maybe I'd get locked up, and I wouldn't be safe here after all. Then, when the judge said I could keep living here and there wouldn't be a trial, I started acting like a brat. After that, when I was getting over it a little, those guys were killed on the plane and I started thinking, what if I die before I do anything I want? So I—" Steve gulped and took a breath. "I don't know, my feelings got all mixed up. It was like I got pushed back to last year or something. How's that brave?"

"You kept going, that's what. A lot of kids—a lot of grownups, for that matter—would have been too scared to keep trying the way you have."

"Like David?" Steve said.

Dad nodded. "Like David. I'll always feel bad about him, that we weren't able to reach him, but he didn't have the strength you have."

"I've been thinking about him a lot since I found out. I feel like I took his place, like I can be happy for him—I mean, instead of him. Is that dumb?"

"Not dumb at all. Hang on a minute, Stevie."

Dad went out of the room and came back a minute later with a rolled up paper. "David liked to draw," he said. "Would you like to have this?"

He unrolled the paper and Steve saw a crayon drawing of a feather with a ringed eye shape in the top of it. At the bottom of the paper was written "PECOCK FETHER. David."

"He didn't spell it right," Steve said, taking the drawing.

"No, he didn't. He never learned to read as well as you have."

"He could draw better, though."

"Yes."

Steve propped the paper on the nightstand where he could see it. Then he fell back against his pillow and yawned.

"I'm going to let you sleep a little," Dad said, stroking his hair. "I'll ask Ruby to bring you up some broth later, and I'm sure your mother will be in with your aspirin soon. You just rest. Everything is going to be fine."

Steve closed his eyes. *But I still wish I had a drink,* he thought.

Chapter 32.

Saturday, May 23, 1959: 10:00 a.m.

Joy

Joy lay looking at the ceiling of her parents' bedroom, wondering why she wasn't happier. The family was about to be all together again. Laurie'd gotten home for the summer a week ago; Jamie would arrive later today. Beth wouldn't have to spend weekdays in Paoli till next fall. Steve and Rob were really catching on as the McAlister Brothers. High school was almost over for the year, and Joy's grades had been great—her English teacher, especially, had told her she showed real promise as a writer. And Steve seemed to be getting over the murder charge scare—he was behaving himself around the house, and he didn't jump every time the phone rang any more.

But there is something wrong, anyway. I know he's still sneaking drinks. And that kiss…

Mom, face down on the bed beside her, reached a hand to Joy's knee. "Did you want to talk about something, Joy May?" Her voice jolted and hitched as Dad's massaging hands chopped down her spine.

I thought I did. But I don't even know how to say what's happening. I don't really know what's wrong.

"No," she said slowly. "No, I guess I have to stew over it a little more. And I can't hear myself think in our room, with Celia's girlfriends there."

"Ask them to move into the spare room," Dad suggested. "That's where they'll be spending the night, anyway."

"Aw, it's her birthday. Or will be on Monday, anyway, but you know what I mean. This is her party, I don't want to rain on her parade."

Mom groaned as Dad kneaded her shoulders. "Oh, Sean, that feels unbelievable. I haven't felt so relaxed since before the hearing."

"How's it going at work?" Joy asked, flopping over on her stomach next to Mom.

"All right, considering. Henderson is going around acting like changing the fosterage policy was his idea, now that he's gotten over the shock of being shown how wrong he was. I shouldn't complain—he felt guilty enough to cover for me today, so I can go along to pick up Jamie at the airport this afternoon."

She stopped talking as Dad went back to thumping on her shoulders with the sides of his hands. She gave a deep, guttural moan just as the partly open door swung in. Joy turned her head to see Steve's horrified face.

What's happened? What's upset him now? Joy pushed herself up and half got off the bed. *Wait, his face is changing. Now he just looks bewildered.*

He was looking past Joy at Mom and Dad. Dad had just started pulling his hands down Mom's back in long, firm strokes as she sighed in contentment.

"Stevie," Joy said gently, "Dad's just giving Mom a back rub."

"Oh," he said. "Oh, yeah, I can see that. It just surprised me, that's all."

Mom craned her head around to see Steve, then turned and sat up, tugging her dressing gown around her legs. Dad pulled his cuffs straight and smiled at Steve. "Come on in, son," he said.

Steve came in slowly. His eyes flicked to Joy and away again. "Do you want me to leave, Steve?" she said.

"What? No, I just—no." He sat down on the end of the bed and tucked his hands under his thighs, looking down. "Hey, what is this?" he said, pulling one hand out to trace a finger along the edge of the patchwork quilt. "This part, it looks the same as Mom's winter scarf."

"It's the McAlister tartan," Dad said. "A special design," he explained at Steve's wrinkled eyebrows. "Every Scottish clan has one. A lot of Americans call the design plaid, though that really refers to a kind of cloak. The tartan was a way of identifying people in battle, and came to stand for the various families, so we thought it would make a good border for the family quilt."

"There's some squares like that, too."

"Those are for the grownups," Joy put in "The rubies are for Ruby, obviously; Dad's the anchor. The funny squiggly green thing is a Greek letter called psi, that's the beginning of 'psychologist,' for Mom."

"And the ones with regular letters? C and L: for Celia and Laurie?" Steve asked.

"That's right," Mom said. "On baby blocks, for our first two babies. By the time Joy came along, though, we were already thinking of adding more to the family, and Ruby and I thought it would start to look silly with letters in all the squares, like a crossword puzzle that nobody could read, so we picked a flower to stand for Joy."

"The angel is Beth, natch," Joy took up the tale, "and the winged sneakers are Rob. The Hebrew letters—what are they again, Dad?"

"They spell *hai*, life, that's also the beginning and the meaning of Jamie's real name, Chaim."

Steve was silent, running his fingers across the squares beside him. *He's figuring out whose the other one is for,* Joy thought, waiting for realization to dawn. His roaming hand stopped on a square with a musical note appliquéd onto it. *He's got it.*

Steve looked up. "For me?" he said.

Mom nodded.

"But this quilt is way more than two years old, how did you know to put this on there?"

"It started, seventeen years ago, with only Laurie and Celia's squares having designs—the rest were just plain colors. As each of you came along, we've added motifs that seemed to suit you. Don't you remember, I said something about it the night your adoption was finalized—that now Ruby and I could add your square?"

Steve shifted his hand back under his thigh again and rocked a little, staring at the quilt. "I didn't know what you meant," he said.

"Why didn't you ask, silly?" Joy said.

Steve whispered, "I thought I was supposed to know, and I might get in trouble if you knew I didn't."

"But you asked today," Joy whispered back. "That's good."

"Yes, it is, sweetie." Mom sighed and pressed Steve's knee, then got to her feet, petting Dad's shoulder as she went by him where he leaned against their dresser. "Despite the fact that your father's turned me into a wet noodle, I have to get dressed or Jamie will be sitting in the airport by himself. Out, kiddos."

Steve and Joy trailed out into the hall and then stood there, turned slightly away from each other. The sound of chatting and giggling came out of Celia and Joy's room. *It's raining, can't go out. Beth's at her piano lesson, Laurie's at that meeting about the poor guy who was murdered by a lynch mob in Mississippi last month.* "Want to go down and play ping pong?"

Steve shook his head. "I think I'll go up and practice with Rob."

Suddenly Joy felt an all-too-familiar sensation. *Drat, I forgot what day of the month it is.* "Uh, maybe I'll come up after a while," she said, feeling her cheeks heating.

Moving away from Steve, she slipped into her bathroom through Beth's room, hooking clean underwear from Beth's drawer as she passed. *Silly, they're all girls in there, I could get my own. But I know them, they'll all smile at me like it's cute that I have my period.*

In the bathroom, she could hear the girls talking. Judy, who was new to Celia's circle, was saying, "But isn't it hard for you and Joy, being the only normal ones with all these—I don't mean this in a nasty way, but—problem kids?"

"Problem kids? That's not how we think about it. We've all been trained since we were little to be almost like a team. We know how to help each other, and we're usually pretty careful not to hurt each other. Though my cloddy brothers, especially, can be jerks sometimes. And if you think Joy's normal...."

The girls snickered and Joy snorted to herself in the bathroom, picturing Cissy's meaningful eye-rolling.

Once she was changed and had a pad on, she went back through Beth's room and headed for the stairs to the music room. The sound of Rob's voice stopped her partway up. *He's mad! Robbie's never mad.*

"So now I'm the one who's grounded," he was saying. "Because I supposedly kept you out after curfew, fooling around after the gig. I lied to them, basically, not telling them what really happened. I hate lying to them. I'm not going to cover for you again."

"All right, all right, I screwed up, ok? Don't make a federal case out of it. Let's just get on the stick and practice." Steve started tuning his new guitar.

Joy quietly backed down the stairs again and went to see if she could pick up any pointers about the care and feeding of boys from Celia's friends.

Chapter 33.

Rob

Saturday morning, hot and thundery. Rob woke up late with a heavy feeling in his stomach that it took him a minute to identify. *Steve. Last night. What am I going to do?*

They'd played a gig at the Navy Depot Officers Club. Mom and Dad had been there, smiling and applauding with everyone else. Afterwards, backstage, Steve had told him the performers were all going to stay on for a party. It was the first Rob had heard about it, but it seemed plausible enough. The parents had left with the usual stuff about being careful and not staying out too late; Rob's more-or-less date pleaded an early-morning appointment and went home with her girlfriends.

But the "party" had turned out to be just one of the bands, five guys in their twenties from Philadelphia. After sitting in the dressing room for an hour, fending off boring teenyboppers and trying to keep his head from splitting in the smoke and clamor, Rob noticed that Steve and the bassist were missing. He'd found them on the floor in the cramped backstage bathroom, passing around a flask and a reefer, with a couple of giggling girls.

"Come on, Steve," he'd said. "Time to go home."

"Hey, Steve, your daddy's here," the bassist had mocked. "Or is it your mommy?"

Steve had looked up, flushed, from behind a giggler perched on his legs. "He's nobody," he'd slurred. Then, at the look on Robbie's face, "I mean, just my brother."

Rob had turned to leave, not looking back but relieved when he heard Steve scuffling to his feet, the girl yelping in outrage as he pushed her off his lap. Steve had maintained a sullen silence in the car home and slipped off to his room in the sleeping house while Rob was still trying to hump their instruments inside without waking anyone up.

So now it's still to deal with. Showered and dressed and nowhere near hungry, Rob set out to find Steve. *At least he doesn't hide in the cabinet any more.* But he did hide in the music room; Rob followed the sound of the beautiful vintage Martin OM Steve had bought from his share of their performance fees after he'd smashed Mom's guitar.

Steve kept playing, his eyes on his fingers, as Rob came in and sat opposite him. "Your B string's flat," Robbie observed. Steve, still looking down, kept working on their new arrangement of "It's All in the Game." He was resting his foot on the case of Rob's new Gibson steel-string. *Is that on purpose?*

Rob reached forward and put a damping hand on Steve's strings. "I said, your B string's flat," he repeated, ignoring Steve's glare. "It was flat last night, too. And you came in late after the bridge on 'Maybe Baby.' In fact, in general you played like crap. And your voice sounded like it came out of a pickle jar. D'you hit the sauce before we even started?"

"What if I did?"

"What if you did? Well, for one thing, I don't enjoy standing in front of a bunch of people feeling like I need to eat crow for what they just heard. I may not be a big talent like you, but I still try to give them their money's worth."

"You're so great, find a new partner," Steve sneered.

"Yeah, well, maybe I could find a new partner, but finding a new brother wouldn't be so easy. And the way you're headed, I could be missing one pretty soon."

"Just pick one off the street. That's what they did with you, right?"

"Nuh, uh, kiddo. You can't throw me off like that. You're heading for a big fall, and I'm not going to hang around and watch you do it. What you're doing is stupid and dangerous. Illegal, too, by the way. If you don't care about yourself or me or the music," *there, that got his attention,* "you could at least think about what it would do to the folks if you got nailed for drinking and doping. I told you last time that I wouldn't look the other way again."

"You're going to tell on me, then?"

"No, I'm not. You are."

"Har-de-har-har. Pull the other one." He started unconcernedly plucking the same few chords over and over.

But look at his eyes. He knows I'm not kidding. "Steve, you're my brother and I love you very much. But if you don't put that flipping guitar down I'm going to wrap it around your neck."

Steve gave an exaggerated sigh and put the instrument back in its case, then fixed Rob with a defiant stare.

Rob put a sneakered foot forward until his toe nudged against Steve's. *At least he's not moving away.* "Who do you want to be?" he asked.

"What?"

"When you grow up or whatever you want to call it, how do you see yourself?"

"I never thought I would grow up."

"Yeah, well, things have changed, haven't they? So, now that it looks like you're going to live awhile unless you do something stupid, who do you want to be? A drugged-out alky who's picked up the clap from some stage-door tramp, a burnout who can't make decent music or—" Steve opened his mouth to interrupt but Rob rode over him, "—or never has a real friend or an honest love? And don't tell me about Bird or Miles or Billie or Hank Williams. They had their hang-ups, you have yours. But they didn't have us, your family. You do."

Steve jerked his foot away and stood up. "All right, so I won't do it any more. Satisfied?"

Robbie stood up, too. "No. That's what you said last time, and it didn't work." *His hands are shaking. Good.*

"I meant it," Steve said, with a hint of a wail in his voice.

269

"I know you did, honey. But you can't do it alone. That's why you have to tell them."

"I can't. I won't."

Time for the atom bomb. "Steve, didn't you tell me Bert used to get drunk all the time?"

Steve's face went deep red, then white as the blood drained from it. He took a step backward. "I'm not like Bert," he whispered.

"No, you're not," Rob agreed, stepping forward to close the distance between them again. "You're not one bit like him. But you need to remember that you can't get a grip when you're drunk. And when you're high on grass you don't care. It's time to straighten up and fly right, honey."

Steve put his hands over his eyes. "I care about the music. I care about you. You gave me the music. Sometimes it's the only thing that keeps me going. I'm sorry I've been messing up the music. I promise I won't any more." He lowered his hands and looked at Rob pleadingly, fearfully. "Why can't that be enough?"

"Do you remember when Mom took you to the dentist the first time?" *Well, at least that stopped him backing away from me.*

"Yeah, so what?"

"It was pretty rough, wasn't it? But your mouth felt a lot better afterwards, right? And you had to tell

Dr. Johnston where your teeth were hurting or he would have had a much harder time fixing them. It would have been stupid not to tell him, even though it didn't feel good when he worked on them."

Steve turned away and starting plunking a piano key. Robbie put a hand over his and gently stopped him. "That's what parents are there for, to help us turn into the people we want to be. They're on our side, remember? But they can't help us if they don't know what's bugging us. Dad's in the study; I heard his typewriter earlier. Just go down and talk to him."

Steve leaned his head against Rob's shoulder. "Is he going to—punish me?"

"Probably. He won't hit you, you know that. In fact, he won't do anything you don't agree to."

"But he'll be mad."

"I don't think so. Disappointed, more likely."

"That's worse."

"I know." Rain splatted against the window. As they talked, Rob was bringing his arm around slowly, as though approaching a wild creature, until he was cradling Steve against him. *He's letting me do it; he must really be scared.*

"Will you go with me?"

"Sure. I've got to come clean about covering for you last week, anyway. He's not going to be that thrilled with me, either. Come on. Just remember how much he loves you. It will be all right, I promise." He turned Steve away from the piano and started him toward their father.

Chapter 34.

Cecilia

Celia stepped through the gap in the low hedge around the vegetable garden, basket and scissors in her hand. Her feet stuttered a little when she came unexpectedly on Steve, bare to the waist, bandana shielding his head from the sun. He was crouched low over the tomato plants, weeding. *Look how brown he's getting. The scars are much less obvious. And he's finally starting to fill out and get some muscles.*

"Good Lord, Steve, are you still being punished? Rob's been off restriction for weeks."

He looked up and grinned at her. "I'm not really sure. I've kinda lost track. Turns out I like gardening better than cleaning, even."

She laughed. "Better you than me. Cutting lettuce for Ruby is about as much field labor as I feel like doing." She started rifling through the plants, looking for leaves that hadn't bolted. "How are the meetings going?"

"Ok, I guess. Boring." He stood up, arching the cricks out of his back, and came over to help her. "AA doesn't seem to have much to do with my actual life, with being in the music world, where everyone is smoking and drinking and there are always girls around." They worked together in silence for a few minutes, then he said, "Cissy, can I ask you something?"

"Go on."

"Do you and Rick—do it?"

Celia gaped at him. He blushed but kept his eyes on hers. *Woo. I guess it's a good thing he feels free to ask.*

Steve swallowed. "You don't have to tell me," he muttered.

"No, sorry, it just surprised me, you coming out with it like that."

"So that's one of those things regular people don't talk about, I guess."

"True, but stupid. Haven't the folks had The Talk with you?"

He stopped picking to look at her. "You mean, 'Sex is good, sex is natural, don't do it'? That talk?"

Celia hooted. "That's the one. But you still have questions?"

He looked away and hunched his shoulders. "I know how it works. That's not the question. I just don't get how—I don't know, what goes on with, like, teenagers. How you feel about it. What kids our age think. I know it's personal, you don't have to say, really."

Celia patted his arm. "It's ok that you asked me. And to answer your question, no. I'm not ready to have sex with anyone, and when I do it's not going to be with Rick Hartzell."

"But you, like, make out, right?"

"Right. You've seen us do that."

"What about Laurie and Linda?"

"You'd have to ask Laurie. I don't think so, though. With Laurie at Haverford and Linda staying around here to go to Dickinson, I can't see them getting more involved when their lives are taking different paths. I think they may even have broken up last week when he was in the Adirondacks with her family. He's been awfully quiet since they got back."

Celia wiped sweat off her forehead with her arm. "I think this is enough lettuce for tonight. If you're finished here, want to walk back to the house with me?" *And please change the subject?*

But after picking up his trowel, dumping his mound of weeds onto the compost pile, and snagging his discarded shirt off the ground, Steve said, "Robbie hasn't had a girlfriend since he broke up with Nancy, but what about Jamie?"

Think fast. "You know, you really should ask—"

"I'm asking you."

Coming into the screened porch, Celia was glad for the time it would take their eyes to adjust to being out of the afternoon glare. *Not sure I really want him to see my face right now. But maybe this is a chance to help out, with him and Jamie both.*

They went into the mudroom and started washing up at the deep sink there, hip to hip, not looking at each other. *Maybe I should check with someone before I tell him. No, this is just being open, right? What Mom's always talking about? I'm going to Barnard this fall; I know what I'm doing here.* "Steve, Jamie's—he doesn't really go for girls."

Now Steve did turn to her, hands hanging limp in the rushing water. "What? What does that mean, he doesn't—you mean he's a fairy? But he and Rima were always—"

"Yeah, *were* always. Mom says he was what they call 'in denial'." Celia was enjoying this. *Maybe I'll be a psychologist, like Mom.*

"*Mom* says? She knows?"

"Mom and Dad both know. He told them last summer. Actually, he told Beth first, and she convinced him he needed to talk to them about it before he went off to MIT."

Celia had put the stopper in the sink to soak the lettuce. Now they both swished their hands in the cool water, agitating the leaves to rinse off the dirt and bugs.

"And where was I while all this talking was going on?"

"You were... having your own problems. It didn't seem like the time to get into it with you. Besides, it's not like we had some big family meeting and didn't invite you. I happened to walk in on their conversation, that's how I know." She started pulling lettuce leaves out of the water and slapping them into the colander beside the sink.

Steve had backed away and was standing behind her now. "Were they mad?"

Listen to his voice. That's not just curiosity. "No, not mad. They weren't happy; Jamie's going to have a rough time of it—as though he needed any other problems in his life. But they're going to stand behind him and help him any way they can." She turned to look at him, leaning against the sink.

"Dr. Benson says homos are sick," Steve said.

Celia sighed, turning back to the sink to shake the colander. "Mom says that's not a helpful way to think about it. All I know is, Jamie had been trying for two years to force himself to be something else, and it hadn't worked."

She led him into the kitchen, set the colander of lettuce on the counter for Ruby to deal with later, and went through into the living room, Steve trailing behind her. Jamie was still there, as he'd been before she went out. He was playing a Bach Invention at the baby grand. He'd been playing a lot since he came home for the summer, always these cerebral, almost mathematical sorts of pieces. *Ok, here we go,* she thought, bracing herself.

"Jamie," she said, "I think Steve has a few questions. About—you know, the way you feel about other guys." For a minute he kept playing. *I'd think he hadn't heard me except for the red in his cheeks.*

But then Jamie looked up at Celia. *Can't read that poker face of his.* Jamie took his hands off the keys and turned to Steve, so Celia did, too. *Easy to read his face.* Steve was aghast. *Oh, God, I've messed this up.*

"I don't, I haven't, I never—" Steve stammered, backing away.

Jamie gave a harsh laugh. "It's the McAlister way, Steve, haven't you learned that yet? There's no problem so complex, no feeling so private, that it can't be made better by endless pawing and slobbering and *talk.*"

Celia felt a wave of heat across her cheeks and a sinking in her stomach.

Jamie pushed the stool away from the piano, slammed the lid down over the keys, and stood up. "So what is it you want to talk about? The prospects for my life, maybe? Let's see: I might go to prison, I can't get a federal job, I could get put in a mental asylum—oh, yeah, let's not forget, Hitler would have killed me twice. Too bad I'm not an artist like Uncle Kevin; he can be a flaming faggot and people just snicker. They expect it from artists. I'm a mathematician. Who's going to hire me? Who's going to want to be around me? Who's going to lo…" His voice had risen till he was shouting. Now he cut himself off and swallowed hard, leaning on his fisted knuckles against the piano cover.

"Oh, Jamie, I'm so sorry," Celia gasped. "I didn't think, I didn't realize you'd feel like this. I should have, I just blundered in with it. I didn't mean to hurt you." She turned to Steve. *He's got to be so upset.*

But Steve looked angry, arms wrapped tight around his torso, jaw set. "I don't care about any of that," he said.

Jamie stood up straight, dropping his hands to his sides. "So why are you glaring at me like that?"

"Why didn't you tell me?" Steve demanded. "We lived in that room together for more than a year. Why didn't I know this? I'm just a stupid kid, right? I'm the one with all the problems, nobody can ever tell me about anything because I might fall apart. I could never help anybody, I'm the one who's broken." His voice cracked. He wheeled away from them and ran out of the room and up the stairs.

Celia and Jamie stood frozen in place till they heard the bedroom door slam. Then Jamie moved out from behind the piano and started after him.

"Jamie—" Celia reached a hand to him as he passed.

He didn't take it, didn't look at her, but he did stop for a minute. "I'm going to be mad at you for awhile, Cissy. I'll get over it eventually, but not yet. Right now I'm thinking about Steve."

"I was trying to help."

"Yes."

She forced back tears as she watched him trudge slowly up the stairs. Then she moved behind him into the front hall and knocked on the study door. Mom and Dad were both in there, working at their desks.

"Can I take your car, Mom?"

Dad glanced at the clock. "It's almost time to start helping with dinner, Cissy. Isn't it your turn tonight?"

"Yes, I won't be long. I have to go to confession."

Mom and Dad glanced at each other. "Do you want to talk about it?" Mom asked, getting the keys out of her purse.

"No, I've talked entirely too much today. But you might want to check in on Steve and Jamie after a while." She reached for the keys, but Mom held her hand for a minute, watching her face.

Celia squared her shoulders and met Mom's eyes. Mom nodded and let her go.

Chapter 35.

Saturday, July 11, 1959: 5:15 p.m.

Jamie

Jamie stood outside the bedroom door with his hand on the knob and his head bent. *Come on, Hymie,* he said to himself. *You can't just leave him like this. Damn Celia anyway.* Expelling a sharp breath of air he straightened up and went into the room.

Steve was on his own bed with his light summer bedspread pulled up over his head. There was no sound or movement coming from the tight cocoon he'd wound around himself. Jamie came around to sit on the edge of his own bed, facing Steve. *Here we are again.*

After sitting a few minutes in silence, Jamie said, "What you said isn't true, you know. You're no more broken than I am. And you have helped me."

Steve's cocoon rocked a little toward him. *At least he's listening.* "I've watched you from the time you first came here," Jamie said. "That was two years ago this week. You were scared and mad and hurt, but you were something else, too. You were stubborn. You had a sort of strength that didn't let you give up, even with all the damage that had been done to you."

Jamie toed off his shoes and swiveled to lie back on his pillows. Looking at the shadows of the trees on the ceiling he went on, "When I made fun of you for crying, you threatened to kill me." The cocoon on the other bed was very still. "Do you know what that did for me? I mean, aside from making me ashamed of what I said? It showed me that you didn't collapse when you were hurt or scared, you pushed back. That's kind of miraculous, you know. When I first came here, if something hurt me or scared me, I would just hide."

"You were little," came Steve's muffled voice from under the bedspread.

"Yeah, but I kept doing it when I got bigger. Those two years I was going with Rima, trying to get my tongue down her throat and my hands down her blouse to the point where it embarrassed our friends, that was hiding. That was me trying to hide, even from myself, who I really wanted to—be close to."

Steve poked an opening in his cocoon and peered at Jamie from inside the bedspread. "Who?"

Jamie swallowed. "Tank Lebo."

Steve scrabbled the bedspread off and sat up, gaping. "Tank Lebo's an idiot."

Jamie made a wry face. "It wasn't his brain I was interested in."

"Oh. Right. So did you ever, uh…"

"No. Hiding, remember?"

"But you told Beth, Celia said."

"Eventually. When I couldn't stand the—I guess I'd have to call it pain, though I don't want to get all dramatic here. But it just hurt something inside me to keep it in, you know? And Beth's easy to talk to."

Steve nodded. "She can't see your face."

"It's not only that, it's that she's just so calm about everything, so accepting." Jamie went on, "But it was you who started me thinking about telling someone. That night when you—you know, the night everything all kind of came to a head for you and you…"

"Cried like a pig and then barfed all over Dad in the bathroom?"

"Did you? I didn't know that part. But yeah, that night brought home to me how you could rip the most painful things out of yourself and put them out there to deal with. And Mom and Dad helping you with the wetting the bed thing: once you could stop hiding it, they could help you deal with it and it got better."

Steve looked down and started tapping on the bedspread. *He hasn't done that in a long time,* Jamie thought.

"It wasn't exactly wetting the bed," Steve said in a low voice. "Or not only that. I mean, it wasn't just pee. Not at first."

Jamie shrugged. "Well, that'll happen. Nothing a guy can do about that."

"Bert thought there was. That's why he tried to kill me finally. He saw my bed. Dr. Benson says it was a sign that I was getting into whaddayacallit, puberty. So he wouldn't be able to—do things to me any more."

Deep water, Hymie. Move carefully. "Do you mean that you were getting too big for him to whip you and burn you and all that, because you'd be too strong?"

"And other stuff." Steve's voice was very small. He was staring out the window across from their beds, but his eyes flicked sideways at Jamie so quickly Jamie almost missed it.

Jamie briefly closed his eyes. "Ah, Steve. Ah, Steveleh. I should have realized."

"Because that means I'm queer, too?" That eye flick again, then back out the window. Steve's face had a deep flush under his summer tan; his fingers were knotted together in his lap.

Jamie sat up and turned toward him. "That's not what I meant. That has nothing to do with it, one way or the other. What Bert did to you has nothing to do with what you want or who you are."

285

Steve ducked his head down and brought his shoulders up to hide his face. "Don't look at me for a minute?"

Jamie got up and moved to the window, putting one knee on the window seat and bracing himself against the casement frame. He cocked an ear toward Steve behind him, but kept his eyes on the barely stirring larch trees outside. He waited. If he hadn't been listening so hard, he would have missed the thin thread of Steve's voice.

"Sometimes I liked it."

Jamie was expecting something of the sort, but he still flinched. He pulled off his glasses and scrubbed at his eyes with his knuckles as if there were sand in them. *Now. Quick. Before you chicken out.* He swung around from the window, stepped across to Steve's bed, and sat down on the end of it, putting his glasses back on. *"Mein harzbruder,"* he said softly. "My heart's brother."

Both Steve's hands were over his face. Jamie pulled them away, gripping them in his own. "How long were you in that room?" he asked. "Eight years? Nine? Who else did you ever see but Bert after your parents were killed in that car crash? Who ever touched you, in any way, for any reason, except to hurt you? When he did that to you, it wasn't love, but it wasn't torture, either. Of course you liked it. You're not made of stone. But that still doesn't say anything about what you want when nobody's forcing you."

Steve bit his lip, then flung his head up to look at Jamie, face flaming, eyes glittering with unshed tears. *God, look at him. Look how fierce, how brave he is.*

"I thought that's why you never touched me," Steve said. "Because you knew I was—dirty."

"You are not dirty. And aside from my little camouflage exercises with Rima, I never touch anybody if I can help it, haven't you noticed?"

Steve looked down at their joined hands. "You mean, because you're queer?"

"What, so you think I couldn't keep from flinging myself at you in the throes of unrequited passion?"

Amazingly, Steve giggled. "I don't know what you're talking about half the time," he said. "But I guess I know what 'flinging' and 'passion' mean. No, dummy, I meant do you not touch anybody because you're like me, you think you're no good and they'll find out?"

"No, that's not why. It's the hiding thing again. If you stay hidden, you can't get hurt."

"Is that really true?"

"No, I guess it's not."

"So… can I hug you?"

"Sweet merciful God, you just keep putting it out there, don't you? Yes, all right, I'll give you twenty seconds."

They held each other hard for a brief time while neither counted the seconds, then disengaged. Jamie moved back to his own bed while Steve wiped his eyes.

"What did you mean," Steve said after a while, "about Hitler killing you twice?"

"It wasn't only Jews the Nazis went after. It was Gypsies, too, and Jehovah's Witnesses. Also homosexuals—maybe ten thousand, maybe more, nobody knows for sure."

"Why kill them?"

"Why, indeed. Why did your cousin decide to lock you up and torment you and molest you for years? Would he have done anything like that if fate hadn't thrown you into his power? If I could explain the nature of evil, Steveleh, I wouldn't have to go to college, I could just set up as a universal wise man. A universal gay wise man."

"Gay means queer?"

"For those in the know, *schmo,* and I'm the original know-it-all, you know." He and Steve both snickered.

Someone knocked on the door. Jamie looked across for Steve's nod before calling, "Come in."

It was Mom. "Cecilia seems to think she said or did something to upset you two," she said, stepping into the room. "Are you all right? Do you need any help from me or Dad?"

Again Jamie silently conferred with Steve, then said, "No, thank you, Mom. We've talked it out."

"Did some pawing and slobbering, too," Steve said slyly.

Jamie huffed a little laugh. "I guess we did, at that. It's ok, Mom," he said to her. "We're all right. We're fine."

Chapter 36.

Thursday, August 20, 1959: 3:00 p.m.

Steve

Steve closed the front door behind himself and leaned against it, eyes shut, head down, feeling the coolness of the dim hallway after the scorching heat of the August afternoon. He was breathing hard. *This changes everything,* he thought.

"Steve? Steve, what's wrong?" came Joy's worried voice.

He opened his eyes and looked at her, confused. "Wrong? Nothing's wrong."

"But you look—I don't know, stunned or something."

"Stunned, yeah," he said. "This changes everything."

"What does?"

"This." He held up the thin, flat, square paper bag he was carrying.

"A record?"

"An amazing record." He pushed himself away from the door and moved into the living room.

Jamie and Laurie were at the side table, with playing cards strewn around and soft drinks at their elbows. "Beth and Celia are out getting stuff for Cissy to take to Barnard. The four of us were playing Hearts, trying to keep cool," Laurie said. "But we can do something else if you—"

"Where's Robbie?" Steve interrupted.

"We're between hands, he just went to get himself a drink. Why, what's up?"

"He has to hear this. I listened to it in the store, and I could hardly wait to get myself back here." Steve opened the cabinet next to the fireplace and turned on the fancy hi-fi set that lived there. *They have to understand this, they have to.*

Joy opened the bag and pulled the album out. *"Kind of Blue,"* she read. "Miles Davis. So it's jazz, what's the big deal?"

"Just wait till you hear it. Where's Robbie?" he asked again.

"Here I am," Rob said, coming through the dining room door, Coke in hand. "Oh, you got the new Miles—have you listened to it yet?"

"Yeah, you've got to hear it," Steve said, taking the album from Joy, ripping off the cellophane and sliding the record out. He put it on the turntable, set the arm, and cranked up the volume.

They all settled back to listen. The record started on "So What," surprisingly slowly, with Bill Evans's soft piano over a gentle bass line from Paul Chambers; they spoke and responded to each other, then brass and percussion joined the conversation. There was a startling cymbal clash, then Miles's trumpet took charge. Cannonball Adderly's alto and John Coltrane's tenor sax took what Miles began and ran with it over Jimmy Cobb's drumming in a freewheeling melodic line, coming back to the original tune.

"See what I mean? It's not thick like bebop," Steve said softly as the piece ended and "Freddie Freeloader" started. "It's not just chord changes, listen, he's using scales, the notes themselves—not just one song, the whole record. It's like a new language. It's just clean melody and different phrases building each other up. Without all those chords, you can just keep going." Laurie and Jamie nodded; Robbie was sitting with his mouth open. *I could listen to this every day,* Steve thought.

Forty-five or so minutes later, after Davis's amazing hand-off to Coltrane toward the end of "Flamenco Sketches," the last notes quietly circled into silence, like water from a stream pooling at its destination. For a full minute no one spoke or moved, then Joy shifted her feet and sighed.

Jamie said, "And I thought I didn't like jazz."

Laurie nodded. "As the only Negro in America with no musical sense, I have to say I'm impressed. I've never heard anything like that."

"No one has," Robbie said in a hushed voice. "You're right, Steve. This changes everything." He got up and walked over to where Steve was carefully lifting the record off the turntable by its edges. He put a hand on Steve's shoulder. "I'm gonna flip to hear what you do with it."

Steve frowned as he slipped the disk into its paper sleeve and then into the cardboard album cover. "What do you mean, what I do with it?"

"You don't just make sounds, you feel 'em in your bones. Remember, that guy from Decca wanted to see something new from us before they sign on the dotted line. Here's your take-off point. Time for you to write something of your own."

Steve swallowed and mumbled something under his breath. *This feels risky.*

"What was that? I couldn't read you," Rob said.

Steve's eyes shot nervously around the room till they caught Jamie's. Jamie gave him a slow nod. *He wants me to be strong. He wants me to trust them.* He cleared his throat. "Actually, I've already written something."

"You have? Let's hear it, sweetheart," Laurie said.

Joy bounced a little in her chair. "Yes, we want to hear it."

"Not now. Tonight, when everybody's here." *Maybe I should rewrite it, now that I've heard—no, what's done is done.* "Robbie, would you come up and work with me on backup?"

"Sure." Rob immediately started out of the room. Steve followed, stroking the new record as though it were a live thing.

That night after supper, the family gathered in the living room to hear Steve's song. It had gotten a little cooler, so the windows were open and gentle air stirred the curtains. The August evening was pink and soft grayish green, with the day's cicadas finally winding down and a few tired birds chirping their quiet late-summer song.

Steve sat on the piano stool, pulled out in front of the empty fireplace, with Rob on the floor in front of him. The lights were off except for the mantel lamps behind and above them. The rich brown of

Steve's prized Martin guitar shone in the lamplight; Rob's blond Gibson gleamed.

Steve had gone over the tune with Rob earlier, but he hadn't shared the lyrics yet. Now, as he looked down at Robbie's golden head bent to his instrument, its fine tone sounding the tentative, slow notes of the intro, the searching, weeping tones of a minor key, Steve ran through the words in one part of his mind while the other part rattled, *What if they don't like it? I'll die if they don't like it. I can't do this, this was a mistake. I'll sing it another time, when I've worked on it some more, worked in some of the things I learned today. But what if they don't like it?*

Yet even as his mind dithered, his fingers automatically came in on the sixth bar, picking a counterpoint to Rob's steady soft beat, and Steve started to sing.

"Like a seed in the ground,
Like a bird in the egg,
Like a child trapped in a dark, locked room,
I was a prisoner and bound
Crying till I begged,
And longing for a bright, warm home;
And longing for a bright, warm home.

"Like a jewel in the earth,
Like a stone in the water,
Like a child kept far too long in the womb,
I was hoping for my birth,
For a mother and a father,
And dreaming of a bright, warm home;
And dreaming of a bright, warm home."

The music built to a mounting progression of yearning, striving chords as they went into the bridge.

"I was hungry,
I was angry,
Choked with tears,
Wracked with fears,
Till your warm arms made me safe
And brought me home
(Safe from harm)."

Their guitars quieted and twined single notes around each other again, repeating the opening theme, now in a major key.

"Like a flower in the light,
Like a songbird in the sky,

Like a child tucked into bed when day is done,
Now my heart fills with delight,
Now I can fly free and high,
Then come back to my bright, warm home;
Then come back to my bright, warm home."

In a few strong, solid chords, the song came to an end. The family sat hushed till Steve dared to look up.

Everyone was crying, even Jamie. They were all looking at him. At his feet, Robbie pressed his cheek to Steve's knee. Mom and Dad were holding hands and leaning on each other. She gave a deep sob. "David," she said. "Oh, all the children." Dad held her.

Steve looked for Joy. Her face was alight.

They liked it.

Chapter 37.

Saturday, October 17, 1959: 2:00 p.m.

Laurie

Laurie was burning leaves, standing over the wire basket in the back yard, enjoying the rich aroma and the feeling of being home for the weekend, but nervous about the girl at the picnic table nearby. She was taking a break from helping rake the lawn, looking casually gorgeous in a coral shirt and black toreador pants, Laurie's high school letter jacket discarded on the bench beside her. *This must seem like another planet to Julia, after growing up in West Philly. Can it really be true that she never knew a white person before she got to Bryn Mawr?*

Beth and Steve came around the house dragging a tarp piled with leaves from the front yard, sweating in the unseasonable warmth.

"Careful, Bethie, there's a rake on the ground. Here, let me move it." Laurie leaned forward and pulled the rake out of her way and put another armful of leaves on the fire. "That's enough for a minute, Steve, we don't want to smother it."

Beth took off the cotton scarf she had wrapped around her hair and used it to mop her forehead. "I think I'm about ready to quit slaving over a hot leaf pile," she said. "How about you, Steve?"

Julia, at the picnic table bench, recrossed her legs and folded her arms over her stomach. *She doesn't like Beth saying "slaving" that casually,* Laurie thought. *She's so sensitive about that kind of thing.*

"Yeah," Steve was saying to Beth. "I want to go back in and work on my new song, anyway."

"You're being awfully mysterious about this song," Beth said, feeling her way to the wrought iron garden bench and collapsing onto it, stretching her sneakered feet in front of her.

Steve looked at Laurie, looked at Beth, looked down at his own hands, looked down the lawn toward the woods, looked at Julia, looked back at Beth. *Something's up.* "Spit it out, sweetheart," Laurie said, smiling at Steve.

Steve shrugged sheepishly. "It's no big deal, it's just that—well, you know Rob and I are going to cut that demo record for Decca, and Mr. Wolfowitz said we needed a B side to 'Bright, Warm Home' and it would be better if that was original, too, and thinking about what I wanted to write about…" He trailed off.

Laurie poked the leaves down into the basket with the iron rake, turning them so the burning embers came to the top and ignited the fresh leaves, which flared up in little spits of moisture and spirals of smoke. *Wolfowitz. That's the promoter Rob told me about, who caught their act in the talent show on WHPL.* "So…" he prompted.

Steve was still looking at Beth. "I wanted to save it for your birthday next month," he said. "But Mr. W. said they need it now."

Beth sat up straight. "Birthday—you wrote a song for me?"

Steve nodded, saw Laurie roll his eyes at him, and hastily said, "Yeah. I, uh, I hope it won't make you mad."

"Why on earth would it make me mad? I'm so honored, Steve, how could I be anything but happy?"

"Well, Beth," Laurie said, "maybe it's a crappy song." He winked at Steve. *Hope he gets that that's a joke. Good, he's giving me that crooked smile.*

"It is not a crappy song, funny man," Steve said. "For your information Mr. W. says it's 'melodically interesting despite the relatively juvenile tone.' Robbie had to explain that to me. He also said it was 'sweet.' It's just, I called it something Beth told me wasn't true about her really. But it is to me."

Beth's head was tilted to one side and she was shaking it a little, half-smiling. "And what is it called?" she said.

Steve mumbled into his chest, "'Angel on the Tree.'"

Oh, boy, Laurie thought. Aloud he said, "Bethie, you'll just have to give in or get mean, one or the other. As long as you're so nice to everybody, angel's what you're going to be."

"G-r-r-r," Beth growled, raising her hands in claws. Laurie and Steve both snickered at the sight of Beth trying to look fierce. Julia smiled disbelievingly.

"All right," Laurie said, "this fire has burned down enough to leave safely. I'll come out later and get the rest of these leaves, just pull the tarp over so they don't blow away. I think we have to go inside and hear this song. Come on, Julia. You haven't been to the music room yet, have you?"

Robbie was already there, working on some key changes. Laurie brushed Rob's shoulder as he and Julia moved past him to the piano bench. *God, I've missed him. This year even more than freshman year. I guess because he's growing up, finding a life with music, with Steve, without me.*

Laurie sat down next to Julia and drew Beth onto his knee. She leaned back against his chest and he wrapped one arm around her, one around Julia. Beth was completely relaxed; Julia felt stiff. *Freaked her out that they all kissed me when we got here last night. Guess she'll just have to get used to it. Or else she won't.*

Steve sat down opposite Rob so they could watch each other's fingers, and pulled his Martin out of the case.

"The new one?" Rob said.

Steve nodded. When he was tuned up they started, an intricate weaving of notes between the two guitars, climbing and climbing for a full eight bars before Steve's voice came in.

"Angel on the tree,
Tell me what you see—
Tell me how you know what's in my heart?"

Rob was singing variations on the last four words under Steve's clear lead.

"When you look at me
I know you'll always be
Watching over me when we're apart."

The melody shifted and they sang in close harmony, their guitars building in a powerful crescendo.

"Look down from far above me,

Look down and say you love me,
Teach me how to live, to make a start."

The instruments dropped back to a soft duet, with Steve singing the melody and Rob echoing the last four words again.

"Take my hand and show me
How to break my bonds and go free
And I will always see my sweet angel on the tree."

They ended, voice and music, together on the last word. *Nice.* Laurie nodded at them. "I like it, guys." He passed Beth his handkerchief.

She blew her nose, glowing. "Oh, that was beautiful, you two. Thank you so much. I love the way you used all that sight imagery, Steve, and it's ok that you made it an angel. It's not me, not really. You've made a song that a lover could sing, not only a brother."

Why did that make him look uncomfortable? Laurie wondered. The thought flew away as Joy climbed into the room.

"I was sitting on the stairs, listening," she said. "Hope that's ok?"

Robbie said, "Sure. We're going to play it for everybody tonight, anyway."

303

Steve said nothing, but shifted to make room for her on the floor next to his chair.

Julia spoke for the first time in what seemed like hours. "That was very nice," she said.

"Thanks," Robbie said, giving her one of his sunny smiles. "Do you dig music?"

"Of course I like music. Why wouldn't I?"

"Well, it's just that you hang around with this gorilla. He can't carry a tune in a bucket."

"Hey," Laurie protested. "Just because I can't make music doesn't mean I don't appreciate—"

"*What* did you say?" Julia hissed. "You called him a *gorilla?* Of all the ugly, racist—"

"Racist! Me?" Robbie was astounded.

Beth turned on Laurie's knee so she was facing Julia, still with her head against Laurie's chest. "Julia, really," she said, "Robbie didn't mean—"

But Julia was pulling away from Laurie. "Is this what you meant about your wonderful family?" she said. "I guess I just don't understand how white people express affection." She got up, brushed between Rob and Steve, almost stepping on Joy, and disappeared down the stairs.

Laurie felt skewered. *Oh, Christ, oh, dear God.* "Robin," he said to his brother's paste-white face. "Robin."

304

Beth slid aside as Robbie got up and came over to Laurie. He took Laurie's face in both his hands and whispered, "You love her, Laddie?"

Do I? Laurie thought over the past year and a half: the loneliness of the first year at Haverford, the sense of light and connection that sparked on when he met Julia this fall, the way she laughed, the things she knew, the look of her walking beside him in the rain arguing politics with fire in her eye. Then he thought of her beauty, and the taste of her mouth. "Yes," he said. "I do."

Robbie nodded, dropped his hands, and turned away.

"Where are you going?" Laurie asked.

"I'm going to fix this," Rob answered. He went downstairs.

The others sat in silence for a minute, then Laurie got up to follow. He stopped on the second or third step, looking back. "Aren't you all coming?"

Joy and Steve stared at each other, then Steve took Beth's hand and they started down after Laurie.

Celia, home on break from Barnard, was just hanging up the phone in the upstairs hall. "Is something wrong?" she said. "Julia went past me a minute ago looking like thunder, and then Robbie came tearing after her—"

"Yes, something's wrong," Laurie said. "Come with us, Cissy."

"Don't you think we should let the two of them…"

"No, I think I want all my brothers and sisters in on this. Steve, you'll have to stand in for Jamie."

They moved, clustered together, down the hall to the larger spare room. The door was open, and they could see Julia sitting on one of the twin beds. Robbie was kneeling in front of her, holding her slim brown hands in his strong, square white ones. Laurie went around to sit on the other side of her bed, leaning forward against her back, looking down at Robbie's face. The others stood in a semicircle around them.

"—since I was a little boy," Rob was saying, all the phony jive talk shed for once. "Dad was still overseas, and Laurie was my rock, my protector, my teacher. He taught me how to stand firm, how to tell the truth, how to be a man. We tease and joke a lot in this family, and I know to some people it looks mean, or—or inappropriate, I guess. But don't think that we don't know about suffering and real cruelty, because we do. And don't ever think we don't know about love. I'd jump in front of a train for Laurie, and he would for me, too. He loves me, and he loves you, so we'd just better get used to each other."

Laurie couldn't see Julia's face, her head was bent. Robbie lowered his to peer up at her. "And part of that means learning that I say whatever comes into my head most of the time, without thinking about how it sounds. I just chatter along like a—like a monkey." He let go of her hands and started hopping on the floor making little monkey noises.

Julia sniffed and raised her head, looking around at them all. "This whole family's crazy, isn't it?" she said in a conversational tone. They beamed at her. She clicked her tongue. "I suppose you're saying that you'll learn to get used to me being prickly and paranoid, too?"

Robbie nodded vigorously, taking her hands again. "Now you're catching on," he said.

"You really, none of you, know anything about what being Negro in America means," she said, "no matter what other troubles you've had."

"So teach us," Laurie said, nuzzling the sweet line where her hair met her neck, the place she'd told him black people called the "kitchen."

"I'll try," she said. "But I'm going to need a little time to get used to a situation where I find out you love me from your brother."

"Welcome to the McAlister family," Celia said. "Embarrassing revelations a specialty."

Julia laughed and stood up. Robbie rocked back on his heels in front of her and kissed her hand with a flourish. "Fool," she said, smiling and shaking her head as she stepped around him. "Laurie, didn't you say you had to finish burning the leaves? Let's get busy before your parents get home and decide I'm an outside agitator, here to make trouble."

Halfway out of the room, she stopped next to Steve. "I'm sorry I ruined the moment for your song," she said. "It's a good song, and I took everybody's attention off it."

"That's all right," he said. "I like watching the way people here know how to make things better. It's like a team, Mom and Dad training everybody how to do it. Anyway, I'll sing my song again later, when Mom and Dad are here, and Ruby. You can make a big fuss about it then."

"I will," she promised, and went out. Laurie followed, taking a minute to look around at the others' faces. *I don't need to say it. They know.*

Chapter 38.

Monday, December 21, 1959: 1:30 p.m.

Joy

It had been almost a year since Steve had kissed Joy on the mouth. He'd never tried to do it again, but she couldn't get it out of her mind. *I should talk to Mom about it,* she often thought, *but it might make trouble for Steve. And it was nothing, anyway.* So why couldn't she stop thinking about it?

She'd tried; she'd had a boyfriend since she'd started ninth grade in the fall, but with Mike it felt like being in a play, pretending to be two kids going steady. They met between classes and walked the corridors holding hands, Joy with her books held against her chest in her left arm, Mike with his against his hip in his right hand, like there was some rule about how girls and boys carried books. After school they'd gone to the drive-in for fries and cherry phosphates till she realized she'd gained five pounds and put a stop to it. They went to dances and leaned against each other, swaying to the music—but more and more often the dances featured the McAlister Brothers, now that Steve was in high school, too, and she'd find herself watching him instead of focusing on Mike.

Now she sat by the telephone in the front hall, feeling miserable and wondering whether she should call Mike and apologize. Last night he'd taken her to a big Christmas party in someone's downstairs rec room where everyone was making out in corners and the record player was blaring and suddenly she couldn't stand it any more. She'd told him she had a headache and made him take her home, even though it was obvious he didn't believe her.

A little while ago she'd slipped out here while everybody else was in the dining room decorating the gingerbread cookies for the tree, but she couldn't make up her mind whether calling Mike would make things better or worse. She fiddled the dial back and forth on the telephone without picking up the receiver. *Maybe if I don't say anything, he'll just—go away. Oh, gosh, is that really what I want? To break up with him?*

Uncle Kevin came into the hall from the living room. "Everyone's wondering where you got off to, Joy," he said. "Are you ok?"

"I don't know," she said glumly.

He perched against the edge of the credenza and gave her an inquiring look. "Can I help?"

"Maybe you can. You've been talking to Jamie about, uh, his situation, right?" His face closed off a little and she said hurriedly, "I don't want to know anything about that, it's just that—you sort of know about, about relationships that aren't exactly normal. No, no, I don't mean it that way, I mean not—regular, not ordinary."

He nodded cautiously. Just then the front doorbell rang. Clucking in exasperation, Joy got up to answer it. *I hope it's not Mike, not right now.*

It wasn't Mike, it was Mike's parents' maid—what was her name? *Bridget, that's right. But why on earth is she here?*

Before Joy even had a chance to speak, the short, brown-haired woman, dark cloth coat over her maid's uniform spotted from the spitting icy rain, pushed into the hall, closed the door, and turned on her.

"I suppose you're proud of yourself, young lady?" she demanded, her Irish brogue stronger than Joy had ever heard it.

"What are you—"

But Bridget was still talking. "Young Michael is crushed. You've broken his heart, that you have, and it's a disgrace, a black disgrace."

311

"I didn't mean—"

"I suppose you think it's all a game, toying with a decent boy's affections. I've heard tales about this family, and now I know they're true. Call yourselves faithful Catholics, I suppose, and you running about lying through your teeth, you ought to be ashamed."

"Really, if you'd just let me—"

"And now he tells me he gave you his granny's ring. I'll have that back, if you please." She held out an imperious hand.

Joy pulled the chain out from under her sweater and unclasped it so she could slide off the gold circlet with its tiny diamond. "I told him not to give me this, it wasn't right," she tried to say, but Bridget cut her off again.

"Not big enough for you, was it? You wanted something fancier?"

"No, that's not what I—"

"He's well rid of you, and so I'll tell him," Bridget said, pocketing the ring and flouncing back out the door in a blast of frigid air.

Joy closed it behind her and leaned her head on it, bumping her forehead lightly against the wood. *Oh, that was awful. What am I going to... what's that noise?*

She turned around to see Uncle Kevin slide off the edge of the credenza onto the floor, shaking, face red, tears starting out of his eyes. *Is he crying? No! He's laughing!* "Uncle Kevin?"

He started to howl out loud. "That was the funniest damn thing I ever saw," he said between hoots.

"Uncle Kevin!"

"Well, it was. That tiny little woman reaming you out over some hulking teenage lout's wounded feelings, and you towering over her, quivering like jelly."

Against her will, Joy had to giggle. "He does have feelings, Uncle Kevin."

He took a breath and calmed down. "I know, Joy, I know, but I'm sure you didn't set out to hurt them. And if you can't see the humor in situations like this, they'll just drag you down." He held out an arm and she came to sit beside him on the floor. "Was that what you wanted to talk to me about, what was going on with this—is his name Michael?"

"Yes. I mean no. I mean, that's his name but that's not what I wanted to talk about. It's why I ran out on him."

"And that was?"

"I kept thinking about Steve."

"What about me?" Steve had come into the hall and almost tripped over their feet. He stood there looking down while Joy could feel her face getting

313

redder and redder. After a minute the blood started to creep up into his cheeks, too. "I have to—" he said, stepping over them and going into the little bathroom that opened into the hall and the study.

What do I do now? Joy hit her fist against her forehead.

"You're going to get a headache if you don't stop banging on it," Uncle Kevin said.

"I wish I could just open it up with a can opener and let the confusion out."

Uncle Kevin patted her back and said, "Here, let's get out of the middle of the floor." He took her hand and helped her up, then drew her into the TV room doorway. As Steve came out of the bathroom, Uncle Kevin said, "Want to join us, Steve?"

"Not really," Steve said. He turned to Joy. "It was just a kiss," he went on. "Robbie told me a long time ago, if you love someone, show them. So I did. Something wrong with that?"

Joy said, "No, but—"

"They're waiting for us in there," Steve said, and walked away.

Uncle Kevin sighed. "I think I'm in over my head here," he said. "You'd better talk to your mother, Joy."

"Yeah, I guess so." *Except I really think I'd rather talk to Steve, if I can get up the nerve.* "Thanks anyway, Uncle

Kev. And thanks for laughing me out of feeling bad over that weirdo maid. Come on, let's go back and do some more cookies."

"All right," he said. "I should, I guess. Jamie was putting little menorahs and dreidels on his, since Hanukkah starts on Christmas night this year. I promised I'd help with the designs."

"Uncle Kevin," Joy said as they moved toward the dining room, "is Jamie going to be ok? Are you? Are you—happy? I mean—"

He stopped and rubbed his forehead. "I know what you mean, Joy, and the answer is I don't know. Things are a little easier for people like Jamie and me than they were when I was young. Am I happy? Sometimes. Not always. Maybe not even most of the time. I hope it will be different for Jamie."

Joy put a hand on his arm so he turned to her. "Have you ever had—I don't know how to say it— somebody special? I'm not being nosy, I just wondered if you're—lonely."

The laughter of a few minutes ago had vanished from his face. "It's all right to ask, Joy. And the answer is yes, I did have someone special once. For about a year, we were happy. Then he went out one snowy night to buy cigarettes and he was robbed and beaten and left to freeze to death in an alley. They call it 'rolling queers.' No one was ever arrested; the Chicago police barely made a report on it."

Joy suddenly felt very young. "Oh, no. I'm so sorry," she said. "And I'm sorry for pestering you with my little problems."

"Your problems aren't little," he said. "I'm serious about you talking to your mother. I wish I'd had parents I could have talked to when I was your age. And when Roy was killed, I was alone. That was one reason I was willing to come back here and make up with Sean when your mother tracked me down. Anyway, we're going to see to it that Jamie doesn't have to struggle alone, and you shouldn't, either."

Joy stretched up to kiss his cheek and they went on to rejoin the singing and laughter in the dining room.

Chapter 39.

Saturday, January 2, 1960: 7:00 p.m.

Cecilia

Celia watched Jamie saying the Hanukkah blessing in Hebrew; the others said "Amen" with him. Then he lit the eight candles on the menorah arms and fitted the servant candle back into the raised center cup, rocking it into the old wax in the socket. He was wearing a white yarmulke with gold embroidery on his head instead of his usual plain black one. The candlelight glinted off his glasses. *He looks like someone out of a book, with his dark hair and deep eyes, and that wonderful nose. My brilliant brother.*

"Who wants to play dreidel?" Celia asked. New Year's Eve at the Navy Depot Officers Club had been a bust for her; her ailing relationship with Rick had finally breathed its last. Even listening to the McAlister Brothers bring the house down with "Angel on the Tree" hadn't salvaged the evening. *I'd rather just be here with the family.*

Still, it was exciting to be at Barnard, and in New York. Nobody had any preconceived ideas about her there; nobody called her Cissy. *The college guys think I'm pretty, and they like it that I'm smart. Mom was right, imagine that.*

Before long she, Jamie, Steve, and Joy had gathered on the settees around the coffee table with their dreidels, a pile of gold-foil-wrapped chocolate coins, and a sheet of paper on which Joy had jotted the Hebrew letters and their meanings in the game for Steve.

Dad came up behind Jamie and leaned over his shoulder, holding out a small package wrapped in blue paper with a white bow. "Happy Hanukkah, son," he said, dropping a kiss on Jamie's head, "from your mother and me."

Everyone watched as Jamie tore off the paper and opened the lid of the little box. His lean face relaxed in a rare smile. "The first Israeli commemorative coin," he said. "Thank you, Mom and Dad." He reached up to clasp Dad's hand and they smiled at each other.

"That should make a good investment for you, darling," Mom said. "Watch it appreciate over the years."

Jamie snorted at her. "I wasn't planning to spend it on a handful of beans, Mother." He leaned over the coffee table to show the coin to Steve. "Look, this is what the Great Menorah looked like, that was in the Second Temple two thousand years ago."

"Those marks under it are Hebrew writing, right?"

"That's right, it means 'Law is Light.'"

"What does that mean?"

"It means that without laws, we'd all be in the dark—clawing at each other till the strongest win."

"Not all laws are so great," Celia said. *Jamie of all people knows that.*

Jamie nodded at her. "Some of them need changing. But without structure, the barbarians take over."

Steve passed the coin on for the rest of the family to admire. "How come only Jamie gets a Hanukkah present? There was that puzzle for everybody, but nobody else got their own thing," he said. "But he got stuff for Christmas, even though that's not his holiday."

"The Hanukkah celebration is about enjoying ourselves together; that's why we get something the whole family can do," Mom said. "And Jamie gets Christmas presents because he's a member of this family, and most of us are Christians. But he's the only Jew, so he's the only one who gets a personal Hanukkah present."

Steve opened his mouth to object while Celia thought, *Pretty shaky logic, Mom.* But Jamie laughed.

"I'll let you in on something, Steve," he said. "When we were kids, everybody envied me because I had presents for both Christmas and Hanukkah. It wasn't till I got to adolescence that I realized it was a zero-sum game, that they were only going to spend so much money even if I could get them to celebrate Ramadan and the Vernal Equinox. I was getting double the number of religious observances for the same number of presents. It was a cruel awakening."

Mom and Dad were both snickering. "I guess our secret is out, Martha," Dad said. "Now that a Catholic's going to run for president, maybe we can parlay our devious religious machinations into a job with the CIA."

"Are we going to play this game or what," Joy said, spinning her dreidel on the coffee table. "I'm hungry for some of that chocolate gelt."

Ruby got up from the armchair where she'd been reading the paper. "Speaking of hungry, who wants some leftover eggnog and the last of the cookies off the tree?"

Robbie went out to help her while the dreidel game went on and the others chatted. After a few minutes he came back in carrying a tray full of filled red glass cups as Ruby set a plate of gingerbread on the coffee table.

Celia sniffed her eggnog. "Hey, I'm over eighteen, can't I have one of the ones with bourbon in it?"

"We didn't make any with bourbon this year," Laurie said without looking up from his book.

"We didn't? Oh." *Shut up, Celia.*

But Steve said, "It's because of me. They can't trust me."

"That's not it, darling," Mom said. "It's just that we don't see the point in making it harder for you. Why keep something in the house that you can't have?"

"Does Ruby still keep that bottle of special brandy in her room?"

Dad's "That's not your business," coincided with Ruby's "No, I do not."

"But I bet you still keep a bag of pork rinds behind the flour canister, and Jamie can't have those."

Jamie said, "In the first place, I don't want them. In the second place, there's no law that I can't have them, outside the laws of my religion that I choose whether or not to follow. In the third place, I could eat pork rinds from now till Passover without it affecting my judgment."

"I wouldn't be so sure of that," Celia said, trying to inject a little lightness into the moment.

Steve ignored her. "So you'll fill up the liquor cabinet again when I'm eighteen?"

Dad sighed. "Son, there may be a law that you can't drink till then, but there's no law that you have to after that."

"Then, that's it for the rest of my life? You think I'm never going to be like a regular person?"

How are they going to talk their way out of this one? Celia thought. It was interesting to sit back a little and watch her family as though she were a stranger, seeing how the dynamics between them shifted and re-formed, sending energy in unexpected directions. *Talking and touching, praying and laughing, with plenty of food and music and poetry. That's the recipe. They just cook it up in different proportions. It's not exactly what I'm learning in freshman psych, but it seems to work.*

Dad had gotten up and come around to stand by the coffee table facing Steve. "What do you see when you look at me?" he said. They all looked at him. He'd taken Uncle Kevin to the airport this morning and then gone in to the Navy Depot, so he was still in his service blues, trim and spiffy, brass buttons and gold commander's insignia gleaming, ribbons bright against the dark navy tunic. His shoes were polished to a high shine, his tie was still perfectly knotted under his crisp white collar, his graying blond hair neatly brushed. His face was kind and grave, his pale-blue eyes on Steve's vivid azure ones.

Steve narrowed his eyes, considering. After a while he said, "I see somebody who's got it all together, somebody in charge." He bit his lip and went on, "I see somebody I'm a little scared of, somebody I trust anyway—somebody I love a lot. Somebody I'm never going to be."

Dad gave a rueful smile. "Yet you've seen me lose my temper, you've seen me uncertain, you've seen me cry. What about that suggests to you that I'm someone who has it 'all together'?"

The room was so still, Celia could hear the fast-burning Hanukkah candles sputtering out in tiny crackles as the little flames subsided into hot wax. Steve looked down at his lap, brows knitted. "You're saying you don't?"

"I'm saying no one does, no matter how they dress themselves up in shiny packages. I battle my demons every day, and so will you, and so does everybody. Am I right?" He turned to Mom and Ruby; they both nodded solemnly. "The problems you struggle with won't go away, and that doesn't mean you're weaker or more broken than anybody else. I told you once you were incredibly strong and brave, and that made you angry then. I hope you can hear me say it again now.

You've overcome unbelievable obstacles; you're a person I'm proud to know. But yes, you'll have to avoid alcohol for the rest of your life."

Steve nodded slowly. Joy, next to him, put her hand on his arm. Mom came over to Dad and gave him a long, deep kiss.

Celia took a slow breath. *I made fun of "The Talk" with Steve that time, but this is what it's about. This bond they have, that's worth working on. Worth waiting for.* Then Mom and Dad pulled apart and their eyes met. *I hope some day I meet a man I can look at like that,* Celia thought.

Chapter 40.

Sunday, March 13, 1960: 12:30 p.m.

Laurie

"Anybody for more pancakes?" Dad poked his head through the swinging door from the kitchen, waving his spatula. When no one at the dining room table spoke up, he shook his head in mock disgust. "Pikers," he said, coming into the room with a plate of pancakes in his other hand and sitting down in front of it.

"They're especially good this week, Sean," said Ruby, passing him the syrup.

"Ah, they're always good," Dad said. "I, madam, happen to be the Pancake King of South Central Pennsylvania. Right, Martha?"

"Of course, dear," Mom said dutifully.

The others smirked or rolled their eyes at the familiar routine. Laurie watched them all, gaze moving from face to face at the long table. Celia and Jamie were talking quietly. Robbie was laughing at something Steve said. Joy and Ruby were head to head, looking at a poem Joy had written; she'd been going around the table with it all through the meal. Beth was sitting with her hands folded in her lap, head to one side, listening to their voices. *It's all so beautifully sappy and sweet,* Laurie thought. *Oh, God, I don't want to do this.*

Dad's finishing his stack. I can't put this off any more. It won't get easier. Laurie got to his feet. Mom looked up at him. "Uh, uh," she said. "Big Men on Campus—or home from it on spring break—don't have to help clear, right, Jamie?"

"Actually," Laurie said, "I was wondering if we couldn't put off the cleanup for a while." He raised his voice a little. "I need to talk to you all."

Mom got up quickly. "Not today, honey," she said. "It's my birthday. I don't want to talk about anything serious today, please. Maybe later in the week?" She was already moving toward the door.

But her face is pale. She's guessed what it's about. "Mom, Mom!" The others were looking around, confused. Dad's brow was creased as he made to follow Mom into the living room. Ruby looked sadly at Laurie across the table, then went after them. "Come on, you guys," Laurie said to his brothers and sisters. "There's something I need to tell you."

Mom had only made it as far as the overstuffed chair by the window. Dad perched on the arm, hand on her shoulder, still wearing his silly flowered apron. Laurie stood in front of the fireplace while the others straggled in from the dining room and found places around the room. *I feel like I'm on stage. Final curtain? Don't be melodramatic.*

Everyone in front of him was sitting down now, quiet and starting to look worried. *Dear Lord, help me.* Laurie took a deep breath. "I'm sorry to do this on Mom's birthday, I should have told you yesterday but I couldn't get up the nerve." He gripped his hands together and started tapping his thumbs against his fists. "I have to tell you all that I'm not going back to Haverford at the end of the week. Julia's taken a leave from Bryn Mawr, too, and we're going down to Nashville with a group of other students to join the sit-ins."

There were gasps and murmurs around the room. Jamie dropped his face into his hands, Celia started to cry, Steve said, "What?" and Joy said, "Oh, Laurie." Robbie, sitting on the floor next to Beth on a settee, said accusingly, "You promised. You promised me you'd never go down there." Laurie gave him a helpless, apologetic shrug and he turned and buried his head in Beth's lap as she bent over him.

327

But Mom's voice carried over everything. "No, you are not," she said firmly. "I won't have it."

Laurie turned toward her. "I have to do this, Mom. The civil rights movement is going to change the face of the South, maybe change the whole country. I've lived here in this safe, comfortable house with my safe, comfortable—" *white* "—family all my life that I can remember. Now I have to take the strength and the resources that you've given me and use them to help in the struggle, help these people." He licked his lips with a dry tongue. "My people."

Dad said, "But there are other ways, son. What you did at Woolworth's in Philadelphia, picketing but in a Northern city where there are limits to how far the police will go. You don't have to go to Tennessee and put your body on the line, risk fire hoses and batons and God knows what. You could stay here and write letters to the papers, organize petitions, even go to Washington—"

"Washington, right. Where the Senate ran a five-day filibuster last week just to try to block a simple voting rights law. Dad, is that what you did after Pearl Harbor? Write letters and organize petitions? Lobby Congress and demonstrate in front of German businesses at home?"

"That's different. That was war." But Dad's voice faltered as he said it. *He knows better.*

"Were you listening to Father Shea this morning, Dad? When he talked about being responsible for each other? But you don't need a homily to know that; you know it in your bones. And you've taught it to me."

"But it's so dangerous!" Celia wailed. "Laurie, think about that man in Texas, not much older than you. They h-hanged him upside down from a tree and beat him with chains and carved his—"

"Stop it, Cissy," Laurie barked. Jamie looked like he might vomit, Steve's face had set in a mask of fear, Beth and Robbie were clinging to each other, Joy just looked lost and bewildered. Laurie went on, "Do you think I don't know that? Do you think I don't lie awake at night imagining the things that could happen?"

Laurie calmed himself and brought his voice down. "But this is important. This is necessary. That guy in Houston wasn't even part of the sit-ins and that could still happen to him. Nobody with a black skin is safe while things like that can go on. Desegregation isn't the answer to everything, but it's a start. And the sit-ins are working. They've already started integrating lunch counters in San Antonio."

"Right, you're right," Mom said suddenly. "He's right, Sean. It is important and necessary. He should go. We'll all go. We're his family. And this isn't only a fight for one race, it involves us all. We'll stand with you, Laddie."

Laurie went and knelt in front of her and Dad. He took Mom's hands and pressed them to his mouth, and she stopped talking as though he'd covered her own mouth. "No," he said softly. "No. This is for me to do. Of course you can help—do some of the things Dad was talking about. But going down there, putting my body on the line as Dad said: I have to do that myself. Please understand. I love you so much. I love all of you so much. But this is about me and I have to do it by myself."

Dad shook his head, shifting on the broad arm of the chair, eyes glistening. "I still don't think—"

"Seanie." It was Ruby's voice. She came forward from where she'd been standing by the dining room door and put her arm around Dad's shoulders. "Seanie, child, you know he's right. He has to go." Dad dropped his face to her breast, tears running down his face. She stroked his hair, looking down over his head at Mom. "I'm going, too," Ruby said. "Not to Nashville or Greensboro; I'm too old and too scared for sit-ins. But I am going to go to Atlanta with

330

my sister Pearl to work for the Movement." Mom put her forehead against Dad's side.

Laurie leaned up to kiss Mom's cheek and stood up. He bent and kissed Dad's half-hidden temple. Then he kissed Ruby's gray head, still bowed over Dad's.

He turned away blindly and hadn't walked three steps before the others all surrounded him, pressing in with patting hands and hugs and kisses till he was in the middle of a close, loving scrum. He leaned down and breathed in the warm, homey scent of his family, felt the dampness of their tears and his own.

But all the while he was pressing gently through till he came out of the huddle. He gave one last close embrace to Robbie and turned to move toward the stairs. Pulling his mind free of the turmoil of emotion, he set it to practicalities. *I have to pack a rucksack and call Julia. Linda, too, if she's really coming along. Tonight I need to—* He was brought up short by seeing Steve standing apart, scowling at him. *Look at him. Can he really be almost sixteen already?*

"Stevie—"

Steve catapulted forward and cannoned into Laurie as though to bring him to the ground. His arms wrapped hard around Laurie's waist and his head buried itself in Laurie's chest. "I don't want you to go,

331

I don't want you to be hurt, you have to stay here," he said fiercely.

Laurie lifted Steve's face and kissed his forehead. "I'm going to do my best not to be hurt, little brother," he said. *God, his eyes are so blue.* "But sometimes you have to risk everything to keep what you have."

Steve said, "You're my brother. You are."

"I know," Laurie said. "I know."

Chapter 41.

Jamie

Jamie came awake with a shout, the taste of Yiddish sour and familiar and comforting in his mouth, like a bowl of schav. But the words he'd been screaming held no comfort.

The full moon through tree branches threw shadow bars across his face and chest; he twisted violently in the bed to escape them, burying his face in his pillow. His chest was pounding, and his head. He couldn't still his brain enough to think.

A hand gripped his shoulder. He tried to get away from it, but it held firm and turned him onto his back. *"Sha,"* said a voice in the dark. *"Sha, Hymeleh, sha, sha, shepseleh."* Another hand moved to his right hand, holding tight.

Then the same voice said, "Steve, come over here. Squeeze his other hand, make him know he's here." Jamie felt his left hand being clasped. "You're ok, Jamie, you're home, you're with us," the voice went on. "Breathe, now, come on, take a deep breath for me, that's it, *shepseleh*." Jamie held on as hard as he could as his heart quieted and his lungs calmed. *Robbie, that's Robbie talking to me.*

The door opened, spilling light into the bedroom, and Jamie's sisters came in and gathered around the bed; this was a familiar routine. Celia and Joy each grabbed one of his ankles through the covers; Beth felt her way to the head of the bed and put a soft hand on each of his temples. After a second she let go, reached for a tissue, and gently mopped his eyes and cheeks, and his sweaty brow. Steve and Rob were still holding his hands. *Anchored. Anchored in reality. Home.*

"Are you here again, Jamie? Can you talk about where you were?" Robbie said.

Jamie cleared his throat and tried to speak but all that came out was a whimper. *Embarrassing.* He took a breath and tried again. "They were hanging them," he said hoarsely. "They used to hang them in the *Buchen,* the beech trees. The singing forest, we called it. Because of the screaming. And that winter it was cold, so cold. I couldn't stay hidden in the barracks, I had to move around. The men told me not to come out, but I had to see w-why the screaming." Jamie's chest was starting to seize up again.

Rob put his free hand on it, pressing gently over his heart, rubbing in small circles. "Shh, easy, easy," he murmured. "It's all over now."

"No, it's not, don't you see? The hate, the killing—I saw…" He choked.

"What did you see, baby?" Beth said, stroking his hair.

Her hand stopped dead when he answered, and the others' hands held harder. "Laurie," he croaked. "They were hanging Laurie. Over and over again, from every tree."

"Strange fruit, like in the song," Steve whispered in horror.

"Yes. The song about lynching, written by a Jew." Jamie brought his knees to his chest, knocking Joy and Celia's hands away as a wave of cramps knotted his gut. "Let me out," he said desperately. "Let me out *now.*"

They pulled back from him and he lunged out of bed and into the bathroom, flinging the door shut behind him, making it to the toilet just in time. He sat, gasping and sweating, head in his hands, waiting to have enough strength to stand up again.

After a while there was a knock on the door. "Jamie?"

"I'm all right, Rob. Please ask everyone to go back to bed."

335

"No, we want to—"

"I know what you want. I'm telling you what I want. Thank you for your help, now *please* go back to bed."

"Well, we'll all leave the room, and I'll wait downstairs till Mom and Dad get home from that meeting so I can tell them what happened. How's that?"

"If you must."

"I must."

Jamie waited till he heard the bedroom door close, then he cleaned himself up and came out of the bathroom. *Steve. I forgot Steve would still be here.*

Steve got up and started toward the bathroom himself.

"I'd turn back if I were you," Jamie said sardonically.

"Oh, yeah, 'cause my shit don't stink, right?" Steve shot back at him. "You're the only one with evil stuff inside?"

"Such a *khokhem,*" Jamie said. "Wiseguy," he explained.

Steve shook his head and went into the bathroom. Jamie got back into bed and curled under the covers, clammy with half-dried sweat, trying to get warm again. Steve came back out and went over to his bed, but

Jamie didn't hear the faint creak of the springs indicating that Steve had gotten in. Instead, after a few seconds, something soft butted against Jamie's hand where it lay on his pillow.

"What's this? Oh." *The bear. Kid thinks I've reverted to infancy. Don't want to hurt his feelings, though.* Jamie took the bear and stuffed it down under the covers next to his chest. *Feels pretty good, actually.*

"Heart's brother," Steve said quietly.

"Harzbruder," Jamie responded.

When Jamie awoke again, he was alone. He put his glasses on and sat up, looking out the window through the bare larch branches, just putting out soft green needles. The sun was glinting on South Mountain in the distance; it must be around eight. *If I hurry, I'll get downstairs before they leave for the day. Do I want to? Might as well face them.* He got up, set the bear back on Steve's bed, and pulled on his old robe.

The kitchen seemed strangely empty without Ruby's bustling presence, even though there were six people already in it when Jamie stepped off the back stairs. Celia and Joy were by the swinging door to the dining room, about to leave. They both stopped when they saw him, came back, and kissed him, one on each cheek.

"Are you still going back to Boston today?" Celia asked. "You could always change your plane tickets, stay a little longer. I'm not catching the train to New York till tomorrow; I'll be back from driving Joy in a few minutes. Maybe this afternoon we could—"

"No, I better get back. Joel, my roommate, said he'd take notes for me, but four days out of class this close to the end of the semester is more than enough."

"Well, I'm glad you got to have Passover at home, anyway," Joy said.

"Me, too, Jo-Jo."

Joy rolled her eyes and the two girls left.

Jamie looked around the room. "Beth already gone?"

"Yes," Mom said, clearing her place and Steve's. "We took her to the train station at seven so she could get back to Bolotin for the rest of the week. She said to give you her love."

Jamie filled the kettle at the sink and put it on the stove. He looked at Rob, who was leaning against the refrigerator next to him drinking orange juice. "*Shepseleh*?" Jamie said, raising an eyebrow.

Rob shrugged, blushing a little. "I've heard Mom say it when you've had a bad dream. I don't even know what it means."

"And I got it from listening to Jamie," Mom said. "Doesn't it mean—"

Jamie cut her off. "It means baby sheep."

Robbie stepped around Jamie to put his glass in the sink, turning his head to hide his grin. "Come on, Steve," he said. "Time to rumble."

Steve slid out of the breakfast nook. He and Jamie nodded at each other.

Rob clasped Jamie's shoulder as he passed. He waited till he was almost out the door to say back at Jamie, "Have a good trip—lambie pie."

Jamie threw a potholder at him. Mom and Dad both laughed as Rob ducked, cackling, and disappeared after Steve.

Jamie retrieved the potholder, made tea for himself, and brought the pot and a box of matzoh over to the table. "Is that all you're having?" Mom asked.

"My stomach's still a little queasy," Jamie said.

"You were asleep when we got in last night," Dad said. "We stopped for coffee with some of the others after the meeting. We didn't want to wake you again, it was so late. But are you sure you're all right to go back? Rob told us what you'd said about your nightmare."

"I'll be all right," Jamie said. *That sounded better than I feel. They don't look convinced, though.* "It was doing the seders that got me going, I think. Especially, you know, that bit in the Haggadah—'In every generation there rises up one who would destroy us...'—I kept seeing Laurie's face, and Ruby's, too, with some redneck Bull Connor type threatening them." He stopped to say a blessing on his matzoh.

When he finished and started to eat, Mom said, "I told you we called Atlanta and talked to Ruby last week, right? Her whole family down there has gotten involved, organizing sit-ins, helping the students get coordinated. And you saw Laurie's last letter; he and Julia are doing fine in Nashville, and he says they're being careful."

"Careful, good. If only they're careful enough, no ravening lynch mob will dare to touch them."

"Son," Dad said.

"I know, sorry. And I'm sorry I went off the rails last night."

"No need to be sorry for that. We're all worried sick."

"Not as sick as I was."

"Don't be so sure about that. Robbie, for one, has thrown up almost every day since Laurie left."

"Poor kid. I know he's closer to Laurie than almost any of us." Jamie sighed, twisting the heavy brass of his class ring around his finger. "How was your meeting last night?"

"A good start," Mom said. "We all got our assignments of neighborhoods to canvass with the civil rights petitions."

"Well, good luck," Jamie said. "I feel bad about being so far away from the family now, but we're doing some organizing at MIT, too, and grass roots activities in Boston."

"Speaking of which, you'd better get dressed if we're going to get you to the airport on time," Dad said.

"Right." Jamie pushed himself up from the table.

Mom got up, too. "I have to get to work myself, so I'll say goodbye now." She kissed his cheek and then rested her palm on it, looking up at him. "Be well, *shepseleh*, my little lamb," she said.

Jamie bowed his forehead to hers. "I will," he said. *I will.*

Chapter 42.

Saturday, May 28, 1960: 4:00 p.m.
Beth

*L*aurie and Ruby are home and safe. That's the important thing. Beth ran her fingers through the sewing kit Mom had arranged for her, picking up a needle she knew would have white thread in it in one hand and a white cotton blouse in the other. She started to stitch on the inside of the collar, a dot that would have three more dots in a vertical line to the right of it: "w" for "white." *So much to get done before I leave for Perkins.*

She breathed in through her nose and rolled her shoulders, trying to relax. *Robbie promised he'd tell them tonight. Everything will be fine, enjoy the moment.* The air on the screened porch was warm, with a light summer rain ticking on the eaves. Mom, Laurie, Ruby, and Julia were sitting around her, Mom helping embroider the Braille on Beth's clothes while the others talked about their experiences.

Ruby had come back after a month in Atlanta, carrying a valise full of printed handouts and a head full of plans for organizing petitions and demonstrations, which the rest of the family had enthusiastically fallen in with. Now President Eisenhower had finally signed the Civil Rights Act, establishing some basic voter protections for blacks. *If Kennedy gets elected, maybe we'll get a real civil rights law, one with teeth in it.*

The Nashville sit-ins had ended two weeks ago. Laurie and Julia had gone from Tennessee to Baltimore to stay with her family, coming on here last night. Mom came home from work early today to be with them. "Can you tell us at all what it was like?" Mom asked now. "I mean, the actual sitting in?"

Laurie said, "We had to sit straight, not laugh, not talk—the toughest part for me was not talking back to people who were taunting us and calling us names, threatening us. This non-violence is hard on the arteries."

"I half expected we'd have to come down there and bail you out of jail," Mom said.

"Julia and I were lucky not to be arrested; lots of students were. Then somebody bombed the lawyer's house—thank God, no one was hurt. That actually raised more support for the protests. We were in the crowd that marched on city hall after that."

"I heard there were four thousand people there," Ruby said.

"I believe it," Julia said. "It was a strong enough showing that Mayor West came out in favor of desegregation. Dr. King came the next day to speak at Fisk University, and after that it was only a matter of time."

Laurie said, "Before we left, we went and had lunch at Walgreen's. It wasn't much of a lunch, but it sure tasted sweet. Though I felt eyes drilling my back the whole time."

"Well, it's a battle won, but not the war, let's not forget," Julia said. "We've joined this new organization, the Student Non-violent Coordinating Committee—they call it 'snick,' SNCC. There's still plenty to do—"

Steve rushed into the room; Beth could hear muffled static and voices accompanying him. *He must be carrying his radio.* "Hey, Ruby and Mom, the Alabama jury just acquitted Martin Luther King on that phony tax charge. I know you were worrying about it this morning…"

"Thank God," Mom said.

"Hallelujah," Ruby said.

Julia said, "One more drop in the bucket."

"I'm going to turn on the TV," Laurie said. He and Mom followed Steve out of the room.

As Beth snipped her thread and reknotted it for the next blouse, she could hear Ruby starting to get up. Then she heard Julia's low voice. "How could you come back here?"

There was a light thump and a scrape as Ruby sank back into her chair. "I beg your pardon?" she said.

"These children call you by your first name, and you're older than their parents. You wait on them and cook their food and wipe their noses. You're an intelligent woman, and you've been to Atlanta and worked for the Movement and seen a bigger world. You could get a white-collar job, with your administrative skills. How could you come back here to be Mammy again?"

The silence that followed had a quality Beth remembered well from childhood. *Julia's about three words away from having her mouth washed out with soap.*

But Ruby's voice, when it finally came, was carefully controlled. "These children call me Ruby because I've asked them to, because we love each other. They know I'm older than their parents; I raised their father. If you think I wait on them, you haven't

345

been paying attention. I do cook for them; I like it, I'm good at it, and it's my job. They did manage to feed themselves while I was gone, you notice, but we're all glad I'm back to do it again. I've had other kinds of jobs, for your information—jobs I didn't need an apron for—when I was married and living in California. And I have a nursing degree; if I wanted a different kind of job, I could have it. I chose this life, this family, instead."

"I didn't know all that about you."

"There's quite a lot you don't know about me, *Miss Hawkins.*" Beth could almost feel Julia's cringe at Ruby's tone on the name. "And finally," Ruby went on, "I wipe their noses because they trust me and I care about them. I am not ashamed of what I do for a living. Dignity comes from inside, no matter what you do in life. Maybe when you're older and know a little less, that will come clear to you. Meanwhile I notice you talking to me like it's just us two here. Beth can't see, but she can hear just fine, can't you, child?"

"Yes, Ruby," Beth said, trying to sound completely neutral.

"Now, if you'll excuse me, Miss Hawkins, I have work to do, and I can hear Steve in the kitchen already, shelling the peas like I asked him to."

Her chair scraped back; she pressed Beth's shoulder as she passed. Beth started sewing again.

She'd stitched two dots and started a third when Julia said in a small voice, "I did it again, didn't I, Beth?"

Beth smiled at her. "Go give her a kiss," she said. "That's what I do when I've gotten in trouble with her. Works every time."

"I hardly know her."

"Time to get started, then?"

Julia hadn't been out of the porch two minutes when Steve came in, rustling the paper bag of pea pods and clonking the china bowl for the shelled ones onto the table. "Ruby's in a mood," he said, "and now she and Julia are sort of hanging off each other and snuffling. I thought I better come out here."

"Good instinct," Beth said. "Do you need help with those?"

"No, thanks, I like doing them. It calms me down. I'm kind of nervous about tonight."

"You mean when Robbie tells them he's not going to college?"

"Yeah. Mom's going to yell, isn't she?"

"And Dad's going to pound on things."

"Are they going to be mad at me, too?"

"Why on earth?"

"Well, it's because of the music, right? And that's sort of my fault."

"It's not only because of the music. Robbie's plenty bright, but he's never been a great student. He's been worried for a while about what he was going to do with his life. When he quit the basketball team so he'd have more time for playing with you, I knew he'd found what he wanted."

For a while the only sounds were the plop-plop-plop of the peas bouncing into the bowl, the soft splatting of the rain on the hydrangeas along the porch, and the tiny groan of the cotton under Beth's fingers as the thread pulled through it.

Then Steve said, "So you think it's ok that he won't go to college, or me either? You don't think we'll be, like, bums or something?"

"I think everyone's life is different, baby. I think no one else can tell you what to do with yours. You know I'm going to Perkins in the fall; nobody's making me do that, it's my decision. I do worry about you two, though, once you start seriously touring."

Beth put her sewing aside and tucked her hands into her armpits, rocking a little, thinking back. "Robbie thinks he's going to be looking after you, the way he always looked after me when we were little, on the street. But I remember how hard that was for him, feeling like everything was on him to do. He would get so wound up taking care of me, he'd forget to take care of himself. Can I ask you to look after him?"

"Me? How do I look after him?"

"Just love him."

"Oh," Steve said. "Ok, I can do that."

Chapter 43.

Monday, July 4, 1960: 6:00 p.m.

Joy

It was a glorious Fourth: hot but not too hot, with a pleasant breeze under the trees and a clear sun shining on Dad barbecuing beef ribs and chicken parts on the stone grill chimney by the picnic table. He would add the burgers in a few minutes. The table in the screened porch was laden with huge bowls of potato salad and Ruby's special slaw; the corn was shucked and ready to plunge into the giant boiling pot on the stove; the blueberry pies were taking up the better part of the center worktable. When it got dark they'd have fireworks.

Joy finished setting out ketchup, mustard, and relish beside the paper plates and napkins, thumping the jars a little as she set them down. *I must be the only person in the country who's in a bad mood right now.*

She scuffed into the kitchen, where Ruby was mashing mint leaves and sugar for the iced tea. "Did you need me to do anything else?"

"No, child, that's fine. It was nice of you to let Jamie off the hook."

"There wasn't that much to do, and I want him to have fun with his friend." *If that's what you call him.*

She and Ruby traded meaningful looks and Joy wandered into the living room, trying to think of something she wanted to do till supper was ready. Jamie was there with Joel, his MIT roommate, fiddling with the piano and talking about some weird mathematical theory.

Joel had a German-Jewish mother and a Chinese-Jamaican father. He was lithe and graceful, with delicate features and café-au-lait skin; he looked like something out of the Arabian Nights. *And Jamie treats him like an exotic butterfly. A butterfly with a mind like a razor.* As for Joel, he called Jamie "Chaim" and followed him around like a baby duck.

Jamie's Joel was staying in the smaller guest room; Laurie's Julia was in the bigger one. *All very proper, but I wonder what they do when they're not here in this house?* She sighed discontentedly. *Everybody's pairing up or moving out or starting their lives one way or another. Everybody but me.*

She decided to go find Steve. Since Christmas, they'd had a couple of conversations about their relationship—or rather, Joy had talked about her feelings while Steve fidgeted. *Maybe I'll try again.*

He was in the music room, surprise, surprise. He wasn't playing, though; he was looking out the window, watching Dad barbecuing down below. She slid an arm around his waist. "What are you looking at?"

"I'm trying to memorize everything."

"You're going to leave, aren't you?"

He looked down at her—he'd grown about an inch a year in the three since he'd come here. "You know I am," he said.

"Right now?"

"Pretty soon. Mr.—oh, he wants us to call him Wolfie—Wolfie says we have to promote the record. He thinks he can get us on Ted Mack, or even *American Bandstand.*"

"Wow. That's great."

"You don't sound that excited."

Joy turned around, leaning against the window so she could face him. "Everybody's going to be gone," she said. "To school or charging around saving the world or becoming international rock 'n' roll stars or something. This fall it'll just be me here, little dumb Joy writing poems about loneliness while three adults give me good advice at every turn."

He raised his hand and ran a finger along her cheek and under her chin. His lips parted a little. He dipped his head toward her. Joy leaned forward and her eyelids fluttered.

Steve stepped away from her so suddenly she almost tipped over.

"Steve!"

"Sorry," he said, moving toward the stairs.

"No!" she said, stamping her foot. "I've had enough of this! Come back here and talk to me."

He stopped at the head of the stairs, his weight hung on one hand grasping the rafter beam at the top of the stairwell. "I can't," he said. "Not now, not like this. Later, when it's dark. When everybody's looking at the fireworks. Dad was taking the meat off just now, we have to eat."

The sky through the music room window was a clear inky blue flecked with stars when they crept back up the stairs after supper. But Steve didn't stop there, he went on through the low door into the attic. "In here," he said, going to his cabinet hidey-hole.

At some point he'd opened the door so the big house fan at the other end of the attic could suck some air through, but the tiny space under the eaves was still stifling hot. Joy wedged herself as far as she could into the angle with the roof so Steve could squeeze in next to her. He craned around and pulled the cabinet door shut after them. It was pitch black.

"Don't you want to turn that lantern on?" *Why am I whispering?*

"No, I don't. Shh, please, Joy, just be quiet for a minute?"

Joy lay there on the rucked-up sleeping bag for what seemed like much longer than a minute, long enough to start to sense thin threads of lighter bluish gray through cracks in the siding, and to hear the distant voices of the family below, oohing and aahing after each thud and swish of a roman candle or crackle of a skyrocket. Steve's elbow was digging into her breast; she shifted minutely to take the pressure off.

With that movement he started to talk, in a voice thready with suppressed emotion. "When I kissed you that time," he said, "and I pushed you away after? What I really wanted to do was punch you."

Did I do something wrong? She tried to think back to that moment. *No, I didn't do anything. He's telling me something about himself, not about me.*

He waited a little, then when she didn't say anything, he went on. "I guess you know Bert used to hurt me. Maybe you don't know he did—sex things to me, too."

In the suffocating heat, she felt a wave of cold flow over her. She held her breath, afraid to move.

"When he was drunk, mostly," Steve said. "If he came in The Room without having a drink first, I knew he was just going to hurt me. If I could smell liquor, he was going to hurt me and also do the other stuff. If he brought in the bottle and made me drink it, too, then it was going to be more of the sex things." He wriggled around till he was turned toward her. "Sometimes he cried, then, Joy. And sometimes he'd pass out and I'd just lie there next to him. And I'd feel dirty and trapped and sore and mad and scared, and I'd also feel— grateful in a crazy way. Because it felt good. But I hated it, and I hated him. And then he'd hurt me again. Mom and Dr. Benson, they have some fancy words for all this. And letters, some new thing—P-something, I forget what it stands for, like what soldiers get. Dr. Benson says I'll grow out of it, and Mom says my feelings are 'normal,' whatever that means. But I can't make sense of it. I can't make sense of me."

Should I say something? If I reach out to him, will that make it worse? Joy could hardly breathe, between the close air in the cramped space and the pressure of Steve's body and the smell of their combined sweat

355

mingled with a deeper odor she didn't recognize, at once alluring and repellent. But she didn't want to speak in case that made him stop talking.

"So when I started getting older," he said, "he would always hurt me after the sex. That didn't use to happen, it mostly used to be before that he'd hurt me. Dr. Benson says Bert was afraid it would mean he was queer, if I was, like, a guy and not just a little kid. So that last night, when he came in and saw that I had messed in the bed in my sleep, he went back out and got the knife, and then he said he was going to cut me. Then he had some more to drink and he said no, he'd have to kill me, I was too bad to live. And I was so scared, so scared, sometimes I think I'll never stop being scared. Then he drank some more and passed out and the knife fell out of his hand and I took it, so shiny, and I put it in his throat and then it wasn't shiny any more. But I was still scared. I am still scared."

Joy thought someone was trying to get into the cabinet, then she realized it was rattling because Steve was shaking so hard.

"So it's all mixed up in my head. And I can't make sense of it. It felt good, sort of, when he touched me, and bad at the same time. Jamie says of course it did, and that helped me some, but really, everybody's so busy telling me nothing is my fault and that's not the point. I mean, it's probably not Bert's fault, either, right? Something probably happened to him to make him like that. But I don't care any more about figuring out who to blame. I care about figuring out how I can ever have sex with anybody without wanting to hit them and hurt them, before they can hurt me. I can love everybody else here now, but I can't love you because I love you so much. And I'm scared of you, too. You might hurt me. And then I'll get mad, I'll get like Bert. If I touch you I'm going to hurt you."

Joy was sad and terrified and filled with love for Steve, all at once. "I don't believe that," she said. "I don't believe you'd hurt me, not really. I'm smaller than you, you don't have to be afraid of me, remember you said that to me once? What have Mom and Dr. Benson told you about this?"

"They say it'll 'take time.' They say be patient. They say I'm too young to worry about it. But I worry about it, every time I look at you. Laurie and Jamie and Rob are my brothers. Celia and Beth are my sisters. I don't think you're my sister."

Joy couldn't tell how much of the wetness on her face was sweat and how much was tears. She waited till she was sure he had stopped talking, then said, "Steve, I'm glad you told me, and that you let me into your special place, but I'm scared, too. Not of you, I mean of everything that hurts you. Maybe a little of you, but not really. I don't know how to say it. I might be able to say it in a poem after a while, but right now my tongue's all tangled up. Could we move out of here now and get some air?"

He opened the door, levered himself out, then reached in and hauled her to where she could get some traction and pull free of the narrow opening. He kept hold of her hand when she stood up. Her knees shook as they made their way back down to the upstairs hall, and she kept hold of his hand all the way into his room.

The fireworks had finished, though there was still talk and laughter in the yard. They got to the seat in the open window just in time to hear Mom say, "Where did Joy and Steve get off to?"

"We're up here," Joy called down. "I was getting eaten alive out there, and we can see fine from here." *Not exactly a lie, since both things are true—if not the whole truth, by a long shot. But I better get into the shower before somebody wonders why I'm so sweaty.*

She turned to Steve. Her whole body was shaking. *I don't know what to do, how can I help him? I'm too young for this. I don't know enough.* "It's going to be ok. I'll take care of you." *But nobody else can save him. I'm the one he came to.* She lifted her face and this time he kissed her.

Her mind went back to that other kiss, more than a year ago. That had been desperate, almost brutal. This time, he seemed both firmer and more tender. *Even though he's still afraid,* she thought, *he's already gained a lot. This is a step forward; I don't want to drive him back.*

In the shower, she kept replaying what he had told her. *I should talk to someone, I can't deal with this. But he's already talking to people, to Mom and Dr. Benson, and they're professionals. He told me because he trusts me, because he wants me to understand.*

She got out of the shower and used her towel to rub a space in the fog on the mirror. She stared at her own face, the way her wet hair lay flat against her head and made her seem smaller than usual. *I'm just a kid. No, I'm not, I'm sixteen. He trusts me. And he's so sweet, so hurt. I shouldn't be afraid. I need to help him. I can save him.*

She turned away from the mirror, went into her bedroom, and sat down on the bed, letting the towel on her head fall over her face. She sat there, enclosed in damp terrycloth, thinking. Feeling. Hoping.

Late that night Joy tiptoed out into the silent hallway, up the stairs and through the moonlit music room into the attic. Steve was there, sitting in the middle of the floor on a pile of old curtains. "I knew you'd come," he whispered.

Chapter 44.

Friday, August 12, 1960: 1:30 a.m.

Rob

Robbie sat hugging his pajama-clad knees on the window seat of his bedroom, staring out at the fog-wreathed three-quarter moon. The summer evening had cooled down enough that the breeze through the open window was making him shiver. *Like on the streets in Harrisburg, when Bethie and I were little. And I knew winter was coming, but I didn't know what to do to keep her safe.*

Steve was sitting on Laurie's bed, pleating the sleeve of his pajama shirt into accordion folds and letting it fall loose again. Wolfie had met them tonight after their performance at the War College Officers' Club over in Carlisle. He'd taken them for coffee and they'd talked for an hour, getting home late and wired on caffeine and anxiety.

By the time they got in, most of the house was asleep; they'd come in here to unwind a little and listen to some sides on Robbie's portable record player. After playing a few old favorites with the volume turned down low, Rob had put on the disc they'd bought today. They'd gone to a record store in Carlisle before the show and blown half a buck on a 45 of a new duo who called themselves Tom & Jerry. Joy had recommended it.

Now, while Laurie showered in the bathroom, Steve and Rob listened to the A side, "Baby Talk." The two voices on the record blended well in the nonsensical song.

I like them better on this than when I saw them on Bandstand *a while ago,* Rob thought. *Cheap Bell Records crap, but they definitely have something.* He sighed and shifted on the cushion. "They sound kind of Everly-ish to me," he said as the record came to an end. "Pretty good, though, I suppose."

Steve started. "What? Oh, yeah," he said, standing up to switch off the turntable. *His mind's a million miles away, too, like mine,* Rob thought.

"Want to hear the B side?" Steve asked.

"Not tonight," Rob yawned. *"Bom ba ba bom," deathless lyrics. Good thing they have some harmony going on. Makes me tired.*

Steve put the plastic disc into its paper sleeve and flipped it at Rob. "Think fast," he said jokily.

Lame. Rob sat unmoving as the small object sailed by and landed on the floor beside him. He and Steve looked at each other for a minute, then Steve retrieved the record and set it on the desk next to the record player in silence.

"What do you think about this Payola stuff?" Steve asked.

Don't freeze the kid out, it's not his fault. "Bunch of crooks, they can all get bent. Musicians are just trying to make some bread, they don't need to be paying off deejays."

"You think Wolfie's in on that kind of thing?"

"I think he's pretty straight, I think he's ok."

Steve sat down again. He took a deep breath. "I'm nervous about Wolfie meeting with the folks tomorrow," he said. "I don't know if they'll go for it, and I'm afraid he's going to piss them off."

"Yeah, he's a shuckster, and Mom and Dad hate that pseudo stuff. I'll try to keep them on track, though, don't sweat it."

Steve's eyes were big. "You will? Rob—"

"It's cool," Rob said, cutting him off. *It's not his fault, but I still don't want to hear about it right now.*

"I just thought—"

"Don't think so hard, you'll hurt yourself." *Great, now he's giving me that wounded puppy look.* "It's groovy, man, I'm not going to fink out on you."

"I'm really scared. What if—"

"You don't have to do it, you know. You don't have to do anything."

"I think I want to. Just, what Wolfie said tonight, it's not how I thought it was going to be."

"Oh, yeah, big news flash."

Steve started drumming his fingers on Laurie's bedspread.

Robbie relented. "Womb to tomb," he said. "Just like we were born brothers, right, honey? I know you like I know me; it'll be copacetic."

Steve's fingers stilled at that but his head stayed bowed. "I'm going to burn my blanket," he said. "The one from The Room. I'm finished with it."

Rob tilted his head back against the window and crossed his ankles. "You send me, kid. That's great."

"I'm taking that picture with me, though. The one David drew of the peacock feather, that Dad gave me. It feels like I'd be like bringing him along, too."

Rob kept his face neutral. *He'll bring some kid he never met along, but...*

Laurie came out of the bathroom in his pajamas, toweling his hair. "You guys done in here? I'm beat. It's time you two were in bed, anyway."

"Yeah, I'm done. I'm way done, I'm gone," Rob said, feeling gloomy again. He got up from the window seat and climbed into bed. "You don't need to do your Junior Dad act, though. We're not little kids any more, you dig?"

Laurie flung his towel into the bathroom and stood facing Rob, hands on his hips. "Oh, I 'dig,' all right. I know you and Steve have it all sewn up together, God knows you don't need me."

Wait, no— "That's not what I—anyway, you don't even know what's going on, I—"

"Right, I don't know what's going on. I'm getting used to that. Steve, was there something else you needed?" Laurie said impatiently.

Steve flinched as he got off Laurie's bed and stood uncertainly by the door. Laurie was still glaring at Rob. Robbie slewed his eyes sideways toward Steve and looked meaningfully at Laurie.

Laurie followed Rob's eyes and his shoulders slumped. "I'm sorry, buddy," he said to Steve. "I shouldn't have snapped at you."

Steve shrugged. "'S ok," he said, and gave Laurie a small smile. "You sure we're ok?" he asked Rob.

Robbie sighed. "I'm pretty frosted about getting shot down, but yeah, I'm not planning on getting all squirrelly about it." He turned over so his back was to the door. "Later," he said.

"Good night, Steve," Laurie said.

Steve lingered a little, then said, "'Night," and disappeared.

Laurie crossed to shut the bedroom door after Steve, and walked back to Rob's bed, looking down at him. *Why's he giving me the fish eye?* Rob wondered. *I can feel it on the back of my head.* Then he thought, *I can never hide anything from him, why try?* He rolled back to look up at Laurie.

They stared at each other in silence for a minute. *Like I did with Steve—but different.*

With sudden decision, Laurie snapped the bedside light off and gray-blue moonlight seeped into the room. "Scootch over," he said briskly.

"Aren't we getting too old for this?" Rob said, scootching over.

"You are, maybe," said his elder brother. "Not me." He slid under the covers next to Rob.

"Just keep your morning woody to yourself," Robbie said. "I don't want any nasty surprises when I wake up."

"Feeling inadequate, baby brother? Overawed by the legendary Great Black Dick?"

Rob punched him on the shoulder. "I think 'mythical' is the word you're searching for, Youngblood."

Laurie snorted and shifted around in the narrow bed to make more room for Rob, who burrowed his head into the shoulder he'd just punched. "You've got your own stuff going on," he said. "All those political plans and everything."

"Never mind that tonight; this is about you."

"Fair warning, I'm prob'ly gonna bawl all over you," Rob murmured.

"That's what they pay me for," Laurie said. "Just try not to get my sleeve all snotty."

"No promises," Rob said.

Laurie snaked an arm under Rob's back and pulled his body away from the edge of the bed to rest against Laurie's solid side, bending the arm up to cup Rob's head in his strong hand. "Talk," he said.

Robbie started talking.

Chapter 45.

Rob

Robbie opened the front door on a perennial Pennsylvania drizzle and Mr. Wolfowitz standing on the stoop. "Hi, Wolfie," Rob said.

"Hi, kid," the promoter said, stepping in, his habitual nervous energy twitching his stocky frame. His short black hair and bushy mustache were both beaded with moisture. "Nice house." He shrugged out of his trenchcoat.

"Thanks. Let me take your coat. The folks and Steve are in here." He ushered him into the study. Mom and Dad hadn't seen Wolfie since the deal for the demo record had been signed at his office. Now there was a flurry of greetings and asking after each other's well-being and offerings of refreshments, which Wolfie declined.

"I'd like to get right down to business," he said, leaning forward to rest his elbows on his knees in the big rocker. *Feels funny to see him in Dad's chair,* Rob thought from his own seat on the other side of the study fireplace. Mom and Dad were on the old blue couch, with Steve between them.

Wolfie went on, "Like I told the boys last night, I've got a nice tour lined up to promote 'Bright, Warm Home': starting in Philly, then Baltimore, then we go on to New Jersey—Palisades Park and Atlantic City, and there's a place called Union Township with a bowling alley that showcases new singers in their lounge. After that, if it's all going the way I hope, I got a couple coffeehouses in Greenwich Village in mind. By then, I expect *Bandstand* to be knocking on the door, so we'll come back to Philadelphia. We start the last week in September."

Mom was frowning. "But that will take weeks," she said. "School starts the day after Labor Day. We've reconciled ourselves to the idea that Rob's not going on to college, but at least he has his high school diploma. Steve can't be running around missing a month of sophomore year."

"He's sixteen, right?" Wolfie said.

"Yes, he turned sixteen last month."

"So the law says he doesn't have to stay in school."

"That's not the point," Dad said.

Steve put in, "I'm as old as Paul Anka was when 'Diana' was number one on the charts. Frankie Avalon never finished high school, and 'Venus' was number one for five weeks last year. Fabian was only fifteen when they made him Most Promising Male Vocalist. And—"

Too much, stop now, Robbie tried to project at Steve, but it was too late.

"Paul Anka! Don't talk to me about Paul Anka," Dad broke in. "I read that his manager got himself named his guardian so he could get a nose job."

"Well, his parents were in Canada," Wolfie said defensively. "There'd be nothing like that with Steve, here."

"In any case, we're not the parents of those boys," Mom said firmly to Steve. "We're your parents, and we need to think about what's best for you."

"Doesn't what I think count?"

"Of course it counts," Dad said. "We're saying we need to think about this with you."

"So are you saying you're my parents so I have to do what you say, or are you saying you're older and more experienced so you're giving me advice, like when I decided to stop going to church? I can't tell which it is."

"You're right," Mom said, "you can't tell. And we're not going to get trapped into drawing that line. You're not grown up, but you're not a child any more, either. You're somewhere on the line, and so are we. We're not forbidding you to go, but we're not just going along with this without question, either."

That calmed Steve down a little. "You know I'm no good in school," he said. "I started too far behind. Some piece of paper diploma isn't going to make me any better at it, and I'm not sure I'd get one even if I stayed in. I am sure I can make music that people want to hear."

Dad said, "Steve, we all think you have a tremendous musical talent. But I'm sure Mr. Wolfowitz would agree that there's a certain amount of luck involved in a career in entertainment. If that doesn't pan out for you, you're going to have an impossible time without a high school diploma. To say nothing of the fact that education will give you tools for life that will broaden and deepen your other experiences."

"Due respect, Mr. M., nobody cares about that any more," Wolfie said. "And I wish you'd call me Wolfie."

"It's properly Mr. McA., actually. Or rather, Commander McA." Wolfie looked bewildered. Dad blew a little exasperated puff of air and pulled himself together. "Call me Mac, if you must," he said.

He looks like he'd like to hold an Admiral's Mast and clap Wolfie in the brig, Rob thought. *Time to tell them what else we talked about at the coffee shop last night.* He cleared his throat. "Speaking of names," he said, "Steve and Wolfie both think Steve should sing under his original name. When Decca releases 'Home' and 'Angel' under his new contract, the label's going to say Steve O'Riordan." *That got them off the high school thing, anyway. Their mouths are hanging open.*

Wolfie broke the silence. "Irish names are getting big—Tommy Makem, the Clancy Brothers. Nobody knows how to pronounce your name: is it mack-a-LISS-ter, MA-kall-ister, mik-Al-ister, what?" He waved his hand as Dad's mouth opened. "No, no, *I* know how to say it, it's everybody else who doesn't. Steve needs a name that—"

"That's not why," Steve broke in. He twisted back and forth to look at Mom and Dad in turn. "Steven McAlister is who I really am. That's my real name. And that's for here, in this house, where I'm real. I don't want all those strangers in here. But Steve O'Riordan, that's that little kid I used to be.

371

Back in The Room, I promised him I'd save him. I know that sounds dumb."

"No, it doesn't," Mom said.

"No?" Steve looked skeptical, then nodded at the obvious sincerity in her eyes. "Ok, well, I'm bringing that kid on stage. That's who's going to be the big deal pop singer. Steve McAlister's staying here."

"Fine, kid, whatever you say," Wolfie said. "Now, about this contract—"

"But how can you have the McAlister Brothers if you're not going to call yourself McAlister?" Dad interrupted.

There was a silence in which Steve looked at Wolfie and Wolfie looked at the floor. *I guess it's up to me.* Robbie cleared his throat again. "There's not going to be any McAlister Brothers. You know I'm not as good as Steve. I've always known that. And our voices aren't really in synch. They don't want me." He tried to joke about it. "I got the royal shaft." *Not funny after all.*

Everybody else spoke at once. Mom said, "What?" Dad said, "Is this true, Mr. Wolfowitz?" Wolfie said, "Don't take it like that, kid." But Steve's voice dominated: "I want you, Rob."

It was to him that Robbie spoke. "I know, Stevie. And you can still have me."

"I don't mean just as a brother, I know you'll always be that, but I want you with me. I thought and thought about it in bed last night. I can't do this without you."

"Now, Steve," Wolfie began.

Rob shook his head. "That is what I'm talking about," he said, "being with you. Wolfie wants you to use this session band of his for recording and performing, but you'll still need a back-up man for working on new material before rehearsals, and for practicing on your own. You'll need somebody to keep track of your stuff, somebody to hold your head when you puke before you go on. Somebody to see to it that you get to AA meetings no matter where you are. That's going to be me."

"But you're the one who taught me to play, without you there wouldn't be any of this. How could you just be—it sounds like, I don't know, my maid or something. It's not fair."

"You know the answer to that one," Rob said. Then he repeated something Laurie had said to him during their long midnight conversation, talking about how his own friends were backing him up in the civil rights struggle. "I'm not going to be your servant, I'm going to be your wing man. And I'm going to be your brother—your big brother, the guy who keeps you in line when everybody else is telling you what hot sh—uh, stuff you are. All right, Mom and Dad?"

Mom was looking at Rob with tears in her eyes and a smile on her face. Dad said, "I've never been prouder of you than I am right now, Robin. And that's saying something."

Steve said, "I really want a drink right now."

Robbie stood up. "I can get you to the three o'clock AA meeting at the community center. Wolfie and the folks can wrangle over the contract. Come on, honey, you're coming with me."

Chapter 46.

Sunday, September 11, 1960: 11:30 a.m.

Steve

Steve and Joy stood outside Mom and Dad's room, hand in hand.

For once, Steve had gone to Mass with them this morning; they could all fit in the Pontiac now, Mom and Dad and Ruby on the bench front seat, Rob and Steve and Joy in back. Steve had tried to pray, to find that clarity and peace Mom talked about without falling into his old numb state, but the church seemed an alien place and inside Steve there was no response to his anxious searching. Sitting in the cavernous space surrounded by strangers, fear had come back to fill him like an old illness he thought he'd gotten over.

Coming home was no better. Everybody else was off at school, and the house was full of ghosts. Steve wanted to go up to his cubbyhole and listen to the rain hitting the roof inches over his face while he stayed dry.

But he had to do this, now. *I should have told Rob, at least. I should have found a way to tell him. He thinks he knows me. And he stood up for me in the big fight about me finishing high school after Wolfie left that day. He's really the one who convinced Mom and Dad. I owed it to him to tell him about this. Too late now.*

When they came in after church, they'd all gone to change out of Sunday clothes before sitting down to Dad's pancakes. *But the way my stomach feels, I'd probably just throw them right up again,* Steve thought. *Oh, God. Joy, too. I can't do this.*

"Maybe—" he said.

"No," Joy said. "We agreed it would be now." She raised her hand and knocked, then opened the door at Mom's call. "Are you guys decent?" Steve could hear the false note in Joy's voice, but Mom didn't seem to notice at first.

"Come on in, darlings," Mom said. "We're about ready to come downstairs. Did you need someth…" Her hands, pinning some stray hairs back into place, faltered as she saw their faces in the mirror.

Dad came out of the bathroom saying, "Are you kids so hungry you can't wait five minutes?" Then he saw their faces, too, and stopped in mid stride. "Whatever it is," he said, "say it fast. Say it." He hadn't raised his voice, yet there was steel in it that reminded Steve that Dad had commanded thousands of men.

Steve put his shoulders back and took a breath to speak, but it was Joy's voice, small but steady, that said, "I'm pregnant."

Immediately, as though responding to something he'd already known, Dad lurched back into the bathroom, slamming the door behind him. They could hear the sound of retching that was half sobbing, the worst sound Steve ever heard.

Mom's face was white. Aside from that, she didn't look like Mom to Steve, she looked like Dr. McAlister, like the concerned but impersonal therapist he'd met at Rolling Meadow, fresh from the carnage of his murdering Bert, when he still dreamed of blood every night.

"Are you sure?" is all she said.

"I'm over two weeks late," Joy said. "You know how regular I am. And I'm throwing up every morning."

"How long—?"

"Since the Fourth of July." The water in the bathroom turned off and Dad came out, wiping his mouth. "It was me," Joy said to him. "He was afraid; I went to him."

Dad looked at her blankly, then turned to Mom. Mom met his eyes, breathed in hard, and said, "You need to leave us alone a little to talk about this. Leave us alone now."

Joy nodded and turned to go, still holding Steve's hand. He hadn't said a word yet. He thought he should say something, but there were no words in his head, just a low, lonely wailing somewhere deep inside.

They went out and crossed the hall, turning left to Joy's room, leaving the door open, sitting down on her bed side by side. The rain blew against the windows and Mom and Dad's muffled voices rose and fell. *I should at least say something to Joy,* Steve thought, but nothing came into his head to say. *And she's not talking, either.* She was crying quietly. Steve's eyes were dry as hot glass.

Eventually Dad and Mom's door opened. Joy's hand tensed in Steve's and he patted it with his other hand. He looked up to see Dad's eyes on that as he and Mom came into the room and sat down facing them on Celia's bed. Both their eyes were red; Mom was mangling a hanky in the hand that wasn't holding onto Dad.

Joy spoke first. "I'm not going to Puerto Rico," she said.

"To get an abortion, she means," Mom said to Dad. "Like the Grayson girl." She turned back to Joy. "Your father and I talked about that possibility, and we feel the same," she said. "You're young but your body is not underdeveloped, you're healthy, and you evidently entered into this of your own free will. Some girls are driven to abortion; I don't think that's you."

Steve couldn't understand what was happening. Mom was talking like a doctor giving advice to a patient, not like an upset mother to a daughter. Dad wasn't saying anything. *If they don't explode pretty soon, I will.*

"So," Mom was saying, "one option would be for you to give the baby up—"

"No," Joy said. "Steve and I don't want that. I'm having the baby, and I'm keeping it."

"All right, but have you considered that your father and I could adopt the baby? We'd tell him or her the truth when the time was right, but meanwhile—"

"No!" Joy shouted. Her face was red. "Can't you hear me? This is my baby, mine and Steve's, it's not yours, it's not Dad's, it's not anybody else's in the family you might think would be a better mother than me. Finally there's going to be something that's all mine, somebody I don't have to share with anybody, and you're not going to take that away from me!"

379

Mom's professional face crumpled and she started to cry out loud, hand over her mouth, bent over as though she had a deadly pain.

Joy took a gasping breath. "I'm sorry, I'm sorry, I'm sorry," she said, flinging herself forward across the space between the beds, ending up on the floor at Mom's feet. Mom leaned down and gathered her up and they rocked together, sobbing.

Dad petted Joy's hair for a minute, then turned to Steve, still with that blank look on his face. "Don't you have anything to say at all?" he asked.

He looked like he was going to go on, but Steve finally found words. "Can I keep my guitar? I bought it with money I earned, not from my allowance."

Mom and Joy abruptly stopped sobbing, though they were still sniffling and hiccoughing. Joy turned in Mom's arms to stare at Steve. Whatever Dad had been planning to say died on his half-opened lips. He frowned and turned to Mom, but she shook her head, brow as furrowed as his. They waited for Steve to explain.

"When you send me back to Rolling Meadow," he said. "Everything else I have, you bought for me, but if I could just have my guitar—"

"Oh, Jesus," Dad said. "Oh, suffering Jesus." He stood up and stepped across, standing over Steve.

Steve shrank away, he couldn't help it. Dad shook his head slowly and sadly, looking down at Steve. Then he sat down beside him and roughly pulled Steve into his arms. *Into his arms? What? What?* "I thought you'd be so mad, I thought you'd hate me."

"Oh, I'm mad, all right," Dad said into Steve's hair. But he didn't sound mad. "I'm furious at both of you. And I'm disappointed and I'm worried and I'm so, so hurt that you didn't come to us when you first started having these feelings for each other. But I could never hate you; I love you. I'll always love you."

Steve drew back so he could see Dad's face. "You mean—I have to ask this, to be sure—are you saying you're not sending me back, I don't have to go away?"

Dad took Steve's chin in his hand. "No, you're definitely going away. You're going on this tour with Rob. You're about to have a child to support, young man, and maybe later when you're a little older, a wife. But this is your home forever, even after you make a home of your own. We're your family, son, now more than ever."

Steve closed his eyes. "I'm sorry," he whispered. "I didn't mean to hurt anyone. Not you, not Mom, especially not Joy. I love her so much, Dad." Dad threaded his fingers through Steve's hair, then Steve opened his eyes and looked across at Joy.

She was in Mom's lap now, and her face was hidden. Mom's cheek was resting on the top of Joy's head. When she saw Steve looking, she said, "Joy's going to be all right here with us while you're on tour, Steve, whether she ends up keeping the baby or not."

Joy pushed herself up, glaring. "I told you, I'm keeping it. What's more, I'm going with Steve. We're going to be on this tour together."

"No, you will not," Mom said, her voice rising.

"I'll take care of her," Steve said earnestly to Dad.

Dad shook his head. "You kids really have no idea what you've gotten yourselves into, do you? Joy is absolutely not going with you. Joy, you are staying here and that's final. This is not some teenage escapade. You've chosen to behave like adults; now face the adult consequences."

"So I should just keep going to school like some kid? That's facing adult consequences?" Joy said.

Mom blew out hard and visibly put a rein on her temper. "They're going to expel you once you start showing, foolish girl, and they're not going to let you back in after the baby's born, either, whether you keep it or not. But you can take correspondence courses to finish high school, and after the baby is born we can think about college possibilities. It's not going to be easy; what the two of you have done will change your lives forever. But we will work it out together."

"Yes, we will," Dad said. "And we won't waste time in recriminations; what's done is done. But I do just have to ask—" he pulled away a little, gripped Steve's shoulders and gave him a shake—"why the *hell* didn't either of you think to use contraception? I know I explained birth control to you, and I'm positive your mother talked to Joy about it."

Joy shifted so her face was half hidden and started fiddling with a loose thread on Mom's sweater. "We only did it three times. I didn't think anything would happen," she said in a voice thick with tears. "I know that's stupid."

Steve bit the inside of his cheek and spoke into his lap, not meeting Dad's eyes. "It seemed like that would make it cheap, like we didn't really love each other." Dad gave a gusty sigh and pulled Steve back into his arms.

"Besides," Joy said, "birth control's a sin."

Mom grabbed the back of Joy's hair and gently pulled her head back to look into her face. "And having sex wasn't?"

"No," Joy said firmly, meeting her eyes. "It was wrong and it was stupid, but it wasn't a sin. God's not mad at us." Dad sighed again, and Mom tucked Joy's head back against her breast.

There was a thumping noise outside the room— Robbie was bounding up the back stairs. "Are we having pancakes today or what?" he called. He pushed the half-open door aside. "Ruby and I are starving, what are you guys—" He looked at their faces, and the way they were sitting, for a long moment. Then he gave Steve a look of betrayal that seared his soul. Without another word he left the door and went slowly back down the stairs.

"Joy?" Mom said. "Would you like us to talk to them, or do you and Steve want to tell them yourselves?"

"You, please, Mom. I think Steve and I are the ones who need to be alone for a little while now. Right, Steve?"

Steve nodded. They all got up and Dad and Mom each kissed and hugged Joy and Steve and went out, closing the door behind them.

Steve slipped to the floor, crossed his arms on his knees and put his head down on his arms. Tears finally started to slide down his face, quiet and steady as the rain. Joy sat on the bed behind him and rubbed his neck.

After a long time she said softly, "Steve, it is going to be all right, you know. I wouldn't have asked for this to happen—no, that's not true, I guess on some level I did ask for it to happen. But we have people who love us and they'll help us. Please don't be so sad. Please don't cry any more."

He looked up. "I think I'm going crazy, or maybe I was always crazy, but I can't stop crying. That's nothing new, you've seen me cry a million times, but this seems different. It's like I'm sad about everything, not only us—sad about the world."

"When you were locked in that room, Bert kept you from growing up. You lived through horrible things, things no kid should even know about, but always as a helpless child," Joy said slowly, still rubbing his neck. "You suffered like a child, you cried like a child. Now you're becoming a man, and you suffer like a man, and you weep a man's tears. You're not crazy, you're human."

"God, I love you." He slid up beside her and they lay down on her bed together, holding each other close. Feeling her lithe young body against his, thinking of how it was about to change, how her world would shift in the coming months, he felt a fresh surge of guilt. *If I'm not honest with her, it will all turn to crap,* he thought. "There's something I have to tell you," he said.

"So tell," she said.

"When Dad said that about me having to go on tour because I'll have a child to support, part of me was glad. I mean, I was already unbelievably happy that they weren't going to hate me or reject me, but I'm talking about something else. I mean I'm happy to be getting away, doing something exciting. It's not fair, I know. You were already feeling bad about being stuck here with nobody but the adults. Now it's going to be worse. They're making you stay here, you won't even be able to go to school after a while, and I'll be out there doing shows and having adventures."

Joy sat up. "You're right, it isn't fair. How about if I carry the baby for the first five months and you take the last four?"

"I was serious."

"I know you were, and thanks for telling me the truth about how you felt. I've thought the same thing, to be honest. But it's just how things are, there's nothing we can do about it." Joy shifted around to put her feet on the floor. "I found a poem the other night, though, that made me feel better in a funny way, I guess because it says what I feel. And it was written by a high school girl, Lois Anne Davison. Want to hear it?"

"You and your poems. Sure, lay it on me."

She went over to her desk, opened her English textbook to a bookmarked page, and read:

"Though the mountains bow to you,
I shall not bow; though the hills prostrate
themselves
At your feet. Though the world be your mirror,
I shall not reflect you. I shall sit alone in the night
While you dance. But when the world
Has marked its vengeance on your face,
Come back to me.
I will make you beautiful with my eyes."

Steve closed his eyes and listened to the rain.

Chapter 47.

Friday, September 23, 1960: 8:15 p.m.

Steve

Steve rinsed his mouth out, wishing Robbie would go away. It was bad enough being with him in Wolfie's car and the hotel when he was acting so cold, attentive but distant, worse than anger. *I really don't need him watching me barf my guts out from nervousness.*

"I'm not going away," Rob said as they stepped back into the shabby green room of the obscure Philadelphia club Wolfie had booked them into. *How did he know what I was thinking?* Steve wondered. "Whatever you do," Rob went on, "I'm going to be here, watching."

Those last ten days at home, Robbie had been tender and protective with Joy. He'd hardly looked at Steve as they'd packed clothes and instruments, his tone calm but detached when they'd discussed details of the tour. Steve went to meetings every day, but he longed for a drink every hour.

Last night Steve had dreamed of the car crash that killed his parents. The dreams were coming more and more often again since Joy got pregnant, along with visions of Bert slumped in the chair with blood down his front like a red bib, and the bloody knife in Steve's hand. He'd gasped awake to find Rob sitting beside him, one hand on his shoulder, the other holding out a glass of water. But after Steve drank and handed the glass back, Rob had gotten up and gone back to his own bed without a word.

Now Steve looked down at him where he sat on the cracked brown vinyl couch with the stuffing leaking out. The back-up band Wolfie hired had already gone out to watch the other acts from the wings; they were going on last. Rob checked the tuning on Steve's Martin, head down near the guitar body, listening intently.

"If you love somebody, show them," Steve said suddenly. "That's what you said to me."

"I didn't mean like that, and you know it," Rob said, not raising his eyes. "And you never told me what was going on. That's what gets me. Day after day practicing, night after night performing, you never said a word."

"Aren't you ever going to forgive me?" Steve said. "I'm really, really sorry. Please forgive me, Robin."

Rob slid Steve's guitar onto the couch beside him and looked up. "I thought you'd never ask," he said.

"What? You mean you were just waiting for me to say it? That's all it takes?"

Rob stood up. "No, that's not all it takes. But it's sure a good start. Stevie, why didn't you tell me, though? I mean, bring me in on the scene? I thought we were tight."

"We are. It's not about that. It's hard to explain, but it was like what was going on between me and Joy was happening in a different world, that didn't have anything to do with you or with Mom and Dad or anyone. It's not that I was keeping it from you, it's that it didn't seem real when it wasn't actually happening. Then she got pregnant, and everything got way too real."

Rob nodded, fingering his lips thoughtfully. "You're not out of the woods yet," he said, "but I'm thinking about it." Shaking his head, he reached out and drew Steve to him, wrapping his arms around his neck. He kissed the side of Steve's head, then pushed him gently away again. "No waterworks," he warned, "you'll wreck your war paint."

"Right," Steve said, breathing in through his nose and blinking hard. "Listen, I've been working on a new song when you weren't around. Want to hear it? It's about Joy."

"A song about the family, a song about Beth, a song about Joy, am I seeing a pattern here?"

He doesn't sound cold any more. "I'm writing about all of you. This is the only one that's finished yet."

"Yeah? What's mine called?"

Steve turned his face away a little. "'Golden Boy,'" he said shyly.

Rob gave a long shaky sigh. "All right, that's it," he said. "You've bought me off. I forgive you."

"For which part?"

"For everything. Forever."

"Oh. Good."

"Do you have names for the others yet?"

"Yes, I've been working a little bit at a time on all of them. There's 'Sweet Cissy' and 'Black Prince'; the one for Jamie I call 'Heart's Brother' because of something he said to me last summer, because he and I are the only ones who really get what's happened to the other one."

Robbie nodded. "So can I hear this new one?"

Steve took the guitar and moved to the table where David's drawing of a peacock feather sat, propped in a new frame. He touched it with his fingertips, slung his guitar strap over his shoulder, took the tortoiseshell pick out of his pocket, then set one foot on the makeup stool. His feathery blond hair gleamed in the lights around the mirror, set off by his soft dark red silk shirt and straight black slacks.

"I finally worked in some of the ideas I got from *Kind of Blue*," Steve said. He started the song with a long sliding glissando up the neck and down the strings, then settled into a standard blues scale in a brisk 4/4 tempo accented on the back beat.

> "You are my Joy, you are my safe place—
> You took care of me
> Now
> I'll take care of you,
> I'll come home to you,
> And you will make me beautiful,
> With… your… eyes."

Steve was picking rather than strumming now, notes carrying the melody on from one verse to the next.

> "You are my Joy, you are my best friend—
> You showed me how to be,
> How
> To be a man for you.

I'll come home to you,
And you will make me beautiful
With… your… eyes."

He went into an instrumental bridge, eyes closed, head bent, pick and fingers dancing over the strings, then returned to the vocal call-and-response.

"You are my Joy, and now I'm far away—
I didn't treat you right;
I know
I need to work for you.
I'll come home to you,
And you will make me beautiful
With… your… eyes."

Steve lifted his head to see, first, Rob's single affirming nod and the quirky smile he knew meant Rob approved, then Wolfie standing in the green room door. Wolfie was smiling, too. "I see we've got Steve O'Riordan's next single," he said. "Come on, kid, you're on."

Rob got up, but Steve stood still a minute, looking at David's picture. *Steve O'Riordan. Yes. I'm going to do what I promised him, that scared little kid I used to be. I'm going to do it for him, and for David. I'm going to do it for Joy, and for the baby. And for me.*

He and Rob followed Wolfie out and threaded through the backstage clutter to the club's shallow wing. Onstage, Steve's backup band was setting up while the applause was still tapering off from the previous act, a couple of guys with electric guitars who pushed past them hauling their amplifiers.

"Here you go, brother," Rob said. "Say hello to the world."

Steve looked back at him. "Ok, lovey," he said. The center spot came up, the audience started to clap. Steve stepped out.

www.ingramcontent.com/pod-product-compliance
Lightning Source LLC
Chambersburg PA
CBHW031419240626
47154CB00001B/111